BREAKING THE BONDS

P.A. WILSON

FREE EBOOK

Claim your copy of Running the Game when you use the QR code below to sign up for my newsletter and cheer on Pen as she vies for a commission in the military.

CHAPTER ONE

Serena caught a glimpse of purple skin and armor as the Meta guards walked into the square. Her heart skipped a beat. In Whitson, you need to have a performing license, or better not be caught without one.

"Run," she hissed at Michal, as the guards turned toward their audience.

Michal nodded and tucked the final spinning knife back into its sheath. Their juggling act was over. Pouring the coins from the hat into his pocket, he gave her a push. "Left toward the pumpkin cart."

She flashed a smile at the remaining patrons. "Until we meet again," she said then spun away in a flash of colored skirts, following Michal through a gap made as the crowd shifted.

The market was in full swing. Carts of produce, house wares and trinkets lined the outer edges of the town square and formed four, more or less, straight lines in the center.

Serena risked a glance over her shoulder. The guards pushed their way through stands and customers. They were almost to the center of the square. Here and there, a cart, or a shopper would obstruct their path.

She turned her attention back to her escape route and stumbled over a display of pumpkins, sending them crashing into other carts, and filling the area with a sweet and earthy scent.

"Sorry!" she called back to pumpkin seller.

Michal tossed a quarter penny in the man's direction and grabbed her arm. As they rounded the corner, she saw the pumpkin seller roll a few more of his wares into the path of the guards who were now forcing people aside to get closer.

The alley was lined with barrows. Here the vendors were selling clothing, sausages, and small handmade toys. Serena's mouth watered at the smell of spiced meat. Michal pulled her to a barrow festooned with bright scarves. He grabbed a handful of cloth from the pile in the center of the display.

"Five pennies," he said to the woman sitting on an upturned barrel.

"In a rush, are you?" she asked.

"Six," Michal held out his palm full of coin.

"Your friends are coming." The woman pointed to the commotion at the mouth of the alleyway. Serena could not see the guards yet, but she knew by the movement of the people that they were close.

"Damn it, how much, before I have to steal them?"

"Take them. Anyone who annoys the duke's guards that much, has earned a few scraps of cloth." The woman waved them away.

Michal laughed and threw half the coins into the barrow. He handed a dark blue scarf to Serena, motioning her to cover her strawberry blond curls. She felt the smooth fine wool catch on her rough hands.

As they ran, Serena watched him build his disguise. Michal wrapped a green scarf around his own black hair, then a long gray one around his waist. He slowed to a walk, hissing to Serena to come back. Michal bent and started to limp. She took his arm and whispered in his ear, "Great idea, grandmother."

They drew into a doorway and stood as though waiting for the commotion to pass. The guards struggled through people standing in the alley entrance. Serena watched them scan the crowds, looking for a sign of her red hair, probably. She held her breath. All it would take was one vendor on the side of the guards. She watched as the woman at the barrel of scarves waved the guards over. Serena prepared herself to start running again, but Michal's grip on her arm tightened. "Wait, there's time. Don't bring attention to us until it's the only option."

"Oh, sirs," the woman sobbed out in a loud voice. "Please, I've been robbed."

"Woman, we are busy," the first guard growled. "We have no time for your petty problems."

"I understand." She bowed her head. "I thought you might be looking for the thieves. Two young people, a man, well a boy really, and a young girl."

The guard stepped closer. "It is possible they're the ones we search for."

"Oh, please, they stole my scarves." The woman sounded relieved. "They took my best white scarves. They ran through there." She pointed to the open door of a butcher shop.

"They are trapped then." The guard looked at his companion. "Go look for them."

"No, you don't understand." Serena was impressed with the volume of the woman's screech. "The shop has a back door. They probably went through to the next street."

"Good. At least you know where your loyalty should lie." The guard gestured for his companion to precede him into the doorway. Serena felt the tension release from her shoulders.

The scarf seller looked toward them, winked, and then turned to the man next to her. They both shifted to block the doorway.

"Now." Michal pulled Serena back into the alley. "Not too fast. Remember I'm an old lady." They limped their way back to the square. Michal tossed a few more coins into the barrow as he passed.

"I don't like this," Serena whispered to Michal. "Can't we go faster? What if someone calls the guards back?"

"No, don't break the disguise," Michal muttered, tightening his grip on her arm. "If there's a snitch in the crowd they would have said something already. It's not likely they saw us change and then saved up the knowledge for later. If they wanted to benefit, they would have spoken up right away."

She tried to dismiss the feeling of eyes crawling across her back. "Okay, I suppose. Let's just get through this and collect our stuff from the inn. We need to get out of town, right?"

"Let's sit for a minute, my dear," Michal said in a high quavery voice. "Here, we can have a cup of tea and rest."

"Are you serious?" Serena asked under her breath as Michal lowered himself slowly onto the chair.

"I need to catch my breath, dear. I'm not as young as I was," Michal responded. He stared at her and then whispered. "An old lady wouldn't be able to cross the square without resting."

"I'll get us a pot of tea." Serena patted his hand and looked up for a waiter.

Michal placed a half penny on the table and whispered, "That's the last of the money we earned today. We won't be able to pay the bill at the inn."

Serena ordered tea from a bored waiter, and then sat beside Michal. "Let's hope the next town isn't crawling with guards." She looked around the square. The merchants were calling their wares, all evidence of the recent disruption gone.

She thought back to her life a year ago. She would have been one of the vendors, standing beside her father as he sold the leatherware they'd created over the previous month. If he hadn't tried to marry her off to Oisin van Mallek, she would never have run away.

Of course, if she hadn't run away, she would never have met Michal, and the last year of living the life of a roving entertainer would never have happened. She knew everyone thought they were lovers, but neither of them felt that way. Michal said his heart was with someone else, and she knew she wasn't ready for anything serious. She knew love always ended, and it hurt, even if she was the one to end it.

She took a sip of tea; the bitter liquid cleared her mind. "I guess we're for a hard bed under the stars tonight."

"You've done that before," Michal answered in his old woman voice. "At least it's summer. Remember last winter? How we snuck into those barns? You should be happy. Tomorrow we won't stink of cow shit."

Serena chuckled. "You always look on the bright side." She didn't mind the hard days. The excitement of the rover's life still held her fascinated. The first time they ran out of money, she'd been surprised that Michal wouldn't steal to support them. She would not have stooped to theft, at least not until she was desperate. But her father had always told her that gypsies would steal anything not locked up. Michal had never considered stealing, even in midwinter when the forest didn't have berries or nuts for them to eat. He said Duke Tirash stole enough of the people's hard work, so he wouldn't add to the misery. She knew if they had to leave the inn without paying, Michal would send the money when they earned it.

"Trouble never lasts," Michal muttered through the steam rising from his cup. "No point in giving it life by talking about it."

"Look." She released her little finger from the cup to point. "They're back."

The guards stomped into the square. They scanned the crowd, and then took up posts again on either side of the main entrance.

"Hmm, looks like they've lost interest." Michal placed his empty cup on the table. "Drink up dear," he said louder. "We should be getting back to the inn, and your father."

Serena swallowed the last drops of her tea and stood, offering her hand to assist the old woman to her feet. "Yes, grandma," she said meekly.

They shuffled to the alley leading to their inn. Serena tried not to look toward the guards, tried not to bring their attention. From the corner of her eye, she saw the closest guard glance at them and then dismiss them. She bent as if to say something to her grandmother, but simply patted Michal's arm. As she straightened, she noticed a tall man, tall and thin, the hood of his brown cloak pulled down, shading his face. He looked away as soon as their eyes met.

CHAPTER TWO

Oisin watched the two women leave the square, the younger one supporting the elder. They shuffled out of sight as the alley curved to the right.

He glanced at the duke's guards. The Metas were dressed in the usual leather uniform. The stiffened texture of the tanned hide contrasted with the smooth purple skin of the aliens. The slight odor of ripe strawberries wafted from them. Twenty-five years after they arrived, the only Meta most people saw were the guards. The duke and the other ruling Meta seemed to prefer life behind the walls of their homes to the crowds of humans.

The guards were watching a dog and a gull fight over a scrap of meat. Oisin slipped into the alley to follow the two women. The younger woman looked familiar and if she was who he suspected, the older woman was a man. Before the guards started chasing them, he'd recognized Serena den Baros as the juggler's assistant. He'd seen the two women stop for tea. As the younger woman reached to pour, a flash of red hair had slipped from under the scarf.

If it wasn't Serena, he'd eat his hat.

"I'll just say hello," he told himself. "No questions about why she disappeared. I won't ask if the thought of marrying me was so horrid that she ran. I won't ask."

There were four inns at the end of the alley, two up against the town walls. The other two closer to the curve of the wall. Oisin tried to breathe through his mouth. The smell of horse dung was the most pleasant of the odors in the alley.

There was no sign of Serena, in disguise or not. Oisin pulled down his hood and turned into the first inn.

The heat and noise from the closed great room felt like it was pushing him back into the coolness of the alley. Oisin moved to the side of the door to get his bearings. The candles burning on the tables and bar did not shed enough light. He needed to give his eyes time to adjust. He felt exposed, vulnerable.

No one paid him the least attention.

He moved toward the bar looking around as he passed. He didn't see Serena or her companion, but his stomach reacted to the savory aroma of stew. He couldn't delay his search to eat dinner, but the food smelled so good that, if he didn't find her, he would return for his evening meal.

"What's your poison, lad?" The barman wiped his hands on the towel he'd used to wipe up the slops. "Beer? Something stronger?"

"He looks like he needs something weaker," a voice called from the end of the bar before Oisin could answer. Catcalls and laughter followed the words.

"Nothing, thank you." Oisin ignored the taunt. "I am in search of someone."

"Information costs money, boy." The barman leaned forward and leered. "Can you afford it?"

Oisin felt as though he was being sized up for robbery. He could see that the men at the bar were waiting for him to pull out his purse. Trying to sound worldly, he replied, "It is possible, but only a fool pays before seeing the goods."

"Fair enough." The cloth passed along the bar again, leaving a larger trail of liquid behind than in front. "Who you looking for?"

"Do you rent rooms?"

"You looking to lose your boyhood?"

Oisin was used to being treated as if he was still in his teens. Perhaps he should try to grow a beard. "I seek two people who have lodgings in one of these inns."

"Ah well, boy, unless you are out to find a companion for an hour, you won't find what you're looking for here," the man at the bar muttered. "There's only one use for these rooms, by the hour, or by the night if you got enough coin."

Oisin gave another bow. "I thank you for the information." He pulled a quarter penny from his pocket and dropped it on the counter.

The man looked at the coin, and then swept it into a pocket.

Making his way to the door, Oisin kept one hand around his purse and the other gripped around the hilt of his knife.

The sign on the inn across the way read The Wild Ram, the picture under the words demonstrating just how wild. Oisin pushed through the curtain that draped the open doorway.

The noise was more subdued than in the first inn. The tables were crowded with men and women speaking quietly. Here and there money exchanged hands. Next to one chair at each table stood a barrel or a large stuffed sack of goods. This was obviously an indoor market. Goods of higher value, or more delicate nature were traded here. As he walked to the bar, the scent of dinner greeted him, a sour and scorched scent. Clearly food was not a specialty of the house.

He looked around for someone to ask about guests staying at the inn. The bartender was surrounded by men carrying trays, but he noticed a serving girl working the tables to his right. "Excuse me." He tried to step into her path, but she dodged him.

Oisin sighed and stepped back against the wall. The woman placed mugs on tables until her tray was empty. She was heading back to the bar when Oisin stepped into her path. This time he managed to gain her attention.

"No rooms for rent," she said in answer to his question. "The rooms got converted to storage when them started working out of here." She nodded to the tables full of merchants.

Oisin thanked her and returned to the street, taking a breath before exiting to avoid breathing in too much of the foul air outside. As he approached the inns that sat against the city wall, the smells intensified, adding vomit and urine to the mixture of horse and dregga dung.

He wondered at how low Serena had fallen if she was staying in such surroundings. Oisin tried to decide which to start with, The Kicking Ass, or The Spitting Goat. Both had stables, both were two floors high, only one had curtains in the windows of the second floor. The other had boards nailed in the window spaces. Oisin decided the Kicking Ass might be slightly better accommodation if the curtains were still intact.

The tables in the great room were crowded with families as well as merchants and other travelers. Oisin made his way to the bar to ask his questions. Children ran around playing some intricate game of tag. The rougher looking clientele seemed to keep to themselves in a corner of the room.

As he approached the bar, the serving woman walked toward him. "What can I get you, son?" she asked.

"I'm trying to find someone." Oisin slipped his fingers into his purse to pull out a few coins. "I thought I saw an old friend come in. I wondered if she was staying here."

The woman looked around the room. "Most of my guests are here, take a look. If she's not here, I can't help you. I don't gossip about the people who've paid good coin to shelter in my inn."

Oisin thanked her and ordered a mug of beer. He needed some time before venturing out again into the alley. Sipping the beer, he turned to look around the room, trying not to appear too nosy as he searched for Serena.

"Enough!"

Oisin turned to face the shouter, ready to duck if a fight broke out.

"I will wring your damn neck." The threat came from a short barrel of a man.

"Gentlemen," the innkeeper said, as she moved to the back of the room where the men at the table were scuffling. "If you must settle this with fists, do so outside."

Oisin didn't think that they would obey such a civilized request. They were still bristling with whatever insult had started the fight, but the four men headed toward the door. As they moved away from the table, Oisin saw why. Against the back wall stood a giant of a man, making shoving motions at them. Clearly, the innkeeper knew how to maintain control in her house.

As the giant stepped back to rest against the wall, Oisin noticed a small table tucked under the stairs. Sitting at the table, staring back at him with fury on her face, was Serena den Baros, his betrothed.

CHAPTER THREE

"What are you staring at? Don't bring attention to yourself." Michal could see the expression on Serena's face. His back was to the room, a position he hated, but Serena had beaten him to the other chair. At least Gordie's presence meant no one was likely to creep up behind him.

Serena broke her concentration and returned her green eyes to his face. "I thought I saw someone in the square," she whispered. "Now he's here. Someone from my past."

"Is he looking at you? Has he seen you?" Michal knew they should have left for the road as soon as they got back to the inn. But Serena had insisted they stay for a final meal – one they couldn't pay for.

"Yes." She sighed. "He is coming over. Don't overreact."

Michal turned as Serena stood. The boy coming toward them looked like every wealthy human Michal had seen before. He was blond, tall, and thin. The only distinguishing feature was his flushed face, that and the bare emotion on it as he looked at Serena. This boy was in love and in pain.

"Oisin," Serena said, smiling to hide her annoyance. "It's been ages."

"Perhaps not ages, but a long time indeed. Many things seem to have changed." The boy, *Osheen* Serena had said, looked toward Michal, and frowned.

"Oh, let me introduce you to my... my friend." The pause did nothing to lessen the jealousy burning in Oisin's eyes. "Michal var Avinon, please allow me to present Oisin var Mallek."

Michal stood and reached out his hand. The boy had a firm grip and Michal refused to enter a contest for hand crushing. "Mallek, are you related to Mallek var Dorian?"

"Regretfully, yes." Oisin inclined his head in a small bow. "He is my father. I hope, though, I have my mother's temperament. I have been known to forgive people who disagree with me — eventually."

Michal laughed. Oisin's father was known to be harsh with his tenants and would drive off the Romany before the caravans could be unloaded. "Would you break bread with us?"

"Stop being so damn formal." Serena motioned Michal to get a third chair for the small table. "Oisin, I hope you don't mind sharing our poor meal."

Michal rearranged the chairs so that Oisin sat with his back to the room. Now Michal was able to see three quarters of the crowd. He felt more relaxed with his back at least partially to the wall.

"Allow me to order and pay for your dinners," Oisin said, looking at the small plate of meat and bread that the others were sharing. "It is a day of celebration for me."

Michal didn't argue. If the boy wanted to pay for the meal, let him. At least the owner would get paid, and they wouldn't have to run out on the meal, just the room cost.

"What are you celebrating?" Michal asked after waving the serving girl to the table.

"Today is my first official day out of school. I have, apparently, learned all there is to teach in the academy. I am taking a few days to travel around before I enter my father's business and start my life."

"I thought you hated the idea of working for your father." Serena poured beer into their mugs. "What changed?"

Michal took three bowls of stew from the serving girl and passed them out. He watched as Oisin breathed in the aroma, a smile crossing his lips.

"Well, one thing happened, and one did not," Oisin said.

"What do you mean?" Michal suspected there was a secret here that Serena didn't want to have exposed. She looked ready to interrupt every time the boy spoke.

"The thing that didn't happen." The boy paused while he chewed a mouthful of stew.

"I'm sure it's not that earthshaking," Serena said into the silence. "How are your mother, and your sister?"

"Perhaps not earthshaking," the boy responded. "But that is the problem. Rebelling against my father is one thing, but not having an option is very much another thing. How am I to say no to the family business when I have no other prospects, or interests? They are fine, thank you for asking."

Michal grunted his approval. "Sensible approach. If you have nothing to run to, no point in going."

"Mmm." Oisin took a sip of beer. "And then my..."

Michal saw Serena's glare, her eyes round and a flush across her cheeks gave her away. He couldn't tell if it was fear, or anger. He could tell it was strong enough to stop Oisin in his tracks.

"I suppose you would call her my friend." Oisin raised an eyebrow at Serena, who nodded. "Yes, my friend left suddenly with no explanation."

"Where else will you travel before going home?" Serena asked.

"I really don't know. I think I might just wander. You never know what I'll learn. Perhaps I'll find the passion I lack in some alternative to life as a merchant."

"Thank you for the dinner." Serena wiped a wad of bread

around the stew bowl. "I'm sorry to say we must leave. I hope you have a good journey."

"Perhaps I can come with you." Oisin looked at Michal as he spoke. "Since I have no definite plans, it would be delightful to travel with an old friend."

"No," Serena snapped.

Michal smiled. Serena was usually so sunny and sweet. It was going to be fun watching these two argue. "Why not? I think it's a great idea." He slapped Oisin on the shoulder. "Where are you staying?"

Oisin shrugged. "I had not booked a room. Perhaps I can share your accommodation. I'll put up the coin, don't fret. I wouldn't expect charity."

"Splendid idea." Michal ignored the daggers that Serena was staring at him. "That way we won't need to find you when it's time to leave. Where are your bags? You should bring them now, before dark."

Oisin said he would send most of his belongings on to his father and bring only what he would need for two or three days of travel. Michal watched him pass money to the innkeeper as he left.

"What the hell was that about?" Serena looked ready to throw the half-empty beer jug at his head.

Michal laughed as he answered, "He's good cover. Besides he has money and until we earn more, we're stuck eating berries and sleeping under bushes if we don't let him tag along."

She put the beer jug down and slumped back in her chair. "Just don't believe this civilized act he's playing. Oisin var Mallek is up to something, believe me."

CHAPTER FOUR

Oisin stretched. The pad of blankets and piled straw had been useless in softening the floorboards.

When he returned to the inn the night before with his newly purchased travel gear, Michal was waiting in the common area to escort him to the room. Serena was already asleep in the only cot. Oisin suspected that she was only pretending to sleep, but didn't say anything. While Michal had slept soundlessly, Oisin had tossed all night.

"Nice to see you up," Serena's voice came from the doorway. "We will be in the common room, so if you want to join us for breakfast, get ready quickly. The convenience is down there." She pointed to the end of the hallway that faced the city wall.

"Ten minutes." Oisin ran to the convenience, and sped through cleaning his teeth and face. His stomach was ready for breakfast. Descending the stairs, he caught the scent of freshly baked bread and frying sausage. He scanned the room for Michal and Serena. It was as crowded as the night before. Despite its location, this inn was a popular.

The two were sitting at a table along the right wall. The empty chair placed so its occupant would be facing away from the room. Other tables filled with laborers, merchants, and families. An off-duty Meta guard sat alone near the door. The noise was subdued compared to his memory of the night before. It might be due to hangovers, but it was more likely to do with the presence of the Meta. No one liked to gain the attention of the ruling aliens.

"Morning," Michal said around a mouthful of lirian sandwich, the grease shining on his chin. "Here, fill your plate. We have plans to make."

Oisin sat, ignoring his prickling nerves. He reminded himself not to be late for meals again. He hated not seeing the room. "What plans?"

"We need to decide where to spend the night on our way to Halm's Town. It's usually two day's walk."

"Is there a chance of a barn, or farmhouse?" Oisin had never spent the night in the open, he was looking forward to the adventure. "What is the weather forecast? Will we need cover?" Serena touched his hand and his face heated with a flush.

"Oisin, one thing at a time," she said.

"Few farmers let my people under their roof," Michal said, his attention directed over Oisin's shoulder. "We'll plan on finding a camp before sundown. That way we'll know what's around us when we sleep."

"Are you often —"

"Get away, damn you," the Meta's shout stopped all other conversation.

Oisin turned in time to see the alien backhand a child. She fell and slid into a table full of merchants. He watched one of the merchants gently pushed the child under the table.

This morning, a man filled the role of innkeeper. He hurried over to the uproar. "I apologize, sir. What is it that the child did that offended you? I will suit the punishment to the crime."

"It did not take the dishes quietly enough. I was disturbed by the noise."

Oisin could feel the human occupants of the room holding their breath. The child had been doing her job. But no one would be foolish enough to stand between a Meta and the child, if punishment was coming.

"I will ensure the child is lashed until she realizes the importance of doing her job quietly," The innkeeper said, keeping his gaze on the floor.

"See that you do, or I shall cut off her hands." The Meta walked to the table of merchants and pushed one aside to aim a vicious kick toward the cowering child, before stamping his way out of the inn.

Oisin watched the innkeeper coax the child out from the table. The merchants offered sweets as an added incentive. Acid turned in his stomach. Lately, it had become common to watch such abuse from the Meta, but that didn't make it easy.

He turned to Serena and Michal. "We should find a way to stop this. It is not right."

"Yes," Michal whispered. "I think it's time something was done about it."

"What do you mean?" Serena's voice was low but Oisin saw the passion shine out in her eyes. Her cheeks were flushed with emotion. He felt the heat of his love for her sear though his bones.

Michal was stabbing his knife into the loaf of bread. "I think you know. I think fate has put us at loose ends at the right moment."

"Rebellion?" Oisin mouthed the word.

"What say you to that?" Michal's stare was burning into Oisin's skull. "Shall we stay and start a fight for freedom?"

Serena put her hand into the center of the table. "I say yes."

Michal covered her hand with his. "It is time."

Oisin placed his hand on top of theirs. "Freedom it is."

CHAPTER FIVE

Serena stood in the doorway of their room watching her companions tidy up. She was still reeling from the incident in the common room. The thought that they might be able to change the way the world worked, both excited and terrified her.

She spoke softly, "Are you sure we can do this?"

Michal turned toward her. "Are you saying you want to back out?"

"No." Despite the heat of the room, Serena shivered. "I just think we are going very fast. And I don't know if we can lead a rebellion. Why would someone follow us?"

"Come inside." Oisin beckoned to her. "Shut the door. We'll make sure no one listens in." He picked up the bed sheet and tied it to the top of the beams on either side of the door. "That should muffle the sound a bit."

Serena sat on the floor near the bed. "Okay, what exactly are we planning?"

Michal leaned forward. "Rebellion. It's time the Meta learned that humans won't be bullied any longer."

"That sounds great," Oisin said. "But don't we need to have some idea of what we'll replace them with?"

Michal shook his head and said, "I think we can work that out when we win. If we try to find an answer to all the questions, we'll never get started."

"I think we should have a plan. Who will join us if we're just going to kill the Meta?" Oisin's voice carried an edge that Serena hadn't heard before.

"Depends on the day, I guess," Michal said. "Today, we'd at least have fifty people."

"Don't count on it. Maybe the merchants, but no one else did anything but cower," Oisin said.

"Fine." Michal sat back against the wall. He flicked a hand toward the other two. "What do you suggest?"

"Before the Meta I think we were run by a council," Serena said. "I remember my father mentioning it once — after a few too many beers."

Michal strode toward the window. "Like the Romany. Even though the king can make major decisions, mostly it's decision by the head of each individual family."

"That sounds more or less like what we learned in history about democracy and communism." Oisin shrugged. "In theory, both have someone who is in charge, makes the big decisions so to speak. And people get a say in one way or another. Other planets still work this way apparently."

"Hush." Serena jumped up and walked to the door, holding her hand up for silence. She moved away the bedding and placed her ear against the wood.

"What?" whispered Oisin, starting to rise.

"I thought I heard..." Serena paused. "It's okay." She returned to them, "Just a couple of kids running up and down. They're gone."

Michal sighed. "So, what are we aiming for?" Serena could tell he was getting bored.

Oisin frowned. "Okay, I guess you are right. We can't pick the new government. So, how do we get started?"

"We gather followers." Michal slapped Oisin on the back.

CHAPTER SIX

"I need some air," Michal said, pulling the sheet off the door.

Oisin closed the door behind Michal and turned to Serena. "Can we talk about—"

"No, I don't want to talk about it."

"That's not fair," Oisin snapped back. "You run out on me after our betrothal ceremony. You just disappear. That hurt."

Serena dropped back onto the floor, pulling her knees to her chest, and burying her face in her skirts.

"Was it something I said?"

Serena shook her head.

"Was it something I did?" He persisted.

Serena moved her gaze to the doorway. Oisin reached out and touched her knee. She slapped his hand away.

"Was it my Father? Did he say something?" He moved to stand between her and the door. Serena returned her gaze to the ceiling.

"Look, I'll keep asking until you answer. Damn it! You agreed to the betrothal. What happened to change that? Am I such a poor catch? I know I'm not handsome, but I would have provided you a good life, a comfortable life."

Serena's eyes blazed. "It wasn't anything you did. Your father described our life to me over the betrothal dinner. It sounded safe, and boring, and desperate. I had to leave. I had to escape. I'm sorry that hurt you. I really am."

"Sorry isn't enough," Oisin muttered. "Look, we're still betrothed —"

"You are what?" Michal stood in the doorway. "You ran out on him?"

Serena spun to face Michal. "You said you were going for a walk."

"Mistress var Mallek." Michal's smile promised a merciless teasing. "I changed my mind." He turned to Oisin. "That explains why you were such a stuffed shirt yesterday."

Oisin felt his cheeks warm. "I am not sure I understand."

"It's okay. No need to be jealous. We're just friends. Aren't we Mistress var Mallek?"

She picked up the thin pillow and threw it at Michal. "Never call me that again."

Catching the pillow, Michal burst into laughter.

"Damn you all." She stamped her foot, acting like a child who didn't know how else to fight back.

"Okay, Michal, I know it seems funny but it's not." Oisin turned to the window.

"Perhaps not to you, but then, I suppose I can understand," Michal said.

Oisin turned back and shook his head, unwilling to continue discussing his love life. "Just drop it. Look, I don't think we are done with the plan."

"No," Michal agreed, his laughter fading. "How are we going to get started? We can't just walk up to people and ask if they want to overthrow the Meta."

"We need to listen to people," Serena said. "We need to take advantage of opportunities. We need to move on from here."

Oisin raised an eyebrow. "It sounds like you have been giving this some thought."

"I can think and argue at the same time." Her eyes flashed as she spoke.

"Okay, okay." Both Michal and Oisin raised their hands in mock surrender.

"It sounds good, but how do you suggest we take advantage of opportunities?" Michal asked.

"It's exactly like being at a party when you don't know many people," Serena answered. "Oisin knows how."

"Hah, you're right." Oisin remembered the etiquette lessons. "You wander from group to group; you listen to conversations. When a familiar topic comes up, you stand close to the group and slip in a comment or two."

Serena nodded. "That's right. Before you know it, you're in the conversation and introducing yourself."

"I missed a lot of education by being born Romany." Michal shrugged. "If that was me, I would have just walked up to a group of pretty girls and introduced myself."

Serena grinned. "Yes, but I'm not sure we can run a rebellion on pretty girls — or only on them. It requires some finesse in society and, it seems, in rebellion."

CHAPTER SEVEN

Kael stood at the entrance to Duke Tirash's dressing room. A bright blue rug cut the chill that rose from the white stone floor. The far wall was broken by vast windows that opened onto a view of the city; concentric circles of streets linked by passages offset from each other. An old Earth design meant to delay invaders long enough to stop them. The design anticipated a vigilant and armed populous. The society on Free Faith had neither. It had not delayed the Meta when they arrived twenty-five years ago. They had simply marched through the streets in the night

"Don't stand there staring, come here and help me." The duke stared at a pile of brightly colored shirts. "I don't know what to wear to the court judgment meeting."

Kael stepped forward, wondering how to broach the subject of the rumors he had received this morning. "Blue is certainly becoming, sire. It also adds a certain gravitas." He held two shirts for the duke to choose, one robin's egg blue, the other a deep sapphire.

"The darker one I think." The duke stood ready to be dressed. Kael helped him into the shirt, then handed him a pale cream tunic.

"I have news for you, sire." Kael held a wide belt for the duke, feeling the softness of the leather on his fingertips.

"News or gossip?" The duke raised his arms so Kael could wrap the belt around his narrow waist. "You are a perfect valet, Kael, but you do love your gossip. And we didn't develop the pigeon mail to speed the spread of gossip."

Kael ignored the slight, he was much more than just a valet, and the duke knew it. When the Meta had taken over, he stayed to ensure two things. One that the Meta would be able to rule effectively, and the other that the humans would be represented in the government. Their rule started out effective, but humans were only represented in the bureaucracy.

"News, I think." He stepped over to the sideboard and picked through a pile of earrings, selecting a large ruby stud. "It concerns an event in Whitson this morning."

"Spit it out, man. It isn't some tale told to pass the evening. If it is news, get it out while it is still at least new."

"It seems your cousin Varais was breaking his fast in the common room of an inn. He reacted badly to the servant who tried to clear the table."

"Varais does have a temper. What of it?"

"The servant was a child of five or six years. Your cousin delivered a rather strong blow and attempted to kick her before leaving."

"Ah, I suppose it didn't sit well with the other diners?" The duke admired his reflection.

Kael noted the contrast of the slightly purple skin to the deep blue color of the shirt. The duke looked like a fresh bruise.

"No, and there was a great deal of angry muttering after he left, without paying for the meal, by the way."

"So? Angry muttering does tend to let off the steam, as you might say."

"I think there might be more steam than can be let off that way." Kael tried to keep the duke's attention, but it was clear that he was preparing to leave. "I am concerned that there will be trouble soon."

"You worry far too much. Now, let's get to the judgment hall. I long to spread my wisdom. Don't fret so. I'm not worried about a little grumbling."

CHAPTER EIGHT

All day was spent trying to make money with their juggling act, but every corner of the market was guarded by an armed Meta. They eventually gave up, agreeing to live off Oisin's funds for a few days.

Now, Serena itched to start gathering followers to the rebellion. She believed people would still be angry and willing to talk about this morning's incident. "Let's get downstairs before people have forgotten about this morning. If they haven't already done so."

"Not yet," Michal said. "I need to understand this technique of inserting myself into a conversation."

He had been practicing for what felt to Serena like hours. Michal may be agile with the juggling knives, but his conversational art was awkward, and far too direct.

"It might be better if you watched us do it. We should start in the market taverns, not here. It is much easier to join conversations when people have had a few drinks," Oisin said, looking at Michal. "If you do it well, that is. The way you do it is likely to cause more fights than confidences."

Michal shrugged. "I'm not making progress practicing. I'll watch the master and mistress."

"Finally! Come on." Serena tied a shawl around her shoulders against the night chill. "I think we should start in that tavern beside the green house. It has always been busy, and a bit raucous, when we've looked in."

"And, I don't remember seeing any Meta there," Michal agreed.

CHAPTER NINE

Duke Tirash dismissed his servants for the night and sat with the final candle waiting for the castle to settle. A night bird's call came through the open window, the scent of the shrubs in the garden rising to sweeten the air of his room.

Five minutes of complete silence later, he picked up the candle and brushed aside the tapestry of fighting dogs on the wall facing his bed. He took a flat medallion from the string around his neck and rubbed it between his hands. When it was warm, he slid it between two of the stone slabs that formed the wall. The medallion vibrated as it cooled. After a few seconds the wall moved silently back two feet, then fully to the right leaving a door wide enough for the duke to slip through into the corridor.

The air in the corridor was dry and cool. The scent of dust tickling his nostrils. The duke stepped in and turned to the left, then left again. Four steps farther, a set of stairs descended, flight after flight down below the foundations of the town. At the bottom, the corridor continued for a couple of kilometers, opening into a large underground room.

The room was lit with bright poles of radiant energy. Inside, ten Meta dressed in uniforms of gray silky material stood at screens, or walked in and out of a spacecraft. The sounds were muted, and the duke's steps rang loudly enough to gain the attention of all the workers. One of the Meta approached the duke.

"Commander Tirash," he said. "It has been some time since you last visited us."

"Have you made any progress, Allorn? Are we closer to the return?"

"Some progress, finally," Allorn answered. "We have been able to create a signal to the waiting transport. One that we can keep open, rather than the sporadic connections we were able to create before."

"That is all the progress you have been able to achieve in over twenty years. When can I expect the next breakthrough? In my lifetime? That is only another two hundred years."

"Commander, I assure you this breakthrough means we are making progress. I anticipate an end to our exile soon."

The duke growled, "I prefer something more specific. Soon is not good enough. You have come perilously close to the end of my patience. We have other technicians."

"This is true, Commander, but might I remind you that none have my expertise in navigation of the command ship?"

"Do you dare to threaten me?" The duke stepped toward Allorn, fist raised.

"Not threaten, Commander." Allorn raised his hand in a calming motion. "It would be a pity to fix the problem with this shuttle, and then find ourselves lost in the vast open space without a navigator."

The duke lowered his fist and stepped back. Allorn was right. As bad as this damn planet was, it was far better than a lifetime searching the stars for home.

"Is this connection two way?"

"It is." Allorn beckoned the duke to the ramp leading into the shuttle. "That is why I believe we are close to resolving the problem."

"Show me." The duke shoved Allorn toward the command screens. "I wish to speak to the transport."

The duke waited while Allorn brought a chair and placed it before the bank of screens. The center screen was lit, unlike the four smaller screens on either side. A blue light blinked in the bottom right.

"How does the connection work?"

"The microphone is live, you simply speak, and the transport intelligence will respond."

"Transport." The duke felt homesick as he spoke in his own language, one he hadn't used for decades. "Report."

"Welcome back commander." The voice of the transport ship was harsh and tinny, designed to avoid anthropomorphism in the commanders. "It has been some time. What I can do for you today?"

"Do you know how to mend the landing shuttle?" He thought a direct approach would be best, and it was unlikely that the technicians had asked so boldly. They liked to project an aura of knowledge, and found it easier to do when no one had clear information.

"I am capable of diagnosing problems with the shuttle. I am also capable of repairing most system problems, but I am not able to repair physical damage."

"We did not crash. What to do you know about the incident?"

"I have not been briefed on the facts. I have not been able to maintain contact with the shuttle systems for a long enough period to conduct a full assessment."

"Why have you not completed an assessment, now that the link is secure?"

"I was not given permission. The last order I received was 'stay out of the damn system.'" The duke winced at the sound of his own voice coming from the speaker.

He turned to the technician. "Why have you not overridden the last command?"

"We made several attempts, but the intelligence would not respond." Allorn shrugged. "Perhaps it will respond to you?"

"Diagnose system," the duke barked into the microphone. "Assess damage, report on potential solutions."

"I require information about the occurrences since being ejected from the system," the tinny voice responded as a series of cubes developed on the screen. Each of them glowed red with a small blue line that started at the bottom corner and crawled along the plane of the cube.

"Very well." The duke motioned for something to drink, and Allorn left the room. "We landed on the planet as we expected. As you know we were scouting for additional water supplies and allowing the entire crew a few days off ship."

"I do remember what led to your leaving. I also remember giving you advice not to remove all Meta from the ship."

"Damn it." The duke pounded his fist on the console. "We had been in space too long. The wives and children needed to feel land. The crew were reporting to sickbay too often. We needed time out of the ship. This planet was not considered dangerous. Now, let us concentrate on fixing the problem and getting back to the ship."

"What happened after the landing?"

The duke assumed the intelligence could read the information in the shuttle databanks. Then again maybe the shuttle had not recorded the events. "We left a small crew with the shuttle to ensure no natives accidentally gained access or damaged it.

We returned with the location of sufficient water to restock the reserves. We intended to depart for the ship and send a scoop to take the water. The shuttle simply did not respond to instructions. We could tell it was operational, because we were able to move it along the ground. It simply would not pull in the ramp, close the door, and fly."

"Thank you, commander," the ship intelligence spoke before the duke continued. "I will concentrate on the systems diagnosis now. The connection is constant, but not strong. I estimate it will take forty-two standard hours. That is two point four days on your current planet."

Allorn placed a cup of tea on the console as the duke responded, "I can convert standard time, thank you."

"Sir," Allorn said. "Perhaps you would like to speak to the crew. They have been working so diligently that it would be kind to acknowledge them."

The duke picked up the cup and inhaled the steam. The sweet scent reminded him again of home. "This did not come from here. Where did you get it?"

"There was a small cache of truna leaves in the shuttle. We have been saving it for a celebration. Would you speak to the crew?"

The duke glanced one more time at the screen. The blue line did not seem to have moved. The intelligence on the ship would have nothing else to report until its scan was complete.

He slapped Allorn on the back. "I think the crew deserves a celebration. We will soon be gone from this damn place."

CHAPTER TEN

Michal followed Serena and Oisin through the swinging doors of the Old Man's Folly. He could hear snatches of conversation. Although, it sounded more like shouting and singing than conversation. He was sure this would end in someone getting a black eye or bloody nose.

"Stay with us; we'll do this together. We only need to convince one person, that person will have friends, and some of them will join," Serena said over her shoulder.

"What are you planning on telling people?" Michal's nerves turned his question into an accusation. It had been a long time since he was the student not the teacher. "We have no concrete plans. We have no weapons. We have no..."

Serena spun around; her face creased in anger. "If all you are going to do is gripe, then go back to the inn. We'll tell you what happened when we get back." Serena stabbed a finger into his chest. "We don't have to figure all that out yet. People who join us can help with the planning. Have some faith."

"Yes, ma'am." Michal tried not to laugh at the fury she displayed. Since Oisin had arrived, Serena had been all prickles and hot temper.

The building was squeezed between a residence and a bakery, making the room long and narrow. One side was warm, the heat from the ovens leaking through the bricks. It looked to Michal as though that was the only heat the room got; no fire burned in any of the hearths. The only light came from candles in sconces along the walls, and on each table.

They made their way to the bar where there was a small space next to the wall. The barkeeper walked the length of it wiping slops with a gray rag as he came toward them. "Beer or cider?"

"Do you have tea?" Serena asked.

"Beer or cider? This ain't a teahouse."

"Three beers." Oisin put a handful of coins on the table.

When the beer arrived, Oisin moved to stand between the bar and a table where two men huddled in conversation.

Michal watched and groaned as Oisin leaned just a bit too much to hear the conversation. "Let me." he pulled Oisin back to the bar. "I think eavesdropping is different to party etiquette."

Oisin grinned at him and leaned against the bar, raising his glass in salute.

Michal turned sideways to the table and stopped listening to the other conversations. The men had their heads bent close together. Michal started to hear individual words, then as soon as he was able to recognize the two different voices, turned his focus completely on them.

"Tomorrow, I think," the one in the green coat said.

"Late, then." The other man nodded his head slightly. "No one'll be expecting it."

"You sure no one will be hurt?" Green coat asked. "I ain't in this for hurtin people. I ain't that hard up."

The second man answered, "We go in, we take the strong box and we get out. The guard will be asleep. The drugs will make sure of that."

Michal released his focus from the table. "Do you think it

would be a good idea to tell the guards about a possible robbery?" he asked Serena.

"You are kidding." She rolled her eyes and laughed. "Not the best place to plan a robbery. Did they say who the target was?"

"No." Michal shrugged. "So, I guess that means the robbers are safe to do as they wish."

"Try another table." Oisin shifted in his seat. "How do you do that? It might be useful later."

Michal shook his head. "Listening is easy if you are close enough. The problem is no one else is close enough to us if we stay at the bar." He pointed at a group leaving. "Let's sit."

Serena took possession of the seats before anyone else noticed the vacancy. Oisin ordered a jug of beer and carried it over. "That should keep the serving girl away for a while," he said as he settled onto the wooden chair.

Serena leaned forward before speaking, "So, do we sit here pretending to talk to you while you listen to all the tables around us? Or can you show us how to do it and let us play spy?"

Michal shook his head. "We can't all listen; it would be too obvious. I can tell you how to do it, but someone still has to make it look like we're talking." He felt relief that they'd stopped trying to get him to learn social conversation.

Oisin topped up Michal's beer. "Tell us the trick, and we can take turns. If we know how to do this, then when you learn our trick of joining conversations, we can split up and cover more ground."

"Okay, it will take you some practice." Michal motioned them to lean into the table. "You have to be able to block out anything you don't need so you can concentrate on one thing."

"I think I can do that," Oisin said, "I've had practice trying to ignore a little sister."

"Yes." Serena laughed. "I've been practicing blocking you out for years."

"Okay. When you've blocked out everything else, you listen

for a word or two from the direction of the table you want to hear. When you have that, you'll start to hear more and more of that thread of conversation."

Oisin looked around. "Let me try first. See that table with the woman in the red blouse?"

"The woman with the bruise on her arm?" Michal asked, remembering seeing her when he walked to the table.

"Yes. What if that bruise came from a Meta? It might make her and her friends angry."

Michal was impressed that Oisin already had a plan. Perhaps this rebellion had a chance. "You focus. Try not to lean into their conversation. It makes it too obvious. Serena and I will chat."

"Thanks for your support," Oisin said. He propped his elbow on the table and put his head on his hand. He looked like he had been imbibing a bit too much of the cloudy, bitter beer.

"Good cover," Michal whispered before turning back to focus on Serena. "So, you are betrothed," he said with a wide grin, knowing she couldn't yell at him.

She rolled her eyes. "You are not going to drop this, are you?"

"No. But seriously, he seems like a decent guy. Why don't you want to settle down with him?"

"It's not him." She looked at Oisin who appeared to be sleeping. "He is a decent guy. We were really close friends when we were kids."

"So?"

"So, I saw the life my mother lived, and his mother. I didn't want to live like that. And, I guess, I didn't think it would happen until Oisin's father explained it to me. It's not that our mothers were beaten or treated badly. It's that they were given everything they needed except for the right to have an opinion. It seemed to me they didn't even *want* an opinion. I know this sounds like I'm an awful person, but I thought they were like domestic animals. You know, they were fed, bred, and content. I wasn't ready for content."

"Were you talking about me?" Oisin blinked and raised his head. "Oh, you were. Anything interesting?"

"No. So what did you hear?" Serena asked.

He leaned toward them again. "It seems they are angry with her lover. He has taken on another woman. The other woman gave her the bruise in a fight over the lover. Sorry, no rebellion. But it was quite easy to listen in when I got the hang of it."

"Fine." Serena sat back in her seat and crossed her arms. "My turn. I'm going for the table of merchants behind Michal."

"This is like a game," Oisin said to Michal as they covered for Serena's silence. "How do we know no one is doing the same to us?"

"Good question. I don't see anyone at the tables close enough who isn't engaged in conversation. You can't do this and talk."

"Yeah, I didn't hear anything but the conversation between the women. So, what were you talking about while I was focusing?"

Michal looked into his beer. "I can't tell you. It wouldn't be fair to Serena."

"I suppose I understand." Oisin shrugged. "Well, we must talk about something. Tell me about yourself. You are a gypsy, right? What are you doing out here on your own? I thought gypsies only traveled in families. At least they did back in my home. I used to love to visit their camps when I was a youngster."

"There aren't too many places where town people let the Romany stay, let alone allow their own children to mix with ours."

"My uncle didn't mind letting the gypsies camp on his land in the winter. It wasn't being used anyway. Your people didn't do any damage. In fact, I seem to remember they helped clear the fields for next season."

"We like to help when someone makes us welcome. I don't remember your uncle, but I have a different memory of your father. And, if we run into any of my people, you shouldn't call them gypsies. We are Romany."

"Thanks, I would hate to offend," Oisin said, no trace of sarcasm in his voice. "So why are you on your own?"

"I felt the need to see the world. I had a disagreement with the head of my family. Nothing really, in retrospect, but enough to make me feel like I should leave."

"Will you go back?"

"Probably." Michal realized he missed his family, even though he had found new friends living on his own.

"I think we have a winner," Serena said leaning forward. "Those merchants were in the Kicking Ass this morning. They were talking about the fact that the Meta shouldn't be able to get away with that. They said someone should do something about it."

CHAPTER ELEVEN

Putting aside his suspicion that it had been too fast, too easy, Michal asked, "What do we do now? This is your area of expertise."

Serena nodded toward the table. "Oisin, you should approach them. You are a merchant's son."

He nodded. "I'll do the 'didn't we meet in...' approach." He stood as though to return to the bar and caught the attention of the serving girl.

"More beer?"

"Another jug I think." He casually cast his gaze over the table of merchants. "I say, do I know you? Are you a friend of Mallek var Dorian? Girl, a jug of beer for my friends here."

"I don't know you boy," the closest merchant growled.

"How do you know var Dorian?" asked the other, shorter, man who was sitting across the table.

"He's my father." Oisin stepped toward the two men. "I'm sure I saw you at the last general merchant meeting. Do you not traffic in fine furs?"

"I do. And I was there," the second merchant responded. "I remember you now, lad. You have grown a mite since then."

"Yes, a spurt in the last semester at college. I have to admit I am relieved. I'm sorry. I also have to admit I don't know your name."

"I be Arthur var Peter. You be Oisin, if memory serves."

Oisin smiled. "It does serve you well, and your friend?"

"I am Zandor var Ivan," the first man said.

"Why don't you join us for a jug?" Oisin shifted his chair to show there was enough room. "This is Michal var Avinon and Serena den Baros. We would be honored by your presence."

"No need to lay it on so thick, boy," Zandor said, his crankiness disappearing. "I'll report to your father that you behaved well. I don't deny that spending time with a pretty lass will be an improvement over Arthur."

When the two men had settled at the table, Serena poured beer and cocked her head as if in recognition. "Are you staying at the Kicking Ass? I believe I saw you this morning."

"There were more than a few people there," Zandor muttered before taking a long drink from his cup. "Not all people either."

Oisin looked down at the table. "No. The damn Meta…"

"Careful, boy," Arthur interrupted. "You don't know who be listening. Don't bring trouble."

Michal watched the two merchants cast looks over their shoulders. The tension released from their faces as they realized no one was paying the table any attention.

"When will it be enough to take a chance," Serena hissed. "That child did nothing, just her job."

"Serena." Oisin made shushing motions. "It's done. We can't do anything about it."

Arthur chuckled. "She's a fiery one."

"She's right," Zandor said. "We don't have to put up with it. There are more of us."

Michal thought he saw how to play the game. Oisin and Serena were giving the merchants the opportunity to pick a side. If they chose Oisin's side, then Serena could be dismissed as a hot-tempered woman. If they chose her side, then Oisin could be easily persuaded over. He saw his chance to help nudge the decision. "Oisin, I didn't think you were so cautious. Where's your heart?"

"I have heart enough." Oisin sat up frowning, his face reddening. "I will happily take you outside and prove it."

"Calm down." Zandor reached over and pushed the beer jug between them. "No one is questioning anyone's manhood. It is one thing to raise fists to each other. It is another thing altogether to face an armed Meta. They have some powerful weapons."

Serena flounced back in her seat, the picture of a sullen child. "If we keep talking about why they can't be defeated, we'll never stop them. Why hasn't anyone tried?"

"Ah, you weren't born back then." Arthur looked around. "This is not the place to speak. Drink your beer and let's go back to our inn."

Michal saw the hook was sunk. He stood and swallowed the last of the beer in his mug. "Which inn would that be?"

CHAPTER TWELVE

The merchants were staying in a much more pleasant neighborhood, Oisin noticed. The stables for their inn were located outside the walls of the town. The air carried the aroma of roasting meat, and a slight trace of sweet perfume.

Entering the inn, Zandor asked for a private room and for dinner, wine, and beer to be brought. The private room was separated from the common area by a long corridor, and privacy was ensured by the presence of a pair of large men who stood at the entrance to the corridor.

The room contained a round table and eight chairs. The door was three inches of solid wood. The serving woman entered, placed the meal and drinks on the table, and then left. Zandor watched her walk away then locked and bolted the door.

"Why were you at the Kicking Ass when you could eat here?" Oisin kept the sudden suspicion out of his voice.

"Had to meet a client," Arthur said. "We will have privacy here. This room has contained more secrets than any other in town."

Oisin burned with curiosity about the night the Metas arrived.

No one would talk about it. The subject simply wasn't brought up.

"Eat." Zandor nodded to the food spread on the table. Oisin's stomach growled with the aroma of roast meat and tubers. He reached for the plates and handed them around.

"You were going to tell us what happened that night," Serena reminded them as she broke her bread into chunks. "Go ahead."

"It's not a long story," Arthur said. "I'll let Zandor tell it. He was there after all."

Zandor grunted. "I regret that trip," he said, pouring wine into a goblet. "I'd traveled to Mont Kinner to discuss trade routes. We operated as a kind of cooperative those days. The council was formed from successful merchants and high scholars. They helped make decisions keeping life simple. Not easy, mind you — simple.

"We were having problems on the road. Some young bucks were willing to steal our shipments rather than work for a living. We were supposed to discuss how best to deal with them." He paused and seemed lost in memory.

"So, when did the Meta come?" Michal prompted.

"That night. They walked into the council hall. They were all dressed in this odd material – haven't seen it since then. They carried these dull gray guns. Didn't look like metal, haven't seen those since either."

Oisin couldn't contain his impatience. "How did they take over? Did they shoot the council?"

"Nothing so simple." A muscle on Zandor's jaw jumped and he continued through clenched teeth. "It wasn't overt, it was just, something they emanated. We knew that they would slaughter us without even thinking. We didn't have any arms on us, because it was a council rule. No arms. No violence."

"You just gave up?" Oisin couldn't believe it. No wonder his father didn't talk about that night.

"No. We were shocked, but not that much. It's not like we didn't know aliens existed. That's why our people came here after all. The craziness of the old world was too much. Too many religions fighting for the position of right. Too many cultures conflicting with each other. Too many species jockeying for power."

"It's better here. Or it was," Arthur added. "The colony ship was open to any being who wanted stability, but no non-humans joined up."

"Well," Michal said, "we got stability. At least until the Metas arrived. Although I guess we still have stability. That's not always a good thing."

The others started agreeing. Zandor waited until the conversation died down before continuing, "I remember watching the council as they offered help. Asked what the Meta needed. The duke just reached out and slapped the head council member.

"They told us they would start killing, if we got in their way. They promised us peace, if we complied. They shot one of the dogs to demonstrate. The poor thing took two hours to die, all the time whining. We cooperated. They were good leaders to start with. It's only in the last few years they have gotten this bad."

Oisin felt the subtle change in the room. A little push and they would go from talking about the past to thinking about the future. "I suppose they haven't lost the weapons."

Arthur shook his head. "No, but they have lost the element of surprise. We are different people now. Less innocent, I suppose."

Zandor nodded. "And they are not protected against blades, or even a well thrown stone. They can die just as we can. It's just a matter of catching them off guard."

"How do we do that?" Oisin asked, trying to keep the momentum of the conversation going forward. "I haven't seen the guards carry weapons other than their staffs. Do they wear armor under the clothes?'

"No. They are overly complacent. They think us sheep," Michal answered. "My people have done a little... I guess you can call it reconnaissance. A few of us left the caravans one night to investigate the Meta household in Halm's town."

"I thought I saw the look of the Romany." Arthur smiled. "It will come in handy, I think. Do you know what your people found?"

Michal nodded. "Skin under the clothes, no armor, nor any hidden weapons. They carry only swords and staffs. The leaders only have those tiny ceremonial knives. If we can get close enough, we can kill."

"Is there no other way?" Serena asked.

"If there were, would you be the one to go beg the duke to share some power? Do you think they will suddenly negotiate?" Zandor's tone made Oisin's hackles rise. There was no need to speak to her like that.

She scowled. "It's not cowardice to think of avoiding bloodshed. No matter the color of that blood." Oisin smiled at her passion.

"Look," Michal said, "let's not fight. We need to be united, or we will fail. How are we going to proceed? How will we gather followers? How will we arm people? How will we coordinate the attack? What will we put in place when we defeat them? There are too many questions to waste time."

"Aye, too many questions, boy. Far too many to answer all at once." Zandor made a motion with his hand to calm Michal. "Let's start with the two important ones. How will we gather followers we can trust? And how will we coordinate them?"

"We have no friends within reach, but we can talk to people," Oisin said.

Arthur added, "We have a good idea of who of our customers will be ready to join."

"How do you know you can trust them?" Serena asked. "We can't afford to have the duke find out what's going on."

"Trust us." Zandor laughed. "We will find the people. You need to be able to whip them up into rebellion. It's something that needs a young hot-head to do. Us oldsters don't have the energy to keep it going."

"When?" Michal and Serena spoke at the same time. "When can we meet people? When can we talk to them?'

"Tomorrow night." Arthur looked at Zandor as if for confirmation. "We can get seven or eight people together by then. If they agree to join, they'll pass the word and gather more. We will need at least twenty rebels from each town. We only have to defeat the duke. The other Meta will spend too much time deliberating who their new leader will be. But the duke has the largest number of guards. Even when we succeed, we will have to consolidate our position before they settle. The Meta between us and the duke are all we have to worry about."

"You've given this some thought." Oisin wondered if his father felt like these two, or was he too cowed, or too comfortable in his life to change it.

"Since the last howls of that dog," Zandor said, slowly. "I have been waiting for this since then."

"And coordination?" Oisin asked.

"Leave that to us," Arthur said.

CHAPTER THIRTEEN

Serena paced the small room in the inn. Her fingers twitched, butterflies fought in her stomach, and she couldn't settle. "How are we going to find twenty people?" she asked. "I don't know that many people in my home town, let alone in a strange one."

Oisin shrugged. "I think we did pretty well yesterday. We found two people, and they brought in more. Why wouldn't we continue with that plan?"

Serena felt her nerves shred. "As bad as they are, we can't count on the Meta beating up children in the next town. I think we need to figure this out in more detail."

Michal laughed. "I wondered when old Serena would surface. I thought you put all that planning and controlling behind you when you left your family. I see it's back at the first sign of trouble. I've told you before, you can't control everything."

"Shut up," Serena snapped. "I just don't want to let people down." She threw up her hands then flopped on the bed. "Fine. I'll stop worrying out loud."

"Look," Michal said. "We need to get out of town tomorrow. We should wait until we get to Halm's town before worrying about what to do."

Oisin started picking up the clothes and other items that had been scattered over the small room. Serena watched as he picked up her small clothes. Blushing, Oisin tossed them to her. "Cleaning up might help to settle your nerves."

She pulled her travel bag from under the bed, getting Michal's at the same time, and passing it to him. "So, when we get there, I guess we need to make some money first. Inns won't be free, neither will food."

"I have enough to pay for a few nights lodging and food, as long as we don't go crazy," Oisin said before sniffing his clothes. "I think I can cover a laundress before we leave. My clothes could walk to Halm's Town by themselves."

Michal bristled. "It's not your responsibility to fund the rebellion. I can make my own way. I always have."

"Look." Oisin put his bag down and turned to face Michal. "You have obviously got the leadership quality. You naturally took over in the meeting. Serena brings her passion, and I have money."

"I bring more than passion," Serena snapped.

Oisin held up his hands in surrender. "I know. I know. We all bring more than one thing to this."

"What's your point?" Michal asked.

"My point is we need to take advantage of everything. Right now, that means using my money until it runs out. If we have to stop and find a way to bring in a few pennies every day, we will have neither the time nor the energy to convince people to join the rebellion."

"I don't like that he's supporting us either," Serena said. "I ran away from that very thing. But today he is right."

She watched as the internal battle between practicality and pride played itself out on Michal's face, his normally open and happy expression changing to a frown that deepened by the second. The fold between his brows tightened so much his eyebrows met.

Then, his smile broke and he relaxed. "I hear my ancestors yelling at me from beyond." He laughed. "A Romany refusing money."

The tension in the room evaporated. Serena relaxed and reminded herself of her promise not to fret.

"How do you want to proceed?" she asked. "Should we split up?"

"I think it would be better to stay together. If we split up, we need to keep checking in, that will make things too complicated," Oisin said, putting all the clothes onto a spread shawl and then folding the shawl to create a bundle. "Is this all for the laundry?"

"Yes, mother," Michal said.

Serena realized she only had the clothes she wore until the laundress returned the rest. It would be nice to have clean clothes for a change, but what if something happened and they had to leave suddenly. She would have one set of clothes and those not too clean. "Take them now. I don't think we should chance the laundry being too busy to do them later today."

After Oisin left, Serena turned to Michal. "Do you really think this can work?"

"No, but I think we have to try."

"What about Zandor and Arthur? Can we trust them?" She was losing the battle with her worry.

"I think so, but we will find out more tonight. If we don't like what happens, we can run. They know who we are, but we can change our appearance."

Oisin slipped through the door. "They said the clothes will be back in the room before dinner." He paused. "What's up? You both look like you've eaten unripe plums."

"If we need to leave quickly, what will you do?" Michal asked.

"Leave with you! I thought we were going to fight this rebellion together. What changed?"

"I'm worried we can't trust Arthur and Zandor," Serena admitted.

She saw Oisin roll his eyes, then look rueful as he saw her reaction. "Okay, you are right. This whole thing relies on our ability to trust people. If it turns out we can't trust them, I'll do whatever you both think the safest. You know you can trust *me*, right?"

"Serena says we can. That's good enough for me," Michal said.

"It's not you, Oisin," Serena said. "Unless you've changed more than I think, you would not agree to be involved unless you were willing to go the entire journey."

Michal rubbed his palms together. "Right, I say we wait until tonight. If we think we can trust these people, then we make sure we stick together. We figure out what to do after we've met them. If we don't like the way the meeting plays out, we'll leave quietly and quickly out the side gate in the early hours when the guards are asleep. We can figure out the next steps on the road."

CHAPTER FOURTEEN

The room was down a small side alley. It looked to Michal as though it was used as a stock room, but when they entered, Zandor led them to the back. Through a hidden door, was a corridor that turned left toward the city wall. It was unlit except for the candles in their hands. The floor was packed earth. The air was humid enough to raise the rank smell of damp dirt.

The corridor was long enough that it must have reached the city wall before a set of stairs descended. Oisin had not seen the step and he stumbled only catching himself at the last second. Michal turned to make sure Serena didn't repeat the act. "Don't break your neck here," he said to Oisin. "Wait for the right opportunity. Maybe you can take the damn duke with you."

"Not funny," Oisin muttered taking the next step.

Michal descended last, worried that there may be a trap. He would be able to pull Serena out if it was, but Oisin would have to take care of himself.

They descended what felt like the depth of a small house. *It must be ten or twelve feet under the cobbled streets.* The staircase turned them around and now they were headed away from the wall.

"We should be able to talk, just don't be too loud," Zandor spoke in a hushed tone.

"Where is this?" Michal asked.

"We are outside the city. Just outside," Arthur said. "It's... well, shall we say, an unofficial gate."

"A smuggler's port, you mean." Michal's estimation of the two merchants shot up. If they were able to bend the rules enough to smuggle, they would be unlikely to stall at the first sign of difficulty.

Zandor chuckled. "You have your words, we have ours. Come, the others are waiting."

"Are you sure the ceiling is safe?" Serena asked, a quaver in her voice.

"It has stood for as long as I have been alive," Zandor answered.

They reached the end of the corridor. A wooden door barred their way, and Zandor knocked a four-beat rhythm before opening it. "It is us."

Michal counted eight people in the room. The candlelight flickered illuminating a stone floor covered in a thick costly rug. There were seven unoccupied chairs. Michal suspected that this room held regular smuggler's meetings.

"So, this is why you were able to find people you could trust. You know their secrets." Oisin nodded. "I hope there is some truth to the honesty among thieves saying."

"Mind your tongue, boy," a brawny woman said from the back of the room. "We ain't thieves. We just don't see why the duke should get a piece of all our hard work. We take care of people with our profit. The duke don't do that."

Michal opened his mouth to smooth the tension, but Oisin put up his hands in surrender before he could speak. "I apologize, a poor attempt at humor. It is brave of you to come."

"So why should we listen to the son of a merchant too complacent to question the system, a lass, and a gypsy?"

Michal stepped forward. "Romany, please. And you? Why should you be part of this?"

Arthur moved between them. "Wait. Before we go ahead, we need to clear the air. Everyone here is thinking it's time for a change. No one is going to argue that. Right?"

With some grumbling, the group agreed. Arthur nodded before continuing, "I suggest we begin by saying who we are, and why we think it should change. I'll start." He waited for the group to settle. "Most of you know me as the fur merchant. What you may not know is that I was once headed for a career as a teacher. I was training in university when the Meta arrived. I had a friend who wanted to join the Meta staff after they took over. He saw it as an opportunity to secure his future. He'd not heard of the events at the council, so he went to the duke and offered his services." Arthur cleared his throat, and then continued. "They laughed at him. They beat him for his presumption and tossed him into a ditch. After that, he was very different. He was broken in his body, and in his mind. He didn't remember me, his ambitions, nothing. No matter what anyone did, he just drifted further away until he finally threw himself into the river midwinter. That has been burning in my gut for twenty-five years. The abuse must stop now."

"You know I was there," Zandor said. "I have no other reason I wish to share."

A tall thin man stood and looked at each of the others. "I am Victor. I have been a smuggler for my whole life. My father and brother were taken by the Meta. They cut off their hands and left them to bleed to death. This happened over year ago. Since then, I've been looking for a way to avenge them." He sat.

"Inka den Oram," the brawny woman said. "My sister disappeared a couple of weeks ago. I since have learned she is in the dungeon of the duke's castle. I wish to free her, and see this as the only way."

"Jane den Zandor, I have watched the pain on my father's face for all my life. I wish to be part of relieving that pain."

Zandor smiled at his daughter.

Each of the others stood and gave their name and their reasons for joining a rebellion. The stories were similar. Missing or killed loved ones, witnessed brutality, and a feeling that the last straw has finally been placed on the camel's back.

Michal stood. "I am Michal var Avinon. I am Romany. These are my friends, Serena den Baros, and Oisin var Mallek. I don't think any of us pretend to have experienced what even one of you have. Even so, we witness this evil every day. We were born into it and have nothing to compare it to, but we know it is wrong. Your stories have made it clear that the brutality is not occasional, it is pervasive, and increasing. I say we stop them. I say they must die."

No one cheered. Everyone stood, raised their fists, and then clapped Michal on the back, and shook hands with each other.

"What do we do next?" Jane asked.

"We are all new to rebellion I think," Michal said. "But I believe we all have some skill that can be turned to that cause." They were looking to him. "My people are skilled at gaining entrance and bringing confusion when needed. I think that many of you have compatriots you can bring to the rebellion. Some of you have weapons. Since you've managed to avoid taxes, I assume all of you have ways to assemble without bringing the wrong kind of attention."

"When do we attack," Inka demanded. "When can I rescue my sister?"

"We need to act quickly, but not without planning," Michal cautioned. "We won't win if we just run at the Meta. We will probably have one chance. Our advantage will be surprise, just like theirs was. If we give the Meta a chance to regroup, we won't win. We'll take the duke's castle then make a plan for the next steps. We are pretty sure other Meta families will try to take the castle back from us, but they are far enough away that we'll have time to build our defenses. Time to ensure we keep what we win."

Michal looked around him, expecting that someone, one of the older people at least, would ask who he was to order them around. All he saw were attentive faces. When his gaze met Serena's, he saw she was smiling at him. Oisin was grinning, too. Zandor stood with his hand on Jane's shoulder nodding in agreement. Arthur simply inclined his head once, as though acknowledging the position Michal had taken. In his heart, Michal wondered at how easily they followed him, a Romany, someone unwelcome in even the most swampy fields.

He continued, "If we plan to attack in three days, could you be ready? Can you bring in at least twenty others in that time? Can we gather in Mont Kinner by then without calling attention to ourselves?"

"I think, despite our high feelings tonight," the one called Alec answered, "and, despite the urgency of our mission, that three days is too soon."

"A week?" Michal asked.

"Yes," four voices answered together.

"A week is too long. My sister has already been in that dungeon longer than that," Inka pleaded.

Zandor stepped to her, placing a hand on her arm. "Inka, you know that we wish to rescue her. She is dear to all of us. But she has already been there a little more than a week. If she lives, and we all hope that is the case, then they are not treating her too badly, and she will be alive in another week."

"I would know if she were dead. I would know," Inka spoke quietly.

"If we can get information about the prisoners we will," Oisin promised. "I would not wish my own sister to spend time in the dungeon. But I do know of two lads who were taken to the dungeon at home. They were ruffians and were sentenced to a month. They came out whole and hardly changed. It is possible your sister is also treated fairly."

Inka nodded, though Michal could see it was because she wanted to believe rather than actual belief.

The candles were burning down and the room would be dark within the half hour. Michal knew Serena would not be able to stay calm if the candles died while they were underground.

"In three days, we must be in contact again. Not in this town. We must leave tomorrow, before we wear out our welcome, and Oisin's purse. Do you have such a place to meet in Halm's Town?"

"Yes," Zandor said. "Meet Jane at the fountain in the market square at four in the afternoon. She will wait there every day starting in two days to bring you to us. So, between now and then, we must find an army of like-minded people, the arms for them to fight with, and a plan."

CHAPTER FIFTEEN

The next morning, Oisin handed Michal enough coins to pay the innkeeper and waited until he took his bag, now full of clean clothes and left the room.

"Let's get going." Serena stood with her bag slung over her shoulder. "What are we waiting for?"

Oisin swallowed his nervousness. "I want to say something."

"Tell me when we're on the road." She took a step toward the door.

"I want to say this before we leave." He took her arm and guided her gently back to sit on the bed beside him. "I need to say it before something happens, before it's too late."

He watched a blush cross her cheeks, as she lowered her eyes to her lap. "Can't we wait? Please, until tonight?" Her voice shook.

"No. I won't have the courage tonight. I barely have it now."

"I think I know what you are going to say." She sat up straight as though to meet her fate head on. "I know you need to break the betrothal. I know you need to find someone, maybe you already have, to have children to continue the line—"

"Sh." Oisin patted her knee. "That's not it at all. When you left, I thought I would never feel anything but sorrow again. But you are right, I have an obligation to continue the family line. And my father is the one who would look for another candidate."

"I'm surprised he hasn't already."

Oisin smiled, thinking he heard regret in her voice that he was not still available. "Well he has paraded some pretty girls before me. I want someone who is smart as well as pretty. I want the family to improve, not just get more attractive."

"Oh. Well, I'm sure if you look hard enough, you'll find someone like that."

Oisin's nerves stole his patience. "I have."

"Oh," her voice dropped almost to a whisper. "Who?"

"You."

"But I left... I thought I was clear that I wasn't coming back. My father disowned me. I saw the notice a month after I left."

"I know. I tried to talk him into forgiving you. I hoped you would come back to your family. I wanted to see you again. Even if you didn't love me, I have loved you since we were children."

"Don't, that's not fair."

Oisin ignored her plea. "Remember when we went swimming in the Galla River? When Aron jumped in too deep? Remember how the other girls screamed and fluttered?"

"Yes, they were like chickens when the fox is around."

"Well, I think you stole my heart when I saw you swimming beside me to rescue Aron. You are brave, and beautiful, and smart."

She shook her head. "I'm not coming back to you."

He could see her thinking through the words, trying to be as gentle as possible. If she cared about his feelings, surely there was hope. "I want you to have the life you desire. I won't tie you to the nursery."

"You won't want to." Tears filled her eyes. "It will happen. It always happens."

"We'll see." Oisin let it go.

CHAPTER SIXTEEN

Kael stood in front of the window watching as the duke finished his breakfast of roast lirian and toasted bread. The sunlight shone in shafts of dust-speckled light. Kael's nose was irritated by the pollen rising from the vase of wildflowers on the broad mantel.

He spoke as the duke wiped the last of the meat juices from the plate, "Sire, I think we should speak more about the temper of the people."

"Kael, do not be such an old maid." The duke rose and strode to the windows, picking his teeth. "I have no doubt that my guards will be able to deal with anything that comes up. Let us talk of more pleasant things."

"I am sure your guards are capable of dealing with a few disgruntled young men," Kael continued. His certainty that something was wrong driving him to uncharacteristic resistance. "I am informed, that the current situation is somewhat more than that."

"I think it is time I find a bride," The duke announced, spinning to face Kael. "It is time to create an heir, time to ensure the blood line."

"An excellent idea, Sire. It will be delightful to have children in the household." He suppressed a shudder at the thought of Meta children running wild in the castle.

"Yes." The duke picked up a sheet of paper from the desk in the corner. "I started a list of likely mates last night. Come tell me your opinion of these."

Kael took the paper and saw that the duke had written the names of the eldest daughters of the three most prominent Meta families. "What is it you desire in a bride?"

"I wish someone who is both obedient and intelligent. I think these three would fit that bill. What would be good for my people?"

The duke's smile set Kael's internal alarms ringing. It was too purposefully wide. Kael didn't know what it was, but the duke was up to something.

"I am sure they would simply wish you to be pleased with the bride," Kael said.

"Come, man." The duke suddenly seemed to lose patience. "I asked you your opinion. You are usually very forthcoming in that area. Which should I invite to visit? Which one will be the most suitable for a duke's wife?"

"It would probably be a good idea to invite all of them to visit," Kael suggested, his mind racing to get back to the rebellion discussion. "That way, none of their fathers will be able to claim favoritism, and you will have an opportunity to see them in your home. See how they treat the servants. Ask them what you wish about how they run households."

"Brilliant." The duke clapped Kael on the shoulder, causing him to jerk forward. The duke was a powerful man. "Arrange for this to happen. When shall we say? A week? In fact, invite all the eligible women."

All of them? Kael swallowed his frustration. "Perhaps a little longer. We want them to be able to fully prepare, to be able to get new dresses, that sort of thing."

"I would prefer not to wait, but you are right, as usual, the ladies will wish to show their very best to me. Splendid."

Kael nodded at the duke's good cheer. "I hope it will be safe for them to travel."

The duke roared his displeasure, "Damn it, Kael. I said not to speak of this unrest."

"As you wish." Kael tried to put as much regret into his voice as possible.

The duke waved his hand in dismissal. "I will tell the guard captain to increase the watch. Now, let that subject be ended."

Kael smiled as he closed the door. The duke would think differently when there was a problem. Kael could feel trouble in the very air of the town.

CHAPTER SEVENTEEN

Michal leaned against the bar while he waited for Oreen, the innkeeper, to total the bill. As usual, the common room was full of people eating breakfast and making deals. Michal would miss the scent of good food, and the quiet murmur of conversations.

"Fifty pennies," Oreen's voice cut into his thoughts. "Covers the room and board."

Michal counted out the coin, passed it to Oreen, and added enough to cover a mug of tea. He was prepared to wait until the other two joined him, and thought a mug of tea would be good cover for a spot of eavesdropping. He quieted his thoughts and let words drift to him from the background noise.

"And she told him she wasn't that kind..."

"A hundred pennies for two yearlings..."

"They are all in an uproar at the duke's."

Michal stopped scanning and focused on the conversation that was coming from a table behind him. He glanced and saw three women gossiping over tea and porridge.

"You know my Alicia's jams are the best in the three cities," A woman in a red hat said.

"Oh, yes, they is indeed." The woman to her right nodded, the feather pinned in her gray hair bobbed with the motion. "We all say that. She's got the touch."

The third person at the table, a large woman with a sour expression on her face sighed, her entire bulk rising and falling with the depth of it. "Yes, so you tell us. I must say her work is sweet and different from anything I have tasted before."

"Well," red hat continued, "it seems that old fussbudget Kael is busy planning a party. The duke has decided it's time to wed. My Alicia got a letter yesterday from the capital."

Michal's stomach clenched. If the duke wed, it would not be as easy to end the Meta rule. Killing the duke was one thing. Killing his wife, another altogether. He looked around. If Serena and Oisin didn't come down the stairs this minute, he would have to go back up. Putting his cup down on the bar, he started to pick up his travel bag and noticed Serena talking to Oisin over her shoulder as they crossed the room. He raised his hand to beckon them over.

"Have a mug of tea before we leave." Michal threw a few more coins on the counter. "Don't look around, but I heard some news from the three graces over there." He flicked a glance at the table of women.

"What? Why can't we get going? It's a long walk to Halm's Town." Serena leaned against the bar her, actions belying the impatience in her words. Michal thought she was arguing out of habit rather than any real objection.

"Just have the tea. You'll be glad of it when we're on the road. It's chilly out there."

Oisin blew the steam from his cup and stared through it to the table. Michal could see his eyes lose focus as he concentrated on hearing the women.

"It seems the duke has decided he needs a mate," Michal murmured just loud enough for them to hear him.

Oisin snapped his attention back. "Damn, when? I'm not

going to kill a woman," he hissed. "It's the duke causing the trouble, not the other families."

"Well, that's not quite true. The Meta are all the same. It wasn't the duke in here the other day," Serena argued.

"True," Oisin said. "It's the duke who makes it acceptable, though."

Michal sighed. "Look, it's not likely that he will get married in the next week."

"Well, the prospective brides might be visiting when we attack." Oisin stubbornly kept to his argument. Michal hoped he wasn't having second thoughts.

"We'll have to make sure that doesn't happen. I think we can figure it out when we are closer to the attack." Michal picked up his bag. "Let's talk on the road."

Serena followed Michal and Oisin through to the street, blinking in the bright morning light that hit as she stepped through the door. The market was set up, but few customers wandered from cart to table to barrow. She was not used to such an open view of the market.

"Come on, don't just stand there." Michal reached for her arm and pulled her a few steps into the street.

She could see Meta guards at the entrance to every street. There were more guards than usually inhabited the center of town. They looked from side to side, as though searching for something specific. Serena ducked her head slightly. There was no use bringing attention herself with them appearing to be on high alert.

"Why do you think the guards are here?" Oisin whispered. "Do you think they are looking for us?"

"Do you think I get their orders delivered to me?" Michal hissed. "There's no reason they would be looking for us. If anyone betrayed us, the guards would have come to the room. We would be in the jailhouse, or on the way to the duke's dungeon in the capital, by now."

"So, we just keep going as usual?" Serena asked. "Just leave as though there were nothing amiss?"

"It seems as good a plan as any." Oisin shrugged then started walking toward Gate Street. "Let's get on our way. Halm's is not getting any closer."

Serena grimaced. "I feel like someone is going to stop us."

Gate Street was across the market square, but it was impossible to walk a straight line to get there. Keeping her eye on the guards, waiting for the moment when they noticed her, Serena followed the boys around and between vendors. She almost fell when she bumped into Michal's back. He had stopped at a rug vendor's table.

"What news have you?" She heard him whisper to the vendor. "Why are the guards here, brother?"

"They are on alert, brother. Seems the duke's man heard whispers of unrest. Orders came this morning for the guards to look for unusual behavior."

"I thank you, brother." Michal went to move away.

"Wait, one thing you should know, the guards have been grumbling about their orders. They would rather be in bed. Take care they do not take out their frustrations on you."

Michal grunted, then left to catch up with Oisin who had nearly reached the opening to Gate Street.

Serena ran after him, her bag bouncing against her back. "Michal, who was that man?"

"Hush." He urged her on with a wave of his arm. "A Romany. Let's get out the gate."

Oisin waited for them inside the street entrance, just out of the sight of the guards in the square. Serena looked down again as she passed the pair of armed Meta. She felt their gaze pass over her, but neither made a move.

The street was shadier than the market. The cool air bringing calm to his mind as well as relief to his body. They had made it out of the square. The gate was only two minutes away.

"I looked ahead," Oisin said as they reached him. "The guards at the gate are inspecting everyone who's leaving."

"Have they arrested anyone?" Michal asked.

"I didn't see anything like that. I was only watching for a few seconds, though."

Serena smiled. "I guess it's a good thing you got the laundry done. Is there anything in any of our bags that will cause problems?"

"Not this time." Michal put on his innocent face.

"Do we go through together?" Oisin asked.

"No point in splitting up." Michal nodded toward the gate. "Be confident. If they ask questions, just answer, but be careful you don't volunteer anything."

Oisin led the way, Serena and Michal slightly behind. The extra inspections had not created much of a line up, or it was a quiet time to be leaving. Serena tried to hear what questions were being asked. It seemed they wanted to know where people were going, what they were intending to do there, and how long they would be gone.

When it came to their turn, Michal and Oisin answered. Serena kept her head down like a good little woman.

"We are going to Halm's Town to visit her mother." Oisin jerked his head toward Serena.

"She needs to be reminded how to behave. We're asking her mother to instruct her," Michal said.

"We will probably be back in a couple of days," Oisin added.

Serena was going to make them pay for that. When the guard came to her he pulled the bag roughly away and opened it. Seeing it was full, he turned it upside down and the contents dropped on the dirt.

"It looks okay to me," the guard said, tossing the bag on top of the pile of previously clean clothes. He stepped on the hem of her blue skirt as he moved on to the next couple waiting in line.

CHAPTER EIGHTEEN

Two hours later, Oisin was regretting the decision to walk.

He had the money to spring for a wagon ride, and now he wished he had made the offer. His feet hurt. He was wearing shoes that were good for a short stroll around town, or school, but not for a hike down the town road.

The road dust had sifted into the heel of his shoe and now several places from heel toe were screaming at him to stop and rest. His pride would not let him ask. Anyway, stopping would only delay the inevitable. Perhaps when lunch time came, there would be a stream. Icing his feet might at least kill the pain.

Serena turned to look at him. "You're limping. Why didn't you say something? We should stop."

Oisin tried not to sound too eager. "I'm not used to hiking. When will we rest?"

Michal turned and looked down at Oisin's feet. "There's blood coming through your shoes. Damn it, you should have said something." He looked around and cocked his head. "Hear that? There's a brook on the other side of those trees. Come on."

Oisin felt close to fainting with relief. He followed Michal and

Serena through the shallow screen of pine trees. The temperature dropped to a more comfortable level as soon as he was out of the direct sun, not enough to ease his feet, but enough to give him hope that they would be okay. The air smelled of cool damp, of ferns, and mud. He hobbled toward the stream, sat, and carefully removed his shoes. Plunging his feet into the water with no hesitation, he sighed as the pain numbed.

"Take care," an old woman croaked. "There's fish in there what will eat your toes."

Oisin pulled his feet from the water and bent to look in the shadows of the bank. Serena and Michal's laughter joined the woman's cackle.

He lowered his feet into the water again, turning to see where the old woman was sitting. Behind her, in the shadow of the trees he saw the colorful wagon of a Romany. "Do you travel alone, mother?"

"Ah, someone who knows his manners." She pulled the pipe from her mouth and walked over; her stride more hale than Oisin's had been.

"Where is your family? Are you alone?" Michal asked as he joined the old woman at Oisin's side.

"They have gone ahead. My old horse needed rest. I'll be catching them up later."

"Where are you headed?" Serena asked.

"Eventually to Mont Kinner. The duke will need help picking a bride. A fortuneteller can be of great help."

Oisin pulled his now senseless feet from the water. "Take care as you journey close to Whitson. The guards are all on alert."

"I thank you for your advice." She looked at his feet. "I'll deal with those as payment." As she walked back to her wagon, the woman looked over her shoulder. "Well, come on. I have a pot of tea on ready and a bit of food. Youngsters like you will likely be hungry. You always are."

They followed the old woman to her small camp. When he saw the smokeless fire under a black pot, Oisin understood how she'd been able to surprise them. No smoke, no evidence. Four mugs and a teapot sat on the ground beside a folding chair and a second large, metal cauldron.

"Pour the tea, girl, then put fresh water in that pot. We'll brew a potion for the boy's feet." The old woman reached behind her for bowls and spoons. She nodded at the cauldron. "It's just an onion and mushroom stew, but you looked like you need some heartiness in you."

Serena passed each of them a mug of tea, careful not to spill the hot liquid. She emptied the rest into a slop jar as directed. Then she ran to the stream with a kettle for more water.

When Serena returned, the old woman poured a green powder into the kettle and then switched it with the black one already over the fire. Oisin passed Serena a bowl of stew, then inhaled the aroma of onion and herbs that rose from his own. "It smells wonderful, mother."

The old woman cackled again. "I'll take your complement, boy, but it's a poor meal. If you find yourselves in a Romany camp one night, tell them you know mother Viella, and you'll eat food that will make this seem like dust."

They ate in quiet while the kettle on the fire boiled. The herbs smelled earthy and complemented the sweetness of the onion stew. Oisin picked up his tea and saw leaves lurking in the bottom. He knew that meant Viella would want to do a reading. He also knew he could not avoid it. Mother Viella would be highly insulted if he tried. He closed his lips and let the tea strain through his teeth as he drank.

"Let me see those feet." Mother Viella held out her hand. Oisin laid his sore feet in her palms. "Good thing I was here. You would have been laid up for days if you didn't fix this." She shook her head and tutted, "Young uns."

She poured the contents of the kettle into a clean mug and mixed the sludge at the bottom into a paste. Taking a mound with her fingers she spread it on the worst of Oisin's sores.

"I'll give you the rest," she said. "You put it on before bed, then when you get up. The sores won't fester. Your feet will be green for a while, but they will survive."

Oisin took clean socks from his pack and gently pulled them on, before sliding his feet back into his shoes. The pain was gone. He walked gingerly to the water downstream from the wagon and rinsed the blood from his dirty socks.

When he returned to the camp, Michal had collected the stew bowls and was swirling the tea in his cup. Oisin watched him strain out the excess liquid before giving the mug a final swirl and passing it to Mother Viella.

Viella looked Michal in the eye. "You know what I see, don't you?"

He shrugged.

"Boy, your destiny will find you. You must fulfill it. The secret will eat its way out, if you don't free it."

"Take care," Michal spoke softly, but with an authority that Oisin had not heard before. "I would keep the secret a while longer. It is not for you to decide my destiny."

She placed the cup upside down on the grass. "True. But you must know it will not be forever."

"Yes." Michal turned to Serena. "You next. We don't have a lot of time, let's get on with it."

Oisin wondered what this destiny could be that turned the normally happy go lucky Michal into this curt and commanding man.

Serena had already spilled the excess liquid from her mug. She passed it to Mother Viella after the final swirl. "Are you going to find my tall handsome stranger in there?" Her voice was light and teasing.

"Yours is not a stranger," Mother Viella said before looking at the tea. "Ah, I see why you travel, child. Your heart is left behind, but you know it will eventually catch you. You can't leave your heart in a box and live your life."

Serena sat straight; a blush crossed her cheeks. Oisin wasn't sure if it was embarrassment, anger, or passion.

"My heart is here." Serena thumped her chest. "I will live my life without giving someone ownership of it, or anything else."

"You know what I speak of," Mother Viella said. "You will know how shallow your life is here when you allow your heart to speak. Until then, you will only half taste life."

"No," Serena muttered.

Oisin sipped the liquid in his cup, the bitter taste puckering his mouth. He swirled the leaves looking at the patterns they created, wondering how the old woman could find truth in the clumps and smudges. But he had seen enough Romany readings come true to put aside skepticism. He handed the cup to Mother Viella, keeping his gaze on her eyes. Willing her to say his fate was what he desired.

"You will do as you wish," she said, turning the mug to see the patterns. "It is within you to succeed at what you fear. You must decide. Only you hold your fate."

The old woman flipped the mug and placed it beside the others.

Michal stood and took all the dishes. "We must be away mother. Is there any other task you require?"

She cackled again. "No, you clean the mugs, boy. Then be on your way."

After Michal left to wash the dishes, Mother Viella grabbed Oisin's arm with unexpected strength. "I would say it to him, but he won't listen. You, boy, you must heed. These secrets will destroy you. It is vital each of you face what you fear. You must. Or at the time of crisis, you will fail."

Serena reached and unlocked the woman's grip from Oisin. "We must do as we think best, mother. I thank you for your advice."

Oisin rubbed the spot on his arm where the old woman had squeezed. There were indents in the skin. Viella had been relentless.

CHAPTER NINETEEN

The duke carried the candle in front of him, cradling the flame with his hand. The door of the chamber was closed, as usual. He knocked the pattern and opened it. Inside the technicians turned to stare at him then looked away.

That does not bode well. Bad news then.

"Status update, now!" he barked, not giving anyone time to hide. "You." He pointed to a thin man bent over some kind of device.

"Commander," the Meta spoke quietly. "I regret to say, we are not on schedule. The intelligence will provide you with the details."

"Why? And no worming out of it." He strode to the Meta. "Speak the truth. Are you incompetent?"

"No." The technician's hands trembled slightly, but his voice was steady. "The problem is in the connection. It is slow. The intelligence has been able to maintain the connection, but it does not support high data flow."

The duke slapped his hand on the counter. "Then I suppose I need to talk to the intelligence. You can stop shaking. It is not your fault."

The technician tried to stifle it, but his sigh was audible as he turned away. The duke strode to the ramp leading to the shuttle. "Allorn, where are you? I wish to be connected to the intelligence."

The head technician popped up from behind the control panel of the set of screens. "Ah, very well. It will take a few minutes. Otherwise, we risk breaking the connection. The intelligence will decide when it is safe to speak."

The duke watched Allorn as he pressed a few keys and then stepped back. "I have sent the request. Please, sit."

The duke did not relish being at the beck and call of the intelligence but knew that a hasty act now could mean starting again from the beginning, and he wanted desperately to be on the command deck of his starship, to be on the way home for new orders. "Tea," he commanded Allorn.

Five minutes after receiving the tea, the duke's thoughts were interrupted by the voice of his ship.

"Commander, it is a pleasure to speak with you again."

"Why has there been a delay?" The duke barked at the machine voice, knowing it didn't have an ego to cow, or ambition to frustrate. Barking simply felt good.

"The connection is weak. When I sense it will fail, I stop the transfer of data and then transfer my energy to support maintaining it. I prioritized the integrity of the connection above the need to complete the task quickly."

"And, your new estimate?"

"Two days."

"Have the data provided any information to this point?"

The intelligence didn't respond.

"Ship, do not ignore me."

There was still no response. "Allorn," the duke bellowed. "What has happened?"

The technician poked his head over the back of the panel again. "The connection is still active." His face was darkened as though he had been hanging upside down. "The intelligence does keep shutting down in order to maintain the connection. It has never been away for more than a few minutes."

"I am short on patience." The duke's voice carried as much threat as he could muster, knowing that no one could do anything about the delay.

"The connection is stable," the intelligence's metallic voice came over the speaker.

"Keep it that way," the duke ordered. He was feeling useless. He could not change anything; he could only snap and shout.

"To answer your question, the following information has been analyzed from the data so far. Please remember that the information is not final, it will be subject to further analysis as the data arrives from the shuttle."

"Yes, yes, carry on."

"The fuel level is sufficient to support three trips. This is subject to the number of adults and the number of children. I estimate two hundred Meta at the average weight of eight five kilos for each trip."

"There are seventy adult males, seventy-five adult females, twenty adolescents, and thirty children and babies. None of the Meta is overweight. This number will fit into the shuttle, not comfortably, but they will fit. We will make one journey off this planet."

"That meets acceptable tolerance for fuel consumption."

"What else have you learned?"

"The shuttle reports no physical damage that would be sufficient to shut the systems down."

"So, you don't know why we were stranded here?"

"That information may be available after the full data is transferred."

"Where would the optimal launch site be?"

There was no response. The duke drummed his fingers on the desktop, trying to keep his impatience under control.

Finally, the intelligence spoke, "The optimal launch site is one hundred meters north of the current location of the shuttle."

"That means we will simply have to open the doors we brought it through to hide it. I will assign guards to the chore of clearing the rubble from the outside," muttered the duke.

"There are no further conclusions."

"End of conversation." The duke could no longer sit through such intermittent communication. "Allorn," he said.

"Yes, commander."

"Would it be wise to send messages to the other families at this point?"

"If you wish my advice," Allorn said, then waited until the duke nodded before continuing. "I would not communicate with the other families until the data has been analyzed fully. If it should be that we cannot leave, then it would be cruel to raise hopes."

"Damn, I am tired of ruling these stupid humans. Did you know they came here from a technologically advanced civilization? They left to live in this backward society. Once they landed, they converted their ship to an incubator for the animals and plants they had brought. One generation later, they had four small villages. Ten generations later those villages have grown into towns. They have no ambition at all. If we had decided to come here, we would have at least one city, and a spaceport."

"It must be difficult, commander."

The duke stood and straightened his tunic. "It is not difficult. It is maddeningly boring. I will return in two days."

CHAPTER TWENTY

Serena sat on the edge of her bed. When they arrived in Halm's town, Oisin had found an inn that they could afford with three beds in the room. Oisin sat on his bed with his feet on the end of hers. The skin of his feet, dyed dark green where the blisters had broken, and light green elsewhere, looked as though they were almost healed. She shuddered to think how bad they would have been if Mother Viella had not been camping at the river.

"I think we should try to make a few more pennies while we're here," Michal said as he returned to the room. "I don't know about either of you, but I'm still not comfortable with the idea of simply living on Oisin's allowance until it runs out."

"It's not an allowance," Oisin said, bristling. "I'm not a child. It was my stipend for school."

"You say stipend, I say allowance." Michal grinned.

Oisin threw the damp cloth he was using to clean his feet at Michal's head.

"Stop it," Serena said. "Whatever you call it, it's still a good idea to have a bit of earnings."

"Yes," Oisin said, "I wasn't arguing that."

"Halm's is a good place to busk," Michal said, looking out the tiny window at the end of the room.

"The last time we were here, no one seemed to worry that we had no license. Those guards didn't seem to notice when we stopped and set up our show."

"The people are generous, too," Serena said. "We earned ten pennies for just that one show."

Oisin shrugged. "Okay, so we busk a bit."

"Not we, me and Serena. You have no talent." Michal's voice was firm. "We busk. You watch for trouble. Maybe you pass the hat at the end."

"Fine." Oisin pulled on his socks. "I would prefer not to make a fool of myself anyway."

Serena shifted on the bed. "So how do we find people here to join the rebellion?"

Oisin grabbed his shoes. "Same way, listen in to the conversations. Go from inn to inn if necessary."

"How well do you know Halm's?" Michal asked.

"I've been here a couple of times," Oisin said. "My father brought me on business."

"Do you know any of the inns? Which might be frequented by the people we want to meet? Which we should stay away from?" Michal had turned to lean against the wall, arms crossed.

"No," Oisin admitted. "My father does not frequent the common rooms of inns."

"We've been here a couple of times," Serena said. "But we stay to ourselves in the evening."

Michal pulled her out of the bed. "Halm's is friendly enough, as you saw today. But the people tire of strangers quickly. I prefer Mont Kinner and Whitson, because bigger towns don't notice strangers as much. What if we wander around today, do a bit of busking, hang around, and snoop a bit on the patrons of the inns. We can figure out where to concentrate our search for the evening."

"We can't just lurk in the corner of an inn," Serena said.

"No." Oisin tied the last lace on his shoe and stood. "But we have enough for lunch at an inn, especially if you earn it. And a beer or two between."

Serena pulled them both to the door. "Then let's get going. If I don't do something soon, I'll go mad."

After eating lunch at an inn and realizing that a place full of grandmothers gossiping about their grandchildren wasn't the best place to recruit rebels, they decided to split up and wander the town.

Michal went west, Oisin and Serena east. Michal was glad for the time alone. He was also glad the other two had stayed together so he didn't need to worry about them getting into trouble. The morning performances had raised fifteen pennies, five of which were in his pocket. They agreed to return to the fountain in good time for the meeting with Zandor's daughter, Jane.

He relished the warmth of the sun baking off the stone street. Voices of children echoing from a courtyard behind the houses raised a smile. The sounds of laughter and sudden shrieks reminded him of the children playing around the camp when he was young. He didn't regret his decision to leave the family— he had reason enough to go. Even so, he missed the comfort, the warmth of a hug from a friend. Evenings were not as good without a fire and a song.

The side alleys looked more promising than the main streets. There were small cafes with people sitting at tables, and stores with clothing and household goods for sale. It was the kind of neighborhood where people gossiped the slow times away.

He turned down the first alley on the right and wandered the length of it, peering in windows, nodding greetings to women sorting soaps and lotions, and to the men making fragrant tea. He knew from past experience, making his face familiar to the locals would be helpful if he found trouble.

The next alley curved around to the city wall. Bakeries were the predominant businesses; the smell of butter and yeast filled his nose. But there were no tables to lounge at, and no one to gossip with, since breads and pastries were generally purchased in the morning. The scents drew him into a bakery called ButterPat Breads. His stomach let him know that it had been long enough since he ate to spend a half penny on a meat-filled bun.

"Your bread looks perfect," he complimented the woman behind the counter when she handed him a bun filled with sliced ham and tomatoes. "Have you been here long?"

"My family built this bakery when the village became a town." She smiled at him and passed him a small sweet bun. "This is our new specialty, sticky buns."

When Michal dug in his pocket for more coin, she waved him away. "Tell people about it. We can always use new customers."

"This seems a nice part of town," he said before biting into the sandwich.

"No problems here," she said, while looking over his shoulder to the door. "The Meta don't come here. They send their servants."

"Are the Meta not appreciated, then?"

She blushed. "Ah, I didn't mean to suggest that. I meant that the servants and us, we know each other—fewer misunderstandings. You know what I mean?"

"I do." Michal realized she would not open up to a stranger; even though there was clearly some animosity toward the aliens. "I thank you for your kindness. I'll tell people about your sticky bun, not to worry."

Michal ate the last of the sandwich and felt better with one hand free. The gift of the sweet bun was appreciated but having both hands engaged made him nervous. Walking across the main street, he approached an alley that curved to the left sharply.

Taking a bite out of the sticky bun, and relishing the toffee taste of the filling, he entered the narrow alley, immediately feeling the temperature drop.

He heard familiar voices coming from around the corner: Romany language. As he stepped into the small side alley, he saw four of his cousins sitting at a table outside a teahouse. Before he could step back, one of them looked directly at him.

"Michal," his cousin Addren called. "Are you free to join us? Or have you left the habit of afternoon tea along with the position of heir?"

"It is good to see you. Of course, I'll share a cup with you."

The other three men at the table shifted to make room for a fifth chair. One scowled and rose as though to leave. "Sit down, Wit," Addren said. "Let's pretend he didn't leave the family. Let's just have a nice visit."

Wit frowned but obeyed. He kept his eyes on the mug in front of him. Michal understood why he was angry, but couldn't change what had happened.

"Iain, Zane." Michal nodded to his other cousins. They nodded in greeting but didn't say anything. He ordered a pot of tea and sat back. "What's the news?"

"If you cared about the news, you would be with the family," Wit muttered.

"Uten is trying to step into your place," Addren answered. "I supposed you knew that would happen."

"I suspected." Michal poured the tea. "Why didn't you try for it?"

"It's your position. I didn't want to just take it until you came back. Will you come back?"

"Maybe, but I have things to do." Michal tried to avoid the topic, but he feared that it would sit on the table like a wild pig, distracting them from what he wanted to talk about, the rebellion.

"What are these things you have to do?" Iain asked.

"Would you hear? Or are you going to keep digging at me?"

Iain shrugged, but smiled as if to soften the words. "Both. No one understands why you suddenly left. We all had arguments with the king. It means nothing. You of all of us should know him, he is your father."

"Let's clear the air," Michal said, pushing his mug to the center of the table. "It was not just an argument. I was not going to do as he wanted. I didn't leave, he disowned me."

"That's not what he says," Wit said. "He *says* you left because he wanted you to marry Lissendra."

"I will tell you the truth once," Michal spoke slowly and evenly, because he could feel his temper rising and didn't want to push his cousins away. "We were close as children. We stuck together. You would have believed me against my father then. Has that changed?"

Wit pushed the mug of tea back toward Michal. "Tell us. It's been difficult to believe you, when you haven't told us what happened. I'm not saying we believe your father, but you're not there, and he is."

"Iain, Addren, Zane, Wit." Michal turned to each of them as he said their name. "If I tell you my side, I want you to keep it to yourself."

All four cousins nodded agreement.

"I can't swear to believe you," Wit said. "But I will listen, and I will keep your secret."

"Do you remember when I went to see Loreen?" Michal asked.

Zane nodded. "The matchmaker? Yes."

"I didn't tell you who. I was nervous, and I didn't want to hear about it for the rest of my life if it went wrong."

"Well, we knew you went," Iain said. "It was expected. You were a man, and the prince of the family."

"But you didn't know who I asked about." Michal wrapped his hands around the mug. He couldn't look at them.

"We figured it was Alana," Wit said. "She was always hanging around."

"It was Lissendra." Michal swallowed as he remembered his nervous request. "When I saw her at the spring festival, she had suddenly become a woman. I thought she was the most beautiful woman I had ever seen."

"So, what did Loreen say? I assume as prince you got what you wanted," Addren said.

"It doesn't work that way. You know it's up to the woman. Same for me as you – same for the king." Michal's tone was bitter.

"So Lissendra didn't want you?" Zane asked.

"It wasn't her." Michal released the tension in his grip, realizing he would soon break the mug if he didn't.

"Loreen went to my father and told him. She didn't ask Lissendra. She went to my father, and he said no. He said to ask Alana. He wanted her as a daughter, not Lissendra."

"So, Alana said yes, I suppose," Zane said. "She always was ambitious. She would have married your father if he were available."

"Yes," Michal said. "He told Loreen to say to Lissendra she should marry Uten."

"So you left," Addren said. "Without telling us, without asking if we would come with you?"

"It was my problem. You had lives." Michal had been so angry about the betrayal he was afraid of what he would do to Loreen. He had gone back to his mother's wagon, packed his clothes in a bag, and left.

"I could have come," Addren said. "I had no ties."

"You did not have a reason. You had a life with the family."

"No more arguing," Zane said, slamming his fist on the table. "I believe you. I have missed you and am glad to take you back as a friend."

"I also believe," Addren said. "I am sorry that I believed your father." He reached across the table and grasped Michal's arm in a Romany hug.

"What can we do now to help you?" Wit asked.

"Yes," Iain said. "You look like you have questions. What do you need to know?"

Michal returned the friendly slaps and smiles. He realized how much he missed knowing he had friends. "I am doing something I never thought I would."

"What," Iain said. "Are you getting a job?"

Michal waited for the laughter to die down, and then leaned in. "Worse. I am recruiting people to join a rebellion against the duke."

"In the name of—" Zane said.

"Idiot," Iain said.

"So, what do you need from us? We don't fight with the *Gadje*."

"No. I don't want you to fight. I want you safe. The world will need handsome Romany studs when this is over."

They all laughed again. "What do you need?"

"How long have you been in town?"

"A week," Iain answered. "A bloody week too long. Three wagons needed replacement metalwork. We're waiting for the blacksmith to fashion the pieces, and trying to avoid getting thrown into jail for the offense of being Romany."

"It seems lucky that you have been successful," Michal murmured, smiling. He looked around the alley. There was still no one else in the sight. "What have you heard? We need to find people who are complaining about the Meta, who might be willing to fight."

"Stay out of it," Iain said. "What have the *Gadje* done for you? Why should you put yourself on the line for them?"

"Who is we?" Zane asked.

"I met a girl who ran from her father," Michal said. "And, I just found out, a betrothal she didn't want."

"Fate," Addren said. "Are you forming an army of the jilted?"

Michal laughed. "It gets even better. We ran into her betrothed yesterday, and he's joined us."

Iain spilled a few drops of tea on the table then drew his finger through and across the liquid. He pointed at the mark. "Fate, in truth. It rings like an omen in my ears."

"We'll have to wait until it's over to see if it's fate," Michal answered. "Tell me if you have heard people complain. Are there inns we should visit?"

"The Orange Gnome is usually full of people griping about something, but I'm not sure that they are the type you need," Wit said. "They are usually grousing about their neighbors or their bosses— human bosses."

"No," Zane said. "You want the Blind Mouse." He turned to Addren. "Remember yesterday. That Meta bastard came in. He didn't do anything, but everyone stopped talking while he was there, like they were afraid to say anything in his hearing."

"Yes, I remember," Addren spat out the words. "As soon as he left, they started talking about him, and his apparent enjoyment of beating his servants. The bastard has killed four this year."

"That sounds like the right kind of place," Michal said. "We will try there tonight. Will you come? I would buy you a meal."

"We stay outside the walls at night," Iain said. "Halm's is not a friendly place for a Romany at night. The *Gadje* think we are going to steal their money, jewels, and daughters."

"And would they be completely wrong?" Michal slapped Iain on the arm.

He laughed. "Perhaps not. There are some pretty girls in this town."

"Thank you," Michal said. He paused, unsure if he could ask the questions close to his heart. "Is my mother well?"

"She was when we saw her last week. Would you like us to tell her we saw you?" Wit asked.

"If you think she would like to know. It would make my heart easy to know she didn't mourn me." Michal felt a weight rise off his shoulders.

"She will know tomorrow night. We leave mid-morning," Wit promised.

"Do you want to know about anyone else?" Addren asked.

"Lissendra? Is she well? Has she married?" Michal held his breath for the answer.

"No," Wit said. "She has refused to marry anyone. It would be a pity if she died a virgin."

CHAPTER TWENTY-ONE

Oisin and Serena walked toward the colleges and book vendors. He watched as she bent to help a mother pick up a toy that her toddler dropped. The mother smiled in gratitude as the child's tears were diverted.

"Do you know anyone who lives here?" she asked when she returned to his side. "Didn't Matt come from here? He lived with his aunt when we were in school together."

"Matt came to the academy with me, but he left school six months ago." Oisin reached out and took her hand. To his surprise, she didn't fight it, just held his fingers loosely in her own. "His father passed suddenly one night. The doctor said it was his heart."

"Oh no, Soren was such a kind man. He always had a candy and a smile for us."

"Yes." Oisin remembered the crowd at the funeral and that he had looked in vain for Serena to arrive. "He will be missed. Matt is working long hours to catch up on the knowledge he needs to run the business."

"He'll do well." Serena gave Oisin's hand a squeeze. "I'm sure of it."

"Do you remember Millicent den Blake? She was that little girl who sat in the corner of the class: mousy brown hair, quick grin, a bit hot tempered."

"Yes, is she married?"

Oisin laughed. "She's too busy. When Matt went to school, she apprenticed with Soren. Her father couldn't afford college."

"But if she got apprenticed, she didn't need college." Serena slowed to look in the window of a bookseller.

"True enough. It turns out she's the one training Matt. I hear there's a bit of romance going on between them."

"Matt?" Serena chuckled. "I can't believe he'll settle down. Didn't he court almost every girl in town?"

"Not quite." Oisin pulled her away from the window. "He didn't court you."

"I have to admit I was kind of insulted he never tried."

"I told him I would beat him within an inch of his life if he broke your heart. Hard to believe, but I think I scared him."

Serena moved closer to Oisin. "My knight in shining armor." She grinned and gave a laugh that made Oisin think of their childhood, when they didn't have to worry about anything.

"We're supposed to be scouting for allies," he whispered in her ear.

A pair of Meta youth rounded the corner of an alley. They were grinning, their widely spaced teeth showing. One wiped his hands on the side of his leather coat. Oisin pulled Serena to the window of an apothecary. They watched the Meta in the reflection of the glass. When the aliens passed out of sight, they casually turned from the window and strolled toward the alley. Staying on the opposite side of the street from where the Meta had exited.

"Stand here," Serena said, positioning herself so that she could look into the shaded entrance of the alley. Oisin watched her squint to try to penetrate the darkness. "I think there is something there. Something piled up on the side of the wall."

Oisin moved to stand beside her. He could see a pile of clothes lying a foot or two inside the alley. "I'll go, you wait here."

"No. We both go."

"You need to keep your eyes out in case those two come back, or some guards. You'll need to let me know."

She looked as though she was going to argue, then sighed and stepped back to keep watch.

Oisin strolled across the wide stone street. The alleyway was one of the larger ones that bisected the main street. He glanced over his shoulder to ensure no one was paying him any special attention — or too obviously not paying him attention.

Slipping into the shadows, Oisin stepped directly to the pile of clothes. The way the Meta had acted, they'd been up to something. It was unusual for them to hide their activity, though. Meta didn't often worry about being caught behaving badly.

When he was only a step away, something in the pile whimpered. Oisin drew a breath, it wasn't human. He gently picked at the top rags, ready to dodge if attacked. As he removed layers, the cloths became damp and sticky, blood soaking in through the dirt.

Under the final layer was a dog. Oisin had anticipated it, but the state of the animal still turned his stomach. The Meta had beaten the animal until it was a mass of blood, with limbs bent at the wrong angle. The dog looked up at Oisin, whimpered again, and then went still.

He used the cloths to bind the dog's body. He didn't want a child to come across it. His own tears fell, his sadness mixed with fury. He knew he would have to tell Serena, but she didn't need to see it. He stood and picked up the bundle before returning to her.

"Oisin," she said, quietly. "What is it? You look like you are going to be sick."

He pulled back as she reached for the rags. "Don't. They killed a dog. You don't want to see it."

Serena looked at the bundle and paled. "Why would they do that?"

"Because they could." His words were forced through the sobs in his throat. "Let's just get it to the refuse pile. I can smell one farther down."

"It's like they're provoking us." She took his arm and led him forward. "I don't remember them being like this. They were never kind, but rarely cruel. Something is happening that we don't know about."

Grunting his agreement, Oisin walked to the wagon and placed the dog's shrouded body down one side. The wagon was almost full. It wouldn't be long until the street cleaners arrived with their horses to transport the wagon to the dump before returning it to be filled tomorrow.

"Wash your hands." Serena pointed to the small tap protruding from a wall, placed there so people could wash after throwing out garbage. "We need tea, or perhaps something stronger?"

Oisin raised a smile. A beer would go down well right now. It wouldn't wash the memory of the battered animal from his mind, but it would refresh his body. They entered a small square that was lined with teashops and taverns. With the three city colleges only two streets away, the tables in this square would be brimming with students and professors in a few hours. Now, they were mostly empty. Only one tavern was popular. Four of the tables were filled with people.

Oisin nodded to the two spare tables. "There," he said. "Let's hear what's going on. Even if we don't find some people to talk to, I would enjoy listening to good conversation."

They sat at a table on the edge of the arrangement. The serving boy took their order and returned promptly with a jug of beer and a plate of spiced nuts.

Serena poured the beer and sat back. "I don't know why, but I feel exhausted. Is it the heat?"

"It's because you always pour your energy into everything,"

Oisin said. "Even when we were really little, you could wear yourself out just thinking about a prank."

"Are you saying I have no stamina?" She poked him in the side.

"No, just that you don't ration your energy." Oisin dodged another finger between the ribs. "Fine, calm down. You are perfect."

She smiled and sunshine came into his life.

"Enough sweet talk." She wagged her finger at him. "Time is passing. We need to be at the fountain soon."

"Okay." He leaned back in his chair. "I think it will be odd for us to sit here facing each other but not talking."

"I've thought of that." Serena shifted her chair to sit next to him. She reached for his hand and took it. "Now, we can gaze into each other's eyes."

Oisin nodded and lifted her hand to his lips. If all he could get was pretending to be her lover, then he would take it. His life seemed to be spent dancing to her rules. He knew it was not manly, but his heart didn't care. He would have to leave her eventually. He didn't hold out much hope Serena would change her mind.

He concentrated on blocking all sounds from his attention. The distant bark of a dog brought a flash of the sad creature they had disposed of. A shiver of metal wind chimes replaced the image with one of home. A child's laugh, and an old man's cough, then silence. Oisin turned his attention to seeking the voices at the tables around them.

"He's a bastard," a young voice declared. "His assignments are impossible."

Oisin remembered complaining about his teachers in just the same tone. He shifted his attention to the older men at the next table.

"It is an interesting problem," one of them said. "Should the duke die before marrying, then one of the other families will take over. I believe it will be the Halm's town baron. If he marries, but has no issue..."

Oisin tightened his focus. If not recruits, there may be news.

"Has a Meta ever died?" a younger voice asked. "It's all fine talking about succession, but if the duke never dies, then there's no point."

"There was that guard who fell from the wall. He broke his neck," the first voice said.

"I meant died naturally," the younger said, a hint of exasperation in his tone.

"Not that I remember," a third voice said. "Regardless, the duke is shopping for a bride."

"Maybe a female will soften him," the first said. "I heard the prospects are set to arrive in a week."

"We could have a duchess in two weeks," the younger said, his voice flat.

Oisin brought his focus back to Serena, and leaned forward. "They are discussing it intellectually, but I think we need to consider moving faster. The duke is hurrying his plans to wed."

"We'll talk about it with the others," she said, drinking the last of her beer and motioning Oisin to do the same. "I don't think we should be rash. It's important we don't make mistakes. This marriage could just be rumor."

Oisin thought it unlikely that someone would dare run out on the duke the way Serena ran out on him.

CHAPTER TWENTY-TWO

Michal watched Serena scanning the crowd the way he had taught her. Making sure no one followed her, keeping her eye on the children who ran in groups. Most were just playing, but there were a few pick pockets running with them. She had proven a fast student, despite his misgivings. When he had found her sitting on the side of the road, shoes off, feet bleeding, he had felt sorry for her. He hadn't intended to get a partner, but she was nothing if not persistent. She had followed him, thanking him for the salve, asking him questions, and generally worming her way into his life until he gave in and taught her the Romany way.

Oisin would have a battle on his hands. Changing her mind on anything was difficult, on something as big as her entire future, maybe impossible.

The crowd flowed like a stately dance. The background noise of deals being made, wares being called, punctuated by the occasional laugh or shout. The fountain sat in the middle of the market, and he could see people resting on the edge, or trailing fingers in the cool water. Jane was nowhere to be seen, but they still had about ten minutes to the rendezvous time.

Oisin and Serena scanned the area around the fountain until

Michal caught Oisin's eye. He tapped Serena on her shoulder and nodded quickly with his chin. She shifted direction, veering around the front of a stall rather than the back.

"Any luck?" Serena asked when she was close.

"Some, but not what we were expecting." Michal kept his gaze on the fountain while he spoke. "I have a place to go tomorrow. We will likely find some recruits there. You?"

Serena sighed. "Just more brutality, and some gossip. I don't think the gossip is important..."

Oisin cut her off. "I think it is. Let's just tell the story, no opinion, so Michal can decide if we tell the others."

"It's too late for that," Serena snapped. "Since we just told him what we think."

Oisin sighed. "Fine. Should I tell him?"

"Since you are the one who thinks it's important." She nudged him and Michal saw a smile pull at her lips. "I might leave out something, and then you'll have to tell it anyway."

"What is the gossip?" Michal turned back to the fountain. This time he saw a familiar, pretty, girl approach and sit on the edge. Jane had made an effort to disguise herself. Her clothes were cut to accentuate her figure, not hide it like at the last meeting. "Tell it now, and fast, we need to meet Jane."

Oisin related the conversation he had overheard, finishing with "I think it means we need to move more urgently."

"Okay, come on." Michal led them to the fountain.

"That's it?" Oisin asked.

"I don't know if it's important, or not. I think we should tell Jane, and let the others know. Let's get their thoughts."

Jane looked up and smiled at the three approaching her. Michal bent to whisper in her ear, hoping watchers would think he was responding to the flirt rather than talking. "We should go somewhere more private."

Jane giggled and gave him a coy push. "Oh, I think we should stay here, sir. I don't trust you to be a gentleman, if we go elsewhere."

Serena pulled Oisin away from Jane, as though she was a jealous wife. She sat next to the girl and made Oisin sit on the other side of her.

"People are listening," Michal whispered again, then took her hand and kissed it.

"As you well know," Jane whispered back, "people listen only to their own interests."

"True," Michal said, flashing a warm smile.

"We have been successful in two ways," Jane murmured coquettishly. "We have found our army. We have thirty men and women eager to join us."

Michal watched a couple stroll by. They were giggling together, not paying attention to anyone outside their tight circle. He used the opportunity to see who might be showing more than casual interest. A woman standing across the market glared at them, and then looked away.

"We are being watched," he said quietly to Oisin and Serena. "Why don't you two walk around? Keep your eyes open for trouble."

They stood and strolled toward a leather goods vendor.

Michal turned to face Jane. "Where are these people from? How do you know they can be trusted?"

"Most are from our trading partners. We've known them long enough to be sure they are trustworthy."

"And the others? We cannot have this rebellion built on the backs of merchants. Whatever replaces the duke's rule needs to represent all interests."

"My father has connections throughout human society. We have gathered four doctors, two lawyers, a few students, and some builders in that thirty. Arthur is speaking to other trades people he knows."

"Good."

"I find this suspicious. It seems to be moving so fast and easily," Jane said.

"It is." Michal nodded and reached to play with Jane's hair. "My grandmother used to say if the time is wrong, the sun will struggle to cross the sky in a day, if it is right, don't blink, the sun will be gone."

"I suppose." She pushed his hand away and giggled for the benefit of anyone who might be watching.

"We'll keep our eyes and ears open, even so. Your other news?" Michal asked.

"We have found a cache of arms." She looked down at her lap. "Inka knew of an old smuggler's cave. She said it hadn't been used since her father's time. She found swords packed in crates. The swords are still sharp."

"It's encouraging to know we will have the means to fight." Michal scanned the crowd again. Two Meta had entered the square. They turned and started walking clockwise. He watched people subtly shift to clear a path. "I hope they don't have easy access to their guns. It won't be an even match with swords, but I think we have a chance."

"A chance is all we need." Jane moved away from Michal. "I think it's time we parted. If anyone is watching they will expect us to leave, together or apart, by now. We will meet again in four days. Mont Kinner. We will find you."

"As much as I would like to leave together, I think it's best we do so apart." Michal leaned forward to kiss her cheek.

"I am not that kind of girl," she shouted and slapped his face.

Michal sat back and grinned. Before he could speak, Jane jumped up and flounced away.

"I could have told you she were a flirt, boy," a woman running a honey stall cackled. "You wasted your time."

"That's true, mother," he called back as he left. "But time is the only thing I have to waste."

CHAPTER TWENTY-THREE

When Michal joined her in the common room of their inn, Serena pointed to the stairs. "You can go to the room to clean up. The water will still be warm. Be quick and I'll order dinner when Oisin comes down."

Michal shook his head, but she was used to how he often did that when she ordered him around, before he did as she'd asked. She smiled as he went to the stairs, and then saw Oisin come down.

"Hang on," Oisin said as he passed her. He went to the bar and said something to the landlady who nodded then passed him a jug of beer and a handful of cutlery before talking to a scullery maid.

"The water was cold already," Oisin said as he put the beer and cutlery on the table. "We can afford a bucket of hot for him."

"You're a good man." Serena felt a tug at her heart when she said the words. Her departure was not about how good or bad Oisin was. It was about how much she would have to give up if she married him.

"What should we order for dinner?" Oisin asked. "If we are going to be planning, we need energy."

"I suppose we could think of it as brain food," she said. "But you're right. We can't afford to get drunk. Tea after this beer is probably a good idea. What do you want to eat?"

"We have a choice for dinner? I guess this place was a great idea. What are the choices?"

Serena repeated what the serving girl had said. "They have roast pig, with roasted vegetables, or sliced meat, breads, raw vegetables, and chutney."

"Hmm, I'm feeling a bit over full of roast. Let's order the sliced meats."

"Fruit compote and custard, or apple and cheese pie."

"Both." Oisin sipped his beer. "We can share."

"We can wait until Michal comes down," Serena said. "Do you see anyone here who looks like they will want to join us?"

They quietly discussed the other patrons for a half hour until Oisin looked up and said, "Ah, here's our fearless leader."

"I feel much better," Michal said, slicking back his wet, black hair. "Thank you Oisin. That hot water was very welcome."

The serving girl came to take their order. When she left, Serena leaned forward. "What did Jane say?"

Michal cocked his head. "Not here."

Serena's gaze followed and she saw that he was pointing toward the dark corner of the room across from her. She glanced and saw a table where four men sat unspeaking. She could see, even from this distance, that they were scanning the room. The men had positioned their chairs so they faced outward, each one swept a third of the room with their scrutiny. They didn't look like hired strong men, there to keep the peace. There was something sinister about them.

"So, we can't talk here." Serena said. "Then we need to eat quickly and move on."

The food arrived and they reached to take meat and bread for sandwiches. The dessert came at the same time. Michal took a fork full of pie after taking a few mouthfuls of his sandwich. "Good pie." He mumbled.

Oisin put a dollop of custard on his plate and topped it with some of the deep red compote. "I don't want to stuff this in, it's too good. Maybe we can talk here if we are careful. So, what did your friend say?"

"That the party guests will fill the hall," Michal answered.

"Is that all?" Serena asked as she picked at the food on her plate. "Did you tell her our news?"

"It isn't all," he responded. "She said they will also have all the tools they need. Are you going to eat that?" Michal pointed at her plate.

"No, I'm not very hungry." She felt sick with frustration.

"It's okay," Oisin said.

"That's not very comforting." She pushed her plate to the center of the table and rose. "Is there anything else you can tell us, or should we just go outside? I think it's getting stuffy in here."

"Sit," Oisin ordered, putting his hand on her arm to push her back to the chair. "Be quiet. Look."

Serena followed his glance. A Meta female was pushing her way past the tables. The sound of chairs scraping along the floor to clear her path echoed off the walls. The low hum of conversation cut off. It was unusual to see a Meta female out alone. They traveled with human servants, and in groups of two or three. This female was dressed as a guard, not in a flowing gown. Her arms were bare, and heavily muscled, her expression grim.

Everyone in the room was watching the Meta's progress. She didn't seem to care. Her path was aimed at the table of sullen men. They straightened up in their seats. One of them started to stand, then dropped back down as she pushed the table toward him.

"Why are you here?" she barked out. "You were hired to guard at the silk merchant's."

"We were ordered here," the man said. Serena strained her ears to catch the words.

"I am in charge of you. Who gave this order?"

"Message came from the capital." The man seemed to want to avoid answering with details. Serena thought he was smart.

The Meta woman didn't seem to care that everyone could hear them. "Who did this message come from? Do not make me ask again. You will regret it."

"The duke's man, Kael var Radborne, his seal was on the message," a second man answered. "It said we were to spend time in the main inns. Watching to see if anything odd was going on."

"What odd things."

"He didn't say," the second man said. "Just to keep our eyes out."

"You will keep your eyes out at the silk merchant's. I do not care what that damn Kael wishes. The duke was clear that the silk merchant was our priority. He has promised his bride the best in beautiful clothes"

The three men jerked up so quickly that one chair hit the floor. "Yes, ma'am." They shouted in unison. The Meta woman followed them to the door.

It took thirty seconds for the conversation to restart when the door closed behind the group. Mostly laughter at the discomfort of the three men, other ribald comments about the Meta woman followed. Serena felt herself let go a breath she hadn't realized she was holding.

"I guess everything happens for a reason," Michal said. "Now they are off the streets, and probably won't be back until the duke himself orders them."

"Let's hope that doesn't happen," Serena said. "I would still like to go for a walk. I'm feeling itchy with the tension in here."

Oisin stuffed the last of the meat into his mouth and rose. Michal nodded at her and stood. "When we go out tomorrow looking for recruits, we should make sure those three are in place at the silk merchant's."

· · ·

Michal took Serena's arm and led them toward a small park he had seen during his walk that afternoon. "It should be warm enough to walk under the trees," he said. "Just keep your voices low."

"So where are we going tomorrow? And why can't we go tonight?" Serena asked him. He knew that she hadn't let go of her impatience.

"It's an inn, the farmers hang out there. You know they won't be back until tomorrow when they can stay overnight. A few beers should loosen them up for talking."

"How did you learn about them?" Oisin asked as he moved to Serena's other side.

"I ran into a few old friends. They have been in town for a week, and they noticed who was grumbling. When I asked them, they suggested that inn."

"Old friends," Serena said. "I thought you didn't speak to anyone from your past."

Michal breathed the cool pine-scented evening air, feeling glad to be outside. "It isn't that. Well, I guess it is. I don't run into them too often. And, when I do, they don't always want to talk to me."

Oisin stepped over the barrier at the entrance to the park. "How do you know you can trust them? I mean, if your people don't talk to you, or are so angry they don't want to see you, how do you know they won't betray you?"

"Not everyone from the tribe is ready to assume I was in the wrong." Michal tried not to go into details, but it was getting harder. He didn't think Oisin was prying, but the casual questions bothered him nonetheless. "I didn't do something I was ordered to do, and so left. There was nothing I could say before I went."

"It's sad." Serena gave Michal's arm a sympathetic squeeze, "I know how it feels."

"What I did was best for the family," Michal said, hoping the firmness in his tone would stop the sympathy, and the questions.

"I guess that's true about the three of us." Oisin stopped as a night bird sang for its mate. "The leaving, I mean. I didn't mean to leave, but I did. Now I'm on a path that could lead to a place I can't return from. I might die before I see my father and mother again."

"Don't think like that," Serena snapped.

Michal spat on the left side of the path and crossed his fingers. "Don't bring a fate you don't want."

"Sorry." Oisin held up his hands. "I didn't think it was that important. I won't do it again."

"Let's talk about something else. Something we can do," Serena said. A small skittering animal caught her eye as it dove into the bushes. The night bird whistled again and this time an answering croak came from his mate. "There's no one here but us," she said. "We wouldn't be disturbing the animals if someone else was in the park."

Michal looked around trying to find a place to sit that was far enough from cover to ensure they weren't suddenly in the midst of a party, or worse a troop of guards. He steered Serena to a wide swath of grass, noticing Oisin sticking to her side.

"Tell us what you meant by that cryptic conversation in the inn," Oisin said. "I think you said the others have found more rebels, and that there are weapons for us."

"Yes." Michal heard a fish jump in the lake. "They found thirty people who will join us, people who they trust. And a cache of swords that no one knew about."

Oisin shook his head. "It's not quite enough, but if we find ten more people that should be plenty to take the duke and hold the castle."

"We are supposed to meet them in Mont Kinner in four days," Michal finished.

"Will that be time enough?" Oisin plucked out blades of grass. "It will take two days to get there unless we catch a ride in a wagon. If we get some recruits tomorrow, we will only have one day to organize them."

"It will have to be," Serena said. "We need to launch the attack before the duke brings his potential brides to visit. We can only just manage the current complement of guards. If the other two households bring their own guards, we are lost."

"I worry that we are moving too quickly," Michal said. He waved off her objections. "I know we have no choice, but it is critical that we don't make mistakes. Rushing means we will make more than we would if we took our time. I'm just saying we need to be more careful."

"Fine."

Serena let go of the subject too easily for Michal's comfort. She would come back to it, he was sure. "If we bring in farmers, that's farmers and merchants and us. The farmers won't want to rule. They will want to go back to their farms as soon as they can. Will we be happy with merchants leading the towns?"

"It's not just merchants," Michal reminded her. "We have smugglers too."

"Oh, they will make much better leaders, I'm sure." Oisin punched Michal's arm.

Serena laughed. "I can see it now. No taxes, no schools, no garbage removal. Until they realize how boring their lives are with no rules to break."

"What about the Romany?" Oisin, serious again, asked. "Will they join?"

"No," Michal said, his voice firm. "They, we I mean, don't get involved in *Gadje* matters. The duke doesn't rule the Romany. He might think he does, but he doesn't. They will probably give us information, some, like Mother Viella will give aid. But, no, they won't join the fight."

"So, smugglers, merchants, farmers, and us? What will they call this rebellion in the history books? The dirt and money fight?" Oisin's voice was hard. "We need everyone involved. If we don't have scholars, lawyers, doctors, shopkeepers, butchers involved we won't have everyone on side when we win."

"The others have brought in more than merchants and smugglers," Michal said. "They had clients and friends. Don't fret, we have good representation. It's not the breadth of the rebellion's forces I'm worried about, it's the fighting ability."

CHAPTER TWENTY-FOUR

Oisin was tidying his bedclothes. "Serena, when we were in the park. When we were talking about maybe not getting home."

"You were not going to say that kind of thing." Serena could tell by the softness and hesitancy in his voice that Oisin wanted to talk about their relationship again. Damn Michal for staying downstairs and giving him an opening.

"No." Oisin turned to face her. "I mean...yes, I know I'm not supposed to jinx us. I didn't mean that. I meant that it made me think."

"Thinking isn't necessarily a good thing when you are planning what we are planning," she said, trying to delay the obvious topic long enough for Michal to join them.

"Well, I don't think that's really true. If we don't think, we'll be sure to lose."

"There you go again."

Oisin sighed and touched her arm, stopping her from shaking out her blanket for the tenth time. "Don't be that way. Let me talk. I need to say this. I need to deal with this."

Serena realized Oisin was determined to speak. She would have to let him, and then try not to hurt him when she told him, again, that she wouldn't marry him. She nodded and sat on the bed.

"It's not easy for me to talk about this," he started. "I've already told you that I love you, and don't want anyone else."

"I know, please..."

"Let me say this." He patted her knee. "When we were talking in the park, I realized I wasn't being fair to my family. Like Michal said, it's best for the family. For me that means I need to marry and provide my parents with grandchildren."

Serena swallowed tears that threatened to choke her. The thought of Oisin marrying anyone else hurt, but not as much as the fear of being trapped. She had been right about him. Here he was, talking about duty to his family.

"I can't marry anyone else if we are still betrothed," he said, then waited for her to respond.

"You want me to formally release you from the betrothal?" she whispered.

"Yes. But not yet, not until we win." He smiled at her. "When we win, we can find a lawyer and have him sign off the papers. Not until then."

Serena ached with the finality of his request. It wasn't fair to him, she knew, to keep him tied to her when she wasn't willing to move forward. It still hurt because she still loved him.

"If that is what you want," she said. "Then of course I will. As soon as we win. I promise."

"Thank you." Oisin turned back to his bed and tunneled beneath the covers.

Serena closed her eyes, but her thoughts kept sleep away. What was she so hurt about? Until Oisin had come back into her life, she had barely given him a second thought. It wasn't like her to be such a dog in a manger. She would have to grow up and be gracious — when the fight was over. It would be better all round for Oisin to marry some good woman who would keep house and willingly give him a child every year. Yes, better all round.

CHAPTER TWENTY-FIVE

Kael handed the duke his hunting jacket. The duke had decided that morning to form a hunting party to capture a lirian boar for the bride's feast. He was a good hunter, but he was supposed to be meeting with his advisers that evening, not hunting.

"Don't look at me that way Kael. You'll sour the wine in my gut."

"We should discuss the arrangements for the prospective bride candidates' arrival." Kael helped the duke straighten his jacket. "There are many details we need to finalize before we can start getting ready."

"I don't want to get into the details. Sod it all to hell, Kael, I have you for the details." The duke's tone had a familiar petulance that Kael knew how to handle.

"Yes, you do have me for that. Do you wish to set a specific date for the arrival? That way I can get the staff prepared, and the cook can stock up on the appropriate sweets."

"Very well." The duke shrugged. "Have I sent the invitations yet?"

"No, you asked me to wait for a few days. But that would be a good step to take."

"Yes, the ladies will want to get prepared to show me their best frippery. Very well, send the invitations today, and we'll have a feast in, oh shall we say, a week?"

"Seven days should allow the ladies to prepare." Kael knew that gossip had already spread the news. He had seen to that detail. So, dresses had been ordered, and jewelry was being designed. "I will ensure that the brides and their parties will have sufficient rooms."

"Good. Now, let me go to the hounds." The duke picked up a whip from the table.

"Shall we arrange for a hunt while the brides are here?" Kael knew full well that most Meta women would not hunt, but their men would enjoy it. Having the men out of the castle for a few hours would make it easier on the staff. Meta were not kind to staff.

"Splendid idea." The duke snapped the handle of the whip against his leg. "Now, have you gathered sufficient information to get about the arrangements, or are you going to keep me here all day."

"Thank you, sire. I think we can get started. I will provide you with an update tomorrow."

Kael watched the duke leave the room. He thought about adding a question about the rebellion but decided against it. The duke would tell him there was no proof and order him, again, to leave the subject alone.

CHAPTER TWENTY-SIX

After an uneventful day, Michal followed Oisin into the Orange Gnome. Wandering the town listening for grumbling hadn't brought any new recruits. An impromptu juggling demonstration yielded enough coin to buy them a dinner and a few jugs of beer. The common room was quiet. The tables were full of what looked like farmers muttering over the day's events.

"Should we stay together?" Oisin asked as they approached the bar.

Michal looked around the room. It was the same as most inns in Halm's Town; square, low ceilinged, warm, and dim. The aroma of dinner answered his stomach's growl. "For now. There's a free table at the back."

As he followed Serena, Michal scanned the tables nearby. Each contained two or three strongly built men and women. If we learn nothing from here, maybe Oisin could go hang out and eavesdrop at the bar, he thought.

When they settled in the chairs, a young boy approached wiping his red hands on his apron. "We have stew of rassam with barley, and chicken roasted with apples. Sweets are a plum pie or lemon cream with grass berries."

"Two rassam stew and one chicken. Do we have to decide on sweets now?" Michal asked.

"No, if you don't care what is left, you don't. If you want to try it, we have some of the new wine. The vines are finally producing enough to bottle. Otherwise, beer, no tea, all out."

Michal looked at Oisin, wine would probably be expensive. Their earnings would likely not cover it. Oisin shrugged, not very helpful.

"How does the wine taste?" Michal asked the boy.

"It tastes a bit sour to me, but then I don't know what it's supposed to taste like."

"We'll stick with beer. Bring two jugs," Michal said.

"It's probably better," Oisin said. "Drinking wine might make us stand out. We want people to talk to us, not gossip about us."

The boy returned with the beer and mugs, and said, "Back in a second." True to his words, he returned with plates and cutlery. "Enjoy."

"Okay," Serena said, moving some of her chicken onto Oisin's plate and replacing it with some rassam. "Eat and I'll listen."

"No, I'll listen, the two of you eat." Michal poured beer. "I can do it faster."

Michal leaned his elbow on the table and placed his head in his hands. He picked up his fork and started poking at the meat on his plate. His attention was floating toward the table to the right when a loud belch erupted from one of the men sitting a few tables away.

"Oy, Brit, what did you have for lunch?" his tablemate said loudly.

"Little enough, thanks to that damn guard."

"Hush," the tablemate said again. "You don't know who's listening. You don't want to spend the night in jail, maybe more. You have a crop to tend."

"Aye, and isn't that one of the reasons why they get away with it? We all have too much to do to stop them behaving like right bastards."

Brit's friend hushed him again. The conversation dropped to murmurs. Michal picked at his food and relaxed. The people at the other tables had grunted as if in agreement before turning back to their beers and dinners.

"Interesting," Oisin said quietly around a mouthful of rassam. "I wonder why they feel so free to speak."

Serena looked around the room. "We are the only strangers in the room, I'd guess."

Michal smiled, and then finished eating the stew. He'd learned to eat fast growing up in a large Romany family. "Finish up. We'll bring them to us. Just follow me." He waved the serving boy over.

Oisin and Serena ate the last few mouthfuls on their plates and handed them to the serving boy. When he left, Michal leaned across the table and said in a loud whisper, slurring his words slightly, "I don't care how much I've had to drink. I'm telling you it was wrong."

"Hush," Serena said quietly, then looked around. "You can't speak about it. You know what will happen if we get caught."

Michal had known she would pick up on the game. He looked at Oisin and waited. The boy blinked and looked at Michal then Serena. She nudged Oisin and whispered in his ear. Michal couldn't hear what she said, but he saw Oisin grin and nod.

"Tell me you don't think the bastard should have killed the dog?" Michal's whisper was louder but still seemed intended to be secret.

"I don't question the actions of my betters," Oisin's voice was slightly louder than Michal's

"No Meta is better than a human," Michal said. "They never were, and never will be."

"Quietly," Serena said. "Think about what you are saying. Don't give anyone a reason to talk to the Meta about you. Rotting in a cell at the duke's castle won't improve your life."

"No one here will turn you in miss," the man sitting closest to their table said. He turned around and nodded to Michal. "You should be careful. Like the lady said, you don't know who's listening. Here, right now, you are safe. Don't know if that will be true in a half hour."

"Leave them be, Rafe," his companion said. "That skinny one didn't seem to have a problem."

Oisin sat up straighter in his chair. "It is not that I have no problem with the behavior of the Meta. I am not sure that anyone in power would act any differently. I don't see any alternative, and without an alternative, why get angry at the status quo."

"Don't know your history, do ya boy?" Rafe said. "Think about where you came from."

Michal looked sideways at Serena, the signal they used to confirm that they had a mark when they worked the three-shell game. "Would you join us? Let us pay for a jug or two of beer to hear the history lesson?"

Oisin stood and shifted his chair to make room for the two men. "Oisin var Mallek." He held out his hand.

"Rafe," the man said moving his chair to their table. "Just Rafe, and this here is Declan var Morris."

"I'm Serena den Baros and our disgruntled friend is Michal var Avinon. Welcome." She waved for the serving boy to bring a fresh jug of beer then poured the last of the current jug into everyone's mugs.

"So, what history lesson are you talking about?" Michal asked.

"You be Romany, am I right?" Rafe nodded at Michal. "You know the way people in control behave, some good, some bad."

"That's the way of power," Michal said. "It seems that's the way of Meta, too."

"Did you learn the reason we came to this planet? They still teach that?" Rafe sipped his beer.

"It is taught in college," Oisin said, raising his voice above a raucous laughter coming from a table across the room. "Not in junior school. Not everyone knows the why. Some don't even know we didn't originate here."

"Tell the story," Michal grunted. "Oisin is the only college boy here. You have an eager audience."

Declan chuckled into his mug. "Don't rush Rafe in telling stories. He's a master. Let him string it out as much as possible. I'll make sure he doesn't drink too much. At least until the story is over."

"Now, Declan, don't be making things up about me." Rafe took another drink. "Okay come in closer. You know that we came to this planet from a highly technical world."

He waited for them to nod then continued, "Well, do you know the reason we left? It was a comfortable world. Do you know why we would choose to come here and live in this simple way?"

Michal leaned toward Rafe, curious for details. The Romany didn't discuss the reasons for coming here. It's not that they denied the journey to Free Faith, they just didn't talk about it.

"No," Serena said. "Come to think of it, I never wondered. But now I'm curious."

Oisin nodded for Rafe to continue, he knew the official teaching, but was intrigued that there was an unofficial version.

"On the old home planet, Ansolm, there were scholars, and technicians, and priests, and common people. The common people lived their lives well. They had all the conveniences of the technology, which was cheap, and they had leisure time. The scholars kept to themselves, and it was a good time to be a scholar because they were able to research everything and anything they wanted. The technicians were able to experiment on whatever they wanted. They developed new toys and medical procedures to make everyone's life better and longer. We were all aliens there. Humans mixed with five other species, no Meta though."

"I don't understand why they left. It sounds perfect," Serena said.

"It was," Rafe assured her. He paused and looked at the jug of beer. Serena poured another mug for all of them. "Then something went wrong in a lab. People got sick. People died."

"How did they stop it?" Michal asked, knowing when to prompt the speaker.

"It burned itself out, but not until two million people were gone. That's when it got bad. Not that two million dead isn't bad. But the bad part came when some people decided that God had sent the sickness to punish them for living an easy life. The priests took advantage of the resulting unrest. They encouraged the fear. It brought people to the church. It brought money to the church, and it gave them power."

Declan leaned forward. "This kind of thing happens all the time in human history. This time was no different from before. People get scared, they look for hope, and then someone takes advantage. If they are successful, more of these predators come and then more. The next thing you know the place is run by vultures, and common people are living grim lives hoping for release."

"Sounds familiar," Michal said. "Isn't that where we are now?"

"Not even close," Rafe said. "This is just the beginning of the cycle. Let me finish the lesson. The priests weren't satisfied with holding hell over the heads of the people who came willingly to the church. They started telling their flock that unbelievers were the reason the sickness was inflicted on humanity. There were riots. More people died."

"That's when our ancestors decided to leave," Declan said, taking over the story.

Michal smiled at the easy way they shared the tale between them.

"They were not willing to pretend faith for safety, and they were able to afford the cost of stocking a colony ship. Before the sickness there was a plan to send a colony ship to explore further, so there was one ship ready."

Rafe spoke again, "All they needed was permission. The priests didn't want to let them go, so they made a compromise. Three priests joined the colonists. The new planet was to be called Souls Rest."

"What happened?" Serena's confusion was clear in her expression. "There're no priests here, and we're called Free Faith... oh."

"Yes, oh," Oisin said and looked to Rafe for permission to take his part of the story. "When the ship landed, the colonists scavenged everything. The ships were made of components that would support life for the first few years. Some of the animals and plants we brought here came from Earth, like chickens and pigs and wheat. We were able to use the ship to analyze which of the native plants and animals were edible.

The priests built a church and tried to gather a flock. No one was interested. Two of them gave up and became farmers. The other died of old age."

Michal nodded. "I guess they changed the name of the planet as soon as they could."

"Yes," Oisin finished. "Then, ten generations later, the Meta showed up. One day they marched into the council chamber, and you know the rest."

Declan turned to Michal. "What do you intend to do about it? And don't play any more games to try and interest us. You have our attention."

"We have people ready to make a change," Michal whispered. "We need more."

"What are your plans, boy?" Rafe asked. "You have a plan, right?"

"Do you have people who can help?" Michal felt leery at the ease of gaining the farmers' interest. "The plan depends on the numbers."

"Yes," Declan answered for him. "We've had enough of them, boy. They take our crops. They beat our children. We won't ask again, what are your plans?"

"We meet in Mont Kinner in three days. We make the final plans there. But now there's a complication," Michal said.

Rafe spoke, "The bride?"

Michal looked down at his empty mug. "We don't want to kill an innocent Meta woman. The duke will be enough to make the difference. The others may be willing to negotiate, if we have enough force on our side."

"Don't be naive, boy," Declan snapped. "Meta women are not innocent, and if you kill the duke the others will get their guns and come for your blood."

"So, we have to kill them all?" Michal's heart squeezed at the thought of destroying the Meta. This was not what he wanted.

"Not necessarily." Rafe made calming motions toward Declan. "But don't count on them folding up and surrendering just because the duke is gone. Don't use all your tricks on the first battle."

"Do you have something to suggest?" Oisin asked.

"Maybe." Rafe looked at Declan. "Maybe we've been thinking along the same lines. Where do we meet you?"

"Come to the market square in Mont Kinner in three days," Michal said, pouring the last of the beer. "If we're not there, we'll be around."

CHAPTER TWENTY-SEVEN

The duke noticed he was forming a trail in the dust on the floor leading to the shuttle chamber. It didn't really matter, there was no way a human would be able to enter the chamber. Even if they could take the key from around his neck, humans were unable to create the resonance in it that was required to unlock the doorway.

He felt an ache across his shoulders from the damp chill. Underground was not a place he enjoyed. There was something about the thought of all the weight of the town resting on his head that unsettled him. The chill seemed to enhance the feeling that there was weakness somewhere, a weakness that would crush him.

Approaching the door, he sighed. Soon he would be back on the bridge of his ship. In a climate-controlled environment, a clear chain of command, and, most importantly, no humans. He would make sure no one brought a pet human aboard. That was one stipulation. The other was that no one stayed here. This planet was off limits for Meta from their escape forward.

Central command would approve that order because this planet made Meta soft.

"Is the diagnosis finished?" he shouted as he entered.

Allorn walked down the ramp nodding. "Yes, we have a result. The transfer of data finished last night. The diagnosis came back five minutes ago. Very good timing, commander."

The duke could see the way Allorn stood, relaxed with a smile gracing his face. The news would be good. He looked the duke in the face, something that had not happened since the shuttle refused to leave the planet.

"What is it?" The duke snapped, unwilling to relax until he had all the facts in hand.

"There are two steps we need to take before the shuttle will leave."

"Get on with it. This is not a story. You don't need to stretch the tension."

"True." Allorn's attitude was so different from before that it annoyed the duke. "Well then, the shuttle did not depart because of an intermittent error in the core functioning. Had we been able to communicate with the ship, it would have been mended in a few hours. Because there was interference, we were forced to hide the shuttle."

"I know this." The duke stepped toward Allorn, pulling himself to the full height, his temper was slipping, and while he had an element of control, he used it to intimidate.

Allorn did not seem intimidated. "Yes, but you need to understand what caused the problem. I thought it would be better to tell you in a logical order than to simply tell you the solution, and then back track."

The duke took a step back, his temper calming. "Ah, friend, you take me back to the days before this. We would spar over everything. It feels as though you are fixing what is broken in me as well. Thank you, I believe I am now fit to command again."

"It does feel good to slip back into the old patterns." Allorn smiled. "Very well, let us continue. The ship's intelligence has identified missing instructions in the core functions of the shuttle. As you know, the shuttle does not have an intelligence. It is capable of following instructions, but not of solving problems."

"Yes, I know we simply tell it to do something, like rendezvous with the ship, and it will follow instructions, and make necessary corrections. The only automated routines required that all Meta on board be rendered unable to provide instructions. Then it will return to the ship, or base, that is closest. If taken by force, it will self-destruct. I had to take flight training because of this."

"Well, the intelligence has determined it will need to delete all programming and reinstall base instructions. Then we will need to recharge the power source." Allorn sounded proud, as though he had repaired the shuttle himself.

"How long?"

"The delete function can be sent in a few minutes and will run automatically with the intelligence observing. Those instructions will contain a reboot code at the end. The download will take three days minimum. If the connection is broken, the process will need to start again. The process will consume the power resources left to the shuttle."

"And the power recharge?"

"One full day in the sunlight of this world will provide sufficient power to return to the ship."

"We will be able to make it in one trip? I don't wish to separate the crew. We cannot take the chance that the same error will happen this time."

"Yes, it will be crowded, and no one can bring anything but the clothes on their back, but we can make one trip instead of the four it took to get here."

CHAPTER TWENTY-EIGHT

The duke gave Allorn a congenial slap on the back. "I need to speak with the intelligence. Wait here." He marched into the control room and sat in what had been, and would soon become again, the control seat.

"Ship," he spoke to the screen, knowing it didn't make a difference, but feeling better that he was talking to something other than air.

"Commander," The ship's voice was stronger than it had been the last time they spoke. "It will be good to have you back on board."

"Yes, it will be good to be back in control. I need to arrange for the rest of the crew to arrive at the launch area in time. We cannot arrive too early. It would arouse suspicions, and I'm not certain it will be completely safe for us to gather in one place. Kael tells me the humans are quite angry."

"There is a clearing within three kilometers of the current location of the shuttle. There will be adequate power left after the reboot to move it along the ground, but not enough to fly. The clearing is large enough to allow sufficient sunlight to recharge the power cells. There is room enough for takeoff with minimal damage to the surrounding area."

"I don't care how much damage we do." The duke smiled at the thought of destroying as much of the planet as possible when they left.

"You may care if the Congress of Beings discovers your actions. You cannot afford another censure on your record. Humans are protected under the treaty of Cygnus."

The duke flicked a hand toward the screen. "I suppose that's true. So, what are the odds that something will go wrong? I do not wish to inform the crew that we will be returning, and then have a delay."

"There is a possibility that the connection will be broken again. When the download is complete, the odds of failure are reduced considerably. After that, the major difficulty will be charging the power cells. If the sun does not come out, we will be delayed. I have analyzed the weather patterns, and over the next two weeks, there is a one percent chance that cloud cover will be heavy enough to delay the power charge by one day."

"And the other possibility is that the humans will find us." The duke drummed his fingers on the counter. "However, they have no technology capable of stopping us."

"It would appear not. There is a possibility of accidental damage to something minor. Should that occur, it will not impede the return of the shuttle."

"So, three days..." He could not take the chance they would fail. "I will inform the crew of the plan when the download is complete. It will take two days for the messages to get to them, and two days of travel, if all goes well. I think it will be best to agree on leaving eight days from today. We will move the shuttle on the night of the sixth day. I will set guards to discourage humans while the shuttle charges its fuel cells."

The duke left the control center and met Allorn at the bottom of the ramp. "Eight days," he said. "I want a progress report every night. Do not enter my chambers before midnight. I will ensure we are alone."

CHAPTER TWENTY-NINE

Oisin picked up the clothes strewn about the room and shoved them into the travel bag. Serena was the messiest person he knew. If they left it to morning it would mean waking much earlier to give them time to clean up and pack.

"I still think we should wait a day," Serena said as she inspected a bright green blouse. "I think it would be smart to meet with Rafe and Declan's friends before we go."

"You don't trust them?" Oisin asked.

"It's not that I don't trust them. I just don't know that they understand exactly what is needed. I worry that they have their own plans, and that they will be more harm than help."

"I agree," Michal said. "I think they're genuine, but when they told the story, there was something there, some hurt they didn't speak about. If they are bent on some sort of personal revenge, then it could cause problems. We need to be in the capital as soon as possible, though."

"Is that why you spent the money on open tickets?" Oisin took another look around the room before closing his travel bag. "So we could stay until the last wagon. We'll arrive in the capital really late, but still be there today."

Michal shook his head as he helped make the beds. "Only one of us needs to stay. I can meet the farmers and take the late wagon. You two can get to Mont Kinner, find an inn, and check out the mood of the citizens."

"Are you certain?" Oisin asked. He didn't like the idea of splitting up the team. This would be the first time they would separate for more than a few hours. He realized that Serena would be alone with him. Up to now, Michal had been an unofficial chaperon. "What would it hurt for us to all stay?"

"We only have so much money, so we need time to find a cheap inn. If we wait until too late in the day, the only choice may be to sleep outside the walls." Serena plumped the pillow and said, "If we are there early enough, I can make some money by juggling, or doing illusions. I can train Oisin to be the straight man for those. The last time you and I were in Mont Kinner, the people were generous."

Oisin watched Michal's reaction. He shrugged and said, "Don't try the shell game. He's not good enough to get away with it."

Serena laughed. "No kidding. It took me a month to learn the tricks. I would feel better if you stayed and talked to them, just be there on the last wagon. We don't want to spend time coming to look for you. If you aren't on the last wagon, we'll start walking back."

Oisin hated the feeling of jealousy that rose in his gut with Serena's words. What was it about Michal that made her willing to take chances like that? She didn't love Michal in that way. He believed that she wouldn't marry anyone, for the same reason she wouldn't marry him. He swallowed the bile that had risen to the back of his throat and didn't speak until he could lighten his tone. "I would prefer not to have to protect her against night creatures and bandits."

Michal grinned. "I swear I would prefer not to rescue you

both from either." He ducked as Serena threw the pillow at his head.

After watching Oisin and Serena leave, Michal wandered through the paths made by the day stalls, casually looking for Rafe or Declan. The cries of the vendors echoed off the stone walls of the buildings surrounding the square: fruit, fresh and sweet; pies, breads, and cakes; fine woolen clothes. The calls overlapped but were still recognizable. He inhaled the smell of warm meat pies and sour pickles.

Arriving at the opposite side of the square, he paused. Leaning against the side of a building, he scanned the market one more time. No sign of either farmer. He turned and followed the twisting street to the ox stable, the smell of dung confirming the location five minutes before he arrived. He heard the oxen bellowing and grinned. The beasts didn't like getting hitched to the wagon. They were reliable but lazy, preferring grazing to working. And who could blame them. Pulling a heavy cart wasn't the easiest job in the world.

Michal stood at the fence and watched as four of the beasts were led to a large wagon that was covered with a white cloth tent. The stablemen hobbled them beside the wagon and led the first one to the halter. The beast tossed its head and resisted the yoke. The resistance didn't matter. The stableman was experienced, and soon returned for the second ox, harnessing it beside the first. Within ten minutes, all four animals were in place. The stableman started tying in the lead straps and finishing the fine work of binding the team to allow them to pull the wagon up the long grades to the farms.

"I thought you were leaving today. What happened?" Declan asked, dropping a strong hand on Michal's shoulder.

Michal pushed away his annoyance at being taken unawares.

Vigilance would be critical to the success of the rebellion, and the safety of the people he was taking into danger.

"I stayed behind for the day. We thought it would be useful for me to meet one or two of your recruits. Just in case something happened to you."

Declan nodded. "In case we were going to join the Meta, you mean. I don't blame you, boy. It's important to be sure. These things can get bloody messy if you aren't careful."

"It looks like you're getting ready to leave." Michal pointed to the stablemen who had started hitching another team of oxen to wagons.

"Not until later," Declan said. "Rafe and me, we like to leave after the rush. It lets us travel at our own pace."

"Rafe is still here, then."

"Aye, he is. Come on, boy. We're meeting some friends in Rafe's wagon for a drink before they head out. I think you'll like them." Declan gestured to a double wagon in the corner. The part covered in white cloth was hitched to a smaller one that looked much like a Romany wagon. It had a wooden roof and a door. It opened as they approached and Rafe stepped out.

"Another for a farewell drink," Declan said loudly, giving Michal a slight shove. "Is everyone here?"

"That they are. Will you stand outside?" Rafe's voice was much quieter. "It would be a terrible problem if anyone listened in."

"I think I'll pass on the drink, old friend," Declan said, heartily. "My head is in poor shape from last night. I'll keep to the perfume of the ox."

Michal climbed the two steps into the small room. Inside, a table was pulled down and two men sat on stools affixed to the floor. He saw a bed folded up and latched to the wall facing the door. The light came from two lanterns on the table, and a small window in the wall that would be behind the driver. The window also acted as a chimney for the lantern smoke.

"Makes you feel at home, does it?" Rafe asked pointing Michal to the far side of the room. "A moving home it is. I built it to save money on inn rooms but ended up liking the accommodation in the inn better. Isn't that always the way?"

"It might suit you with a bit of decoration." Michal laughed. The walls were bare wood, sanded enough to remove the splinters, but not enough to paint.

"Joseph and George," Rafe said, pointing to the other men. "I'll leave it at first names. This be Michal."

Joseph and George were alike enough to be twins, both redheaded, both with gaps in their front teeth. One was shorter, and the lines on his face showed he was more used to laughing than scowling. The other had belligerence written all over his face.

"Michal, I'm George," the smiling one said. "I guess you can figure out that means he's Joseph."

Michal shook George's hand, and then reached toward Joseph who refused to shake.

"Joseph," both Rafe and George spoke. George let Rafe continue. "What the hell is the matter with you? Shake the man's hand."

"He's not a man, he's a gypsy. I'm not having anything to do with something that includes a filthy gypsy." He sat back, brows furrowed, arms crossed over his chest.

George sighed. "I'm sorry. My cousin is a stubborn ass."

"I have a few cousins who could top him in the being an ass department," Michal said. "What is your problem, Joseph?"

Joseph looked away.

"His mother left when he was a child. His father said she ran off with the gypsies." George reached over and punched his cousin in his arm. "It's not true. You know that. I saw her in Whitson. She ran away with that silk merchant. She didn't like the way your father used her as a punching bag."

"Damn, it's not that. What do you take me for? He hit me

enough to make me want to leave as soon as I could." Joseph shook his head while he spoke, and Michal could see the raw emotions flood the boy's pale face.

"I respect your decision. I regret whatever the Romany have done to make you angry."

"Their bloody king," Joseph spat. "He refused to let my mother come with him. I remember damn it. She tried to take me with her. He said no. Too much trouble would come from it."

"And you hold all of us responsible for this?" Michal kept his voice low. "Would you risk your family for the sake of a Romany child?"

"My mother let them stay. She kept my father from burning their camp. She protected them. He should have taken us." Joseph clamped his lips closed.

"Yes," Michal said. "He should have helped. I am sorry. We have few friends in the *Gadje* community. The king does not always understand the value of loyalty to people outside the family."

"I'm sorry too," George said. "She should have come to us. We would have done something." He turned to Rafe and asked, "Is it still possible to talk about this thing?"

"You do not know?" Michal looked at Rafe, who shook his head.

"No," George said. "Declan said we should hear it from Rafe in quiet, where we wouldn't be interrupted."

"Joseph, if you want to leave, the time is now," Rafe said. "I'll trust you not to say anything about meeting here. But, if you stay, you are committed. I need to be able to trust you."

"How do you expect us to agree to that?" Joseph asked. "Why should I say anything but no?"

"Wait, Joseph," George said. "Think about what you are saying. Before you met Michal, you were ready for whatever Declan and Rafe suggested. They asked if you wanted to make a change, if you were happy with the way things are."

"So," Joseph said, the anger easing in his voice. "I trust Declan and Rafe with my life. I've done it enough to know they wouldn't lead us down a wrong path. We've always made money on their ventures. It's just the gypsy. If they are getting in with them, then I don't know them anymore."

Rafe touched Michal's arm. "You go wait outside with Declan. Let me talk some sense into these two before they make a decision."

Michal nodded. "I'm clouding this issue. Let me know what you need."

He stepped outside and saw Declan walking around the wagon, checking the ties holding the sheet onto the sides. "Are we done?" Declan asked.

"No, there's a problem. Joseph doesn't like Romany. Can we trust them to keep quiet, if they don't want to come into the rebellion?"

"We wouldn't have brought them this far if we were worried about their loyalty. Don't worry. Joseph would rather cut off an arm than betray a friend. No matter what he thinks of you, he's Rafe's friend, and mine."

"Do you think Rafe will bring him around?" Michal hoped so. Young men as passionate as Joseph were needed.

"It might be uncomfortable. It will take a lot for Joseph to work with you. He hates that king of yorn."

"He's in good company. I hate him too, and he's my father."

Declan laughed. "Ah, well that's probably not something to share with George, or Joseph, until they trust you. Fate seems to be playing a hand in this game too."

"If Joseph doesn't want to follow my lead, he can work with Rafe instead. I know it looks like I'm running the rebellion, but it's not true. Nor is it something I sought. If we are going to win, we will all need to be responsible for leading."

"If Rafe can talk him into listening, Joseph will be able to bring most of the young farmers into the rebellion." Declan kept his eyes on the people in the yard as he spoke. Michal had also been keeping watch for anyone showing interest. No one was.

"You know," Michal said. "If my father had taken them in, Joseph would have grown up with me, not with Rafe. He would still hate my father, though. I don't see any real meanness in Joseph, just a stubbornness that looks more like pride than anything else."

"You might get an opportunity to tell him if he joins. He's smart enough to see the irony." Declan looked up as the door opened.

Rafe nodded for Michal to join them.

"I'll agree to join," Joseph said as soon as the door was closed. "I hate the Meta almost as much as I hate that king."

"If it would make it easier, you should know I'm not leading this rebellion. I'm just one person."

"I'll join you on one condition," Joseph said, looking in Michal's eyes as he spoke. "When we win, and I assure you we'll win, or die. When we're done, you don't form the government. You leave and go back to what you were doing before."

"It will be my pleasure." Whatever Rafe said to the boy had done the trick. "I have no desire to do anything else. Now, what do you know?"

George answered for both cousins. "Rafe told us it was rebellion. He said the Meta would be destroyed, and the humans would take back control of Free Faith. We're ready to fight."

"How many people can you bring in?" Michal asked.

"We'll bring ten," George said, eying Joseph who nodded. "No, fifteen strong farmers. People like us. We only have pitchforks and scythes, but we have strong hearts."

"You'll be given a sword. Can you use one?" Michal hoped there would be no delay for training. If the plan he had in mind worked, they would only have to stick the sword forward and push. The confines would be tight. No need for finesse.

"I can," Joseph said. He looked up from the table where his gaze had been glued during the conversation. "I learned from books. I haven't used it on anything but a pig carcass, but I know how to hold a blade. I can show the others. If we fight in close quarters, then it's like using a long knife. Most of us know how to do that."

"We will get you the weapons in the next few days. It won't be me. Likely a merchant will come by. He'll know you. You'll ask him if the market in Whitson is still thriving. He'll say not so good as the old days, but not bad as it could be."

"When will we fight?" George asked the question but Joseph looked eager for the answer.

"Within the week. You'll get the call to come to the capital. We'll strike in the morning and will be sleeping in the castle that night."

"You're a cocky bastard. I'll admit I like that about your kind." Joseph stood. "Let's get going. We've got a long journey home, and work to do by tomorrow."

Michal looked at Joseph, seeing an intelligence and stoutness there that would have made them friends if there wasn't so much hatred clouding the boy's mind.

"I look forward to working with you," he said, shaking George's hand, and bowing slightly to Joseph. "You might make a good council member when we're done. Try not to get killed."

When the two left, Rafe beckoned Declan into the caravan. "Keep your voices down, and no one will be able to hear." He rapped on the wood. "Stout new oak, two inches thick, many a secret has been kept here."

"Most of them women," Declan said. "Ah, well not for years since, I suppose."

"Don't put money on it. I've still life in me." Rafe bent and opened a cupboard that must have backed under the driver's seat. He took a dark bottle and three small cups from the shelf. "We'll have a toast to the adventure."

"Only one," Declan said. "I have to be off. I'll share a bottle with you at the mid station."

"This be good aged wine." Rafe poured. "We only just started selling to the inns, and what we sell them is not great. The good stuff is precious, and we keep that for ourselves."

Michal looked at the red liquid and sniffed. He could smell berries and something woody. He looked up to see Declan and Rafe swilling the liquid around in the cup. They sniffed, smiled, and sipped. Michal followed suit. The taste of ripe summer plums lay on his tongue for a moment, but it was followed by a tartness that left his mouth feeling stripped.

"I think this might be an acquired taste. One beyond my skill of acquiring." He passed the cup back.

"More for us then." Declan shared the liquid between the other two cups. "Now, we'll make sure that those two act according to the seriousness of the adventure. We'll be in Mont Kinner within the week. Who will we be meeting?"

Michal hesitated. "I'll get word to you. I think the less we talk about the other groups the better."

"That's a good idea. I bet even you won't know everyone." Rafe looked at Michal. "What else do you have to say? Come on, I can see you're bursting."

"I told Declan, but you should know too. I'll leave it to your wisdom whether to tell Joseph. I am the son of the king. I wasn't there when Joseph and his mother came for sanctuary, but he's better for not getting it."

Rafe took a sip of his wine. "I think we'll leave that until after we win. You'll need time to explain it to him."

"As you decide. I don't think there was anyone else there when they came, either. If you could find that out and tell me I would appreciate it."

Rafe looked up at him. "Why is that important?"

Michal was surprised at his feeling of regret. His hatred for his father was so deep and so old that he'd forgotten he'd once loved and respected the man. "In Romany law, there are two rules that are never broken. Family is important above all other things. My father violated that one when he ordered me to obey or leave. And you never refuse sanctuary. I hope my father was alone when he broke that one. He will have to pay for both when I am done with the Meta."

"Vengeance is a sharp needle, boy," Rafe said. "I understand what you feel, but you must keep your head. It's not a long way down that road to become what you hate."

CHAPTER THIRTY

Serena took her bag from the back of the wagon and thanked the driver. Rubbing her backside as they walked into the capital, she regretted the nine hours sitting on the hard seat of the wagon. The padding provided by their cloaks had done little to protect her bones from the jolts.

She turned to Oisin and said, "How much can we afford to pay for an inn?"

He tapped his pocket. She sighed. She'd have to teach him to be more cautious when out in the street. Pickpockets always had an eye out for clues to where purses were carried. "We have sixty pennies left. If we can get the room for forty for the week, we should be able to make it last."

She glanced around the busy square. "Well, that rules out the market inns. I think we're better off in the outer streets, and we're less likely to see your father if he's in town."

"He's not likely to be in town for another month," Oisin said. "He stays in Richlow until the festival, you know that."

She wondered if that was still true. She had not seen Oisin's father for almost a year. Serena increased her pace as they reached the market, not wanting to catch the eye of anyone who might recognize them. It was not unusual for her parents' friends to spend a week in the capital. It was going to be awkward while they were here, but she'd learned how to disguise herself with a scarf and change in posture. Perhaps Oisin could learn too.

The second alley was lined on both sides with homes and small craft shops. Here and there, narrow side alleys cut into the wall. She heard the noises of homes; crying babies, complaining old men and women, pots being scrubbed, children laughing and parents yelling. It would be comforting to be surrounded by such hominess.

"Do you think this would be a good place to set up a business?" Oisin broke into her thoughts.

"Why? Is your father planning to open another store?" She looked around. "I think this would be a great place. Look at all the people in such a small area."

"I'm thinking of myself," Oisin said, pulling her to a stop to look in the window of a small cafe. "After this is done, I want to set up a life somewhere. I can't go back to my father and take over. I've seen too much of the world. It wouldn't be fair to Rosa anyway. She's done all the work while I've been gone. Father should let her take over; it would be a good reward. She has no other prospects."

"I think you shouldn't make decisions you can't undo until after the... well after."

"I can't be like you and Michal. I need to think about the future. I can't just live from day to day, not knowing where I'll sleep, or if I'll eat."

"You make it sound worse than it is." Serena pulled him along again. "We've never been hungry. Michal always knows where to find food if we're on the road. We've slept rough, true, but only for a night or two."

Oisin stopped her and turned her to face him. "What happens when he goes back to his family? He will, you know, eventually."

She shook off his hands. "I know. He has to eventually. I don't know what I'll do. Maybe go with him, if they will let me. Or find a job. I don't know. Oisin, things are going to change; I can't plan until we're done. The world will be different. Who knows what opportunities there will be after ... well after we succeed."

He dropped his hands from her shoulders and sighed. "I wish I could be like you, but I can't be."

"It takes all kinds, Oisin. Don't try to be what you are not." She turned and started walking. "Hey look there's an inn." Shrugging her bag higher on her shoulder, Serena tugged his arm. "It looks clean and the patrons look respectable."

CHAPTER THIRTY-ONE

Michal saw Oisin lounging near the gate, hidden from sight by shadows of the watch house. He was not obviously hiding, but no one would notice him if they weren't looking. It seemed he'd learned a few skills. There was no sign of Serena.

He stepped away from the wagon and watched Oisin peel himself from the shadows to follow. Halfway down the street, Oisin stepped to Michal's side.

"Did you have a good journey?"

"Bumpy, but uneventful, as usual," Michal answered. "And do we have an inn?"

"It's on the other side of town. The Jolly Wagoneer. It's clean and it's cheap, the food's not great but I don't think it will poison us." Oisin steered Michal through the market square.

Michal checked the square for promising places to set up. "I'll make some money for us tomorrow."

"We still have money," Oisin said. "The room is only thirty pennies for the week. There's no bed, so we'll sleep on the floor. Serena and I made a few pennies with a juggling act."

The boy sounded proud of himself. Michal figured that he had a right to be, it wasn't an easy thing to earn money on the street. Oisin had been trained to provide for his loved ones, and he must be feeling good that he was contributing. "Well, then, I guess we can concentrate on important things over the next couple of days."

Oisin pointed. "Through here."

Michal looked up and saw the castle looming over the square. The street, alley really, ran around the side of the wall. The houses on the left backed onto the castle fortifications. Anyone in the castle would be able to see into the street as long as there was light.

"It's pretty close to where we need to be," Michal said. "I don't know if that's good or bad. Close makes for shorter travel when we move, but danger of being caught if we meet with people in the room."

"Serena and I have already figured out a plan." Oisin stepped aside as a boy chased a dog out of the alley and into the square. "There're several taverns where we can get a private room for cheap. If we are careful not to use the same one too often, we should be able to do what we need to without raising suspicions."

They entered the common room of the Jolly Waggoneer and crossed to the ladder that led to the second floor. Oisin knocked on the door immediately to the left of the ladder, Serena opened it as though she had been waiting.

Inside, the room had three sets of bedding on the floor, no chairs, no table. The two travel bags were piled in the corner. Serena had managed to spread her clothing around the room as though she'd been there for days, not hours.

"Good, you're here," she said, reaching for his bag. "Now tell us what happened. Did you meet anyone?"

"Hello to you, too." He recognized the signal that Serena wasn't in the mood to wait in her impatient toss of his things on the floor. "I met two of the new recruits. They will bring in more.

They're eager, and a bit hot tempered, but Rafe will keep them in line."

"I guess there's no going back," Oisin said. "Not that I want to. I just think it's important to mark the turning points."

"What have you learned?" Michal asked, ignoring Oisin's prattling.

"Nothing," Serena said. "There really isn't much going on. We've seen some likely places to listen in, like we've been doing. There's not a lot of love of the duke, if the gossip I've overheard is representative. The problem is, there doesn't seem to be a lot of hatred, just grumbling."

"Have you looked at the castle?" Michal felt the skin on his shoulders shiver with the thought that the castle was behind his back. Only a wall protecting him from the duke.

Oisin nodded. "The forecourt is open during the day. The building is not. There are six or seven places where we could sneak in, if the guards weren't looking. It will have to be at night."

Michal thought through the process. "Night doesn't work. They will be roaming the streets. Remember last time we were here? But very early in the morning does work; the guards will be tired. If we can slip an advance force in to start the attack, the rest of the army can storm the castle when the guards react."

"How many in the advanced guard? And who?" Serena had a glint in her eyes that Michal knew very well. She was eager for action.

"Probably no fewer than ten and no more than twenty. We'll want to rush the duke's chamber if we can, so half to do that, the other half to draw the guards into the building."

"And who?" she asked.

"Me, you, Oisin if he wants. Then the farmers and smugglers. I figure they'll be the most effective. One of our farmers can handle a sword, if you can believe it."

"Maybe the others will have some ideas." Oisin's stomach grumbled. He patted his belly and asked, "Did you eat?"

"Yes, Rafe gave me food for the trip. You go ahead and eat; I'll try to sleep." Michal figured it would take quiet and time to get over the feeling that the duke was listening to them through the wall.

CHAPTER THIRTY-TWO

"You can trust me to catch the pins," Oisin said as they set up to juggle in the square. "Serena has been practicing with me. I can't juggle, yet, but I can catch at the end."

Serena laughed. "Yes, he's not as bad as you expect."

"We need to be sharp to get paid for our act. If the duke has really removed the licensing requirements, by tomorrow the competition will be overwhelming, and there will be fights over places to set up." Michal was unrolling the wooden pins from the blanket they used to mark their space. "We might only have today to make money."

Serena was tucking a scarf around her curls and tying it off so her strawberry blond hair wouldn't attract attention. Oisin checked his own disguise. He wore baggy clothes and lots of layers to fill out his skinny frame. A hooded shirt allowed him to keep his face in shadow, and he was forced to stoop by a set of suspenders that were too short for his long frame.

"So, I get to collect the pennies." He tried not to sound too disappointed.

"Oh, Michal," Serena said. "Let him catch. We might get more money if there's some comic relief. Either he catches them and the act works as usual, or he doesn't and the act is funnier."

Oisin could see that Michal was reluctant, but he didn't want to simply stand by while others did the work. "Look, why don't you try me out while Serena sets us up? We can pretend you are warming up."

Michal capitulated. "Go stand at the edge of the blanket." When Oisin stood facing him, Michal continued, "Now, I'll say 'hut' when I'm ready for you to catch. When I say it, you reach out your hand, and I'll place the pin there. Trust me, you won't have to reach for it, just keep your eye on me."

Oisin focused on Michal who started tossing the blue and red pins in the air. The noise of the crowd faded as he listened to Michal's patter draw in an audience. The young Romany walked in circles, pretending to trip over Serena, passing the pins under his raised leg and behind his back. The act was mesmerizing.

Michal faced him. "Hut." Oisin put out his hand and the narrow end of a pin smacked right into the center. All he had to do was wrap his fingers around it.

"Hut." Another flew his way. He caught that one, too.

"Hut." Then he flipped one pin into his left hand and grabbed with his right.

Michal bowed and pointed to Oisin, who held up the pins and bowed low. A few pennies were thrown onto the blanket. Oisin was amazed that he hadn't dropped a pin. Michal held out his hand and nodded. Oisin took one pin and tossed it to Michal, making it spin. The other two pins followed, and the juggling began. Serena took the role of coin gatherer. When he wasn't focused on Michal, Oisin noticed she was scanning the crowd as she collected. He thought she was looking to see if anyone they knew was coming close, but no one did.

After an hour of juggling, Oisin did drop a few. The crowd, not realizing it was a mistake, applauded. When they had gathered enough money for two days' worth of meals, Michal called for a rest.

"I think I saw Jane," Serena said as she joined them in the center of the blanket. "Let me go get some tea, I'll try to find her again." She took enough coin to buy a snack along with the tea. Oisin watched her go. Even in disguise, he thought he would recognize her in a crowd.

"Don't pine," Michal said. "She'll not come to you out of pity."

"I know, and I wouldn't want her to." Oisin sighed. "I know she has made up her mind. I hope she won't be too stubborn to change it."

"She might be if you push too hard. Let her see that you aren't your father. Let her think about how life might change after we do this."

"It feels different now we're here." Oisin rolled his shoulders. "I don't know if it's just because we're closer to the castle, or if there's more Meta around, or what. But I feel like I'm being watched all the time."

"I feel it too." Michal looked up. "Here she comes."

Serena handed them each a mug of tea. "It wasn't Jane, and I didn't see anyone else we know."

Oisin sipped the tea and watched the crowd of people move together and apart. There was a musician setting up a few stalls away. She was tuning her instrument, the notes shifting from sharp nerve ripping to smooth and soothing. A man stood on a small wooden crate on the other side of them. He waved his arms and called to the crowd. "Sore feet? Stomach ailments? Dull hair?" he called. "Your complaints can all be cured. Come witness the powers of the elixir."

"I don't know why people fall for that pitch," Oisin said to Michal. "Look they're crowding around. There's no way one liquid can cure all ailments."

"People want to believe," Michal said. "And, if there's any Surra oil in the potion, it will give them some relief from pain.

Enough will cure stomach problems. I don't know about the hair though."

"Are we going to put on another show?" Serena asked. "It's getting crowded. Another juggler will be here before we know it."

"I suppose we should do one more." Michal stood. "Oisin you want to catch again?"

"Probably not a good idea. I was dropping more than I caught at the end." He knew Serena would be a more active part of the show. If they could make a bit more money, then they could manage for a week.

"We'll do the scarves and knives then." Michal bent to get the equipment and said to Oisin, "Stand well out of the way. I wouldn't want to cut your ear off by mistake."

The patter began. This time Michal's voice competed with the cure-all merchant and the cello music. Somehow, Michal made it all sound like a coordinated performance. People crowded around, eating meat pies or holding bags of shopping. Laughing, and clapping and enjoying the show.

Oisin scanned the crowd. The suspenders made it difficult for him to see over the heads of their audience, so he sidled through the small gaps. In a clear space off to the side of the entertainers, he saw a man standing with three Meta behind him. The man was clearly in charge of the Meta, so he must be high in the court.

The man was stocky but held himself as though he was tall. He glared at the crowd. Oisin couldn't help but think the man was staring directly at him. Out of the corner of his eye, he saw the man move toward them, the Meta following in lock step. Suddenly feeling he didn't want to be noticed, Oisin slid between two housewives, and slumped a bit further.

"What are you doing?" A short thin woman asked, pushing him away and turning to look. "Ah, Kael var Radborne, time to move on. He won't like the crowds. Got a burr up his ass about people getting together. Thinks we're up to something."

The crowd started to thin. The man with the cure-all stepped off his box, put his wares inside, and walked away. The cello player kept up her performance, and so did Michal and Serena. Oisin took his place behind them, watching the knives fly between him and the approaching Kael. As the crowd thinned, Kael slowed. In the middle of the market, he came to a halt, said something to the two Meta, then spun on his heel and returned to his original path.

The two Meta followed the cure-all merchant who began running toward the gate. He had a good head start on the two guards and the crowd shifted to let him pass. People moved the wrong way and bumped the Meta. A drunken man stumbled into the path of the aliens. They lost their prey before they had crossed the market.

The show ended. Moving around the edge, Oisin gathered the tossed pennies, and listening to people as they left.

"That damn, Kael, he's taking all the fun out of life. It's not as if anyone believes in a magic potion."

"That poor man, he was only trying to make a few pennies."

"I bet the duke is getting an earful now. Kael don't like the fuss, but the duke is enjoying it. Wonder who'll win out."

"My niece says Kael is worried someone is plotting to overthrow the duke."

"That's what he says, but I think he just likes breaking up the fun."

Oisin thanked the crowd and returned to where the other two were packing up their equipment. "I think we have another problem."

CHAPTER THIRTY-THREE

Michal clenched his fist to control his frustration. The townspeople didn't want to talk to strangers. There was no grumbling, but he knew from the way they twitched at the sight of a Meta, or scurried aside when someone in the castle uniform approached, that they were more than just on edge.

He watched as Oisin wandered around the edge of the square scoping out the taverns, Serena walked through the market square, pretending to look for bargains as the remaining stalls closed for the night. They didn't need more rebels, what they needed was information. When they'd investigated the forecourt of the castle earlier, it had been plain to see that they would not be able to launch an attack from there, no cover, and only one door.

"I'm sure we'll find someone," Serena said, returning to his side. "You saw how people reacted this afternoon, they're not happy. They are just more frightened than we've seen so far. We'll need to be patient."

Michal shrugged. "It feels like we don't have the time for patience." He held up his hand to halt her reaction. "I know, I know. Don't look at me like that."

"It's time for us to eat. Get some hot food in you, and you'll feel better." Serena pulled Michal away from the wall. "Look, Oisin is trying to get our attention. Maybe he's found a likely candidate."

Michal noticed the difference in the way Oisin held his shoulders. He strode with confidence, keeping his disguise firmly in place. They had all matured in the last few days. He saw Oisin nod toward a tavern. Hoping there was good news, Michal took Serena's hand, and they veered to join him. He noticed a ceramic man's face peered out of an arrangement of carved leaves. The tavern was called The Green Man.

"I think this will be a good place to eat," Oisin called as they approached. "They have meat pies and roasted potatoes. Remember when we would have that for dinner, Serena. At the end of a school week, when we were free from the oppression of lessons. When we were children?"

"Memories of a kinder time are always welcome," Michal answered.

Serena let go of Michal and slid her arm around Oisin's waist. The two led the way into an open courtyard with a lattice roof covered in vines. This time of year, it provided the tavern with twice as much room for diners. In the winter, Michal thought, it would be empty of tables, the cold driving people into the smaller, inside rooms.

Oisin found them a table in the center of the courtyard. People watched them as they passed, but no one spoke.

"Three meat pies, a plate of vegetables and a platter of potatoes," Oisin ordered. "A jug of water and a jug of beer, please."

The waiter returned with the beverages immediately and promised the hot food in five minutes. Michal poured beer into their mugs.

"Well," he murmured, a sigh escaping despite his efforts to control it. "Is there something we should be noticing? Or is this really just about the food?"

"Are you okay?" Oisin asked.

"He's just tired," Serena said.

"You don't need to make excuses for me," Michal said, then realized his tone was sharp. "Sorry, Serena's right. It feels like we've been at this forever. I know it's only been a few days. I know everything is moving fast, but it doesn't feel fast enough. I just have this weird feeling that time is running out. I don't know where it comes from, but my grandmother would tell me to pay attention to my weird feelings."

The waiter slid the plates of food into the center of the table. "Enjoy," he said before turning to a group of women waving for his attention.

"I heard someone saying there'd been some upsets in the castle," Oisin said, his voice barely above a whisper. "It seems four people were fired today. They questioned something that Kael wanted. He told them to pack their bags and leave. A scullery maid, two upper housemaids, and a gardener."

"Are they here?" Michal asked, not looking around. "Did you hear them talk, or were they being talked about?"

"They were here. All but one has gone home. The gardener is in the far corner. He's been drinking since early this afternoon. We should be able to get some information from him, or from his friends, if we don't wait too long." Oisin pushed food toward Michal.

Michal picked up a meat pie and placed it on his plate. "If he's too drunk, he won't be much use to us. He'll regret telling us anything and might turn us in to get his job back."

"So, it's useless?" Serena asked. "I guess we'll eat and go somewhere else."

Michal recognized the sarcasm. "No, I didn't mean that." He finished his pie. "I mean we can't use him. We can get some information and use that to find someone."

A mug crashed to the floor across the room, and one man swore while another laughed. Michal turned at the sound, taking the opportunity to glance at the corner where Oisin said the gardener sat. A small group of people gestured angrily, but no one was shouting, or making any noise.

"Anything more?" the waiter asked as he took the stacked plates from Oisin.

"Send a jug of beer to the table over there," Michal said. "I hear he lost his job."

"Yes, things are changing at the castle. Used to be a man had a job there and kept it for life. Now you keep your mouth shut, or you're gone."

"Sounds like you have experience," Serena said, smiling.

"Used to work in the kitchen." The man shrugged. "The duke didn't like the way I sliced his meat. He had me chucked onto the street then they locked the front door."

"It's good you have this job." She encouraged him with another smile. "Were you out of work for long?"

"No," the man said. "Dorsey is a good woman. She's the owner here and she takes in strays like me, and the two chambermaids. And that gardener. She'll see he has employment when he sobers up."

The waiter returned to the kitchen.

Oisin said, "I guess we've found someone. The waiter will know how we can get into the castle."

Michal leaned forward before speaking. "Not the waiter. Dorsey is the one we need to talk to. She's already running a little war against the duke by taking in his rejects."

CHAPTER THIRTY-FOUR

Kael watched the duke and his secretary finish the correspondence. The duke wiped the nib of his pen and pressed blotting paper to his signature. He turned to the other man. "Thank you, Edmond, you may go." The door closed behind Edmond leaving Kael alone with the duke.

"Sire, I think it is time for you to decide which of the candidates will be selected as possible brides. There are, after all, several eligible Meta women from the families, and you've invited all of them to visit."

"I suppose." The duke sighed. "They are all sufficiently beautiful. I would prefer a companion who can join me in the hunt, and one who is intelligent enough to challenge me in conversation."

"Elisiette is said to have a quick mind," Kael suggested.

"She will not join me on the hunt. The damn girl is a vegetarian."

"Mautine will certainly join you on the hunt."

"She's about as bright as an unlit candle."

"Her sister, Launielle?"

"Yes, she is young, but well suited to running the castle." The duke nodded. "Add her to the list."

"The twins Ysllin and Moste," Kael suggested. "Either of them will join you in the hunt."

"I do not wish to be bested by my wife. Both of them are far better at blood sports than I."

"Jullinda?"

"Yes, a good choice." The duke paced the room. "How many more will I need to add?"

Kael wondered at the duke's response. It was as if he had lost interest in the brides. "It would be best to have three. Why not add Ponsollyn. She likes hunting and will bear you strong sons. She has already done so for her other husband. It was an unfortunate accident that left her a widow."

"She is strong willed as well. Excellent! Three perfect choices."

"Now, the banquet menu has been set pending your approval. If you would look it over?"

"Just tell me what you've decided." The duke walked to the window.

"To start, a selection of meat morsels and cheese on crackers, served with the new wine. The meal itself will begin with a chilled vegetable platter and a clear soup to follow. The main course is roast pig and root vegetables. We'll provide a vegetarian selection. And, for dessert, we will offer sweet honey cake, savory honey cake, and iced cream."

"Sounds delightful. I knew you would take care of it."

"Thank you, sire." Kael paused. The duke was in a good mood, perhaps it was time to talk about the unrest.

"Is there anything else?" the duke asked. "You seem distracted."

"I believe that the people are unhappy, sire."

"Why would I care about that?"

"When the other families arrive, surely you wish them to enjoy the experience. Would you have them compare the peace in their towns to the unrest in yours?"

"Would they dare?" The duke spun on his toes. "I think they would not."

"Not to your face, perhaps," Kael said. "You know they will afterward, in their own home."

The duke smiled. "True, that's what I would do. Well, how do we stop this unrest you see all around you?"

"I am not sure we can stop it. I think we must acknowledge it and try to contain it."

"I tire of your innuendo. What exactly have you seen?"

"Rumors in the taverns," Kael started to explain. "Grumbling in the market."

"This is not rebellion, its normal." The duke turned to look out the window again.

"It is not normal, sire. Yes, people grumble, but this is more open, and it often doesn't stop when the guards come near."

"I still do not see this danger. This revolt." The duke strode to the fireplace and poked at a log. "If we put down a rebellion that does not exist, we may incite the very thing we are trying to stop."

"It does exist, sire. The staff you let go this morning know too much about the castle, they can tell people our weaknesses."

"I have no weaknesses," the duke snarled. He bent, picked up the poker, and advanced toward Kael. "Any weaknesses that exist are in your people."

Kael stepped back and raised his hands in a gesture of placation. Fear gripped his stomach. This was not like the duke. He was a hard man to please and changeable, but never this angry.

CHAPTER THIRTY-FIVE

Serena leaned back in her chair. They had napped in their room for the afternoon, and then returned to the common room of the Green Man for their discussion with the owner.

They ordered tea and waited. Serena watched the crowd while her two companions chatted. The drunken gardener was gone, but she could see some of his companions still sitting at the tables against the far wall. There were two different servers, both young women, working the room. Serena wondered if they were the ex-maids.

Outside, the courtyard was chilly, a breeze rustled through the leaves of the vines. Inside, the room seemed cozy. There was a fire burning on each of the three walls. The warmth came with a peppery scent of well-seasoned Mola wood. She sighed and closed her eyes, letting herself enjoy the familiarity of the scent, and the memories that came along with it.

"More tea?" one of the girls asked. "We have pastries, honey cake, nut cake, and dried fruit."

Serena looked at Oisin who nodded. "A plate of pastries and another jug of tea, please."

"If we drink tea and eat pastries all night, you might have to put on another performance in a couple of days." Oisin looked around. "Are we going to talk to the owner soon?"

"She's busy," Michal said. "I'll wait for an hour or so. She'll be closing then."

"What about us?" Serena asked. "Should we try to get the girls talking?"

"Do you think they will? They seem pretty shy to me. I thought you might want to try with the drunks in the corner."

"Okay, but won't that look weird?" Oisin asked.

"Yes, probably, but it will give you something to do. It's going to be a long wait."

Serena could see that Michal was interested in only talking to the owner of the tavern. Their plan was solid. If she gave jobs to the people who had displeased the duke, she might be interested in talking about getting rid of the Meta. Serena was trying to think of a more appealing alternative to pass the time, when a man entering the restaurant caught her eye. She recognized him from the morning. What had Oisin called him? Oh yes – Kael.

"This might be interesting," she said. "It looks like the castle food is not to his taste."

"Don't stare at him. Don't bring his attention to you," Michal hissed. "Pay attention to what happens. Who seems upset he's here. Who seems to pay attention to him."

"He's sitting down at a table by the door," Serena reported. "Oisin, if you shift your chair a little, you can see him. We can tell you what's going on, Michal."

Oisin shifted his chair closer to Serena. "The waitresses are not going to serve him. That woman who came from the kitchen must be Dorsey. It looks like she's going to save them the effort."

"He knows the menu. She didn't have to tell him what they have," Serena said. Looking around at the other tables, she noticed that the other diners were all concentrating on their meals. No one was looking at Kael, only at their own plates or mugs. The buzz of conversation had died, the only sound coming from the table of drunks. They were muttering but not moving from their table.

"His food has arrived. That was fast. He must be a regular. That might not be a good thing," Oisin said.

Michal waved one of the waitresses over. "A jug of beer, please." He smiled at her, and Serena watched the wariness lift from the girl's face.

When she returned with the beer, Michal took the jug. "Thank you, I hope the presence of your former employer is not too distressing."

The girl looked at Kael's table. "Ach, he's just an old maid who follows orders. It's the duke who sacked us. You never know where you are with that one."

"It's good that you got work so fast," Serena said. "Is Dorsey a good boss?"

"She's okay." The girl looked at Kael's table again. "She gives us a bit of time to adjust, you know. It's nice not to have to worry. I'll be leaving you now. Take care. Kael is paying attention to you. He may be an old biddy, but he can still be dangerous if he takes a dislike to you."

Not so shy after all, Serena thought as she watched the waitress walk away. She tried not to look at Kael. If he was watching their table, she didn't want him to read too much into their conversation with the waitress.

The drunks in the corner were getting noisy again. She hoped it was bravado caused by too much beer. It would not help anything if their potential rebels were locked up for disorderly behavior.

Oisin pushed his mug to the side and reached for the teapot. "She was right. He was watching us, but his attention has moved on. I think we might want to keep to ourselves a bit until he's gone."

"Let's hope it's not too long," Michal said. "I can't talk to Dorsey while he's here. If he noticed us talking to the waitress, he will be getting suspicious. If Dorsey thinks we brought the wrong kind of attention, she'll be unlikely to help." He took a set of dice out of his pocket and shook them before dropping them onto the tabletop from his opened fist. "This might be more fun than just sitting here trying to look innocent."

Serena looked at the dice and saw the two face-up symbols were Lion and Snake. Oisin put both his elbows on the table and rested his head in the palms of his hands.

"Fortune telling," Oisin said. "Don't you think that's going to bring attention to us?"

"Not fortune telling for anyone else." Michal chuckled. "Let's see if Serena can teach you to tell fortunes."

Serena groaned. This was her downfall. She found it difficult to keep the meanings of the symbols clear enough in her head to tailor the reading to the client. "Okay, before we start you should know that the order of the dice is important, and the symbol will mean different things depending on the question asked."

She glanced at Kael's table without moving her head. "He's lost interest in us. He seems to be focusing on the food. I think he's pretending to not listen to the grumbling."

She pointed at the dice. "Look at the dice. If we were doing the reading for you, Oisin, the snake is closest, so it's prime, meaning it will be more important to the answer. The lion will be about how you obtain your heart's desire. The snake will tell us if it is possible. The same would apply if the reading was for me. If Michal was the client, the lion would determine the possibility, but the snake would determine the how."

"Well done," Michal said. "If Oisin were the client, what would the snake mean?"

"Should I think of a question?" Oisin asked.

"You can, but the dice weren't thrown for you. Why don't you hold onto your question until we actually do a reading?" Serena thought she knew what Oisin would ask and didn't want to answer what the dice might say about his future marriage prospects.

"Okay." Oisin stretched back in his chair then leaned forward again. "Kael is staring at the drunks. I don't know if he'll do anything, but Dorsey is going over to the drunks' table."

"Good," Michal said.

"Now the snake is about the possibility of an answer. When it is in the prime position it means that there are ways of getting what you want. Some ways you follow may get you what you want at too high a cost. Other ways will get you what you need, not what you want."

"Is that ambivalence true of all prime symbols?" Oisin asked.

"No, some will tell you directly that your heart's desire will cost too much. It is up to you whether the desire is stronger than your reluctance to pay the price," Michal said. He pointed at the lion. "When Serena explains the reading from my perspective, you'll see what I mean."

"So," Serena continued. "The snake doesn't really help you. The lion tells you that you will have to stand bold, and not back down in the face of adversity to achieve your goal. The two together could mean that you will have to stand firm in your desire, but compromise on the end result."

Oisin smiled. "And if this reading was for you?"

"Pretty much the same." She pointed again to the dice. "You can see that the position puts the symbols the same distance from me as they are from you. The meanings don't change from man to woman. It's the questions that change."

The grumbling from the table of drunks subsided. Serena saw Dorsey heading back to the bar. Kael had finished his meal and sat sipping his mug of beer.

"If the reading was for Michal," Serena continued, keeping an eye on Kael. "His decision would be clearer. The lion in this position symbolizes strength of decision. There is no maybe, no multiple ways to the path. The lion tells him he must do what it takes, or not act at all. If he is willing to do what it takes, he will succeed. The snake represents the barriers he will face in his journey to achieve his goal. The snake will be difficult to avoid."

She saw Kael place a stack of coins on the table before leaving.

"What would this reading mean for Kael?" Oisin asked as he watched the man leave.

Serena looked at the dice and then at Kael's seat. "A good question. The lion and snake are both in the prime position. It means he is capable of achieving his goal but doesn't know what it is."

Oisin put his hands in his pocket to finger the coins. Twenty pennies. He mentally calculated the costs of living over the next week. If they were still alive after that, they wouldn't need to worry about money. The problem was twenty pennies wouldn't last more than three days at this pace.

The noise level in the tavern had steadily risen since Kael left. The grumbling came from every table.

Michal laughed. "It looks like the whole crowd is ripe for recruitment."

"Let it settle for a while," Serena said, shaking her head. "It's only been a half hour. We won't know who is just grumbling, and who is really angry, until people start to leave."

Oisin's stomach growled. He tried to ignore it, but it growled a second time.

"We should order something more to eat," Michal said. "It's been too long since we had real food. Pastries don't count."

"You'll need to make more money if we have more than one meal a day," Oisin said. "I can go hungry if it's just me."

"It's not just you." Serena patted his arm. "You're too skinny as it is. There's no point in saving pennies for the future. If we can't make money, we'll go hungry later."

"We meet the others tomorrow," Michal said. "If we have to, we can ask them for some money."

Oisin felt an echo of Michal's reluctant words in his own

heart. Neither of them liked the idea of borrowing money from merchants and smugglers. He raised his hand to catch the eye of a waitress, but they were both running back and forth between the bar and the tables. He saw Dorsey nod at him and hold up a finger to indicate she'd be there in a minute.

"We might have to split up after Dorsey talks to us," Michal suggested. "There are too many people grumbling for us to work together."

"Look, the space around us is clearing." Oisin jerked his chin to the room. "Maybe Dorsey can take the time to sit and talk to us."

The woman stepped up to their table, wiping her hands on her apron. "What can I get you? The kitchen is closed, but everything is still available if you order fast."

"A couple of your pies will be greatly appreciated, and a few minutes of your time if you can spare them."

"I'll be back. The girls can take care of the room." She nodded at the dice. "I'd like to get a reading if you can."

"Of course." Serena smiled at Dorsey, who turned and walked back to the kitchen.

"Perfect," Michal said. "Build the rebellion into the reading."

"Won't she suspect?" Oisin anticipated a problem if the woman believed she was being manipulated.

"I'll be subtle," Serena assured him. "Most people who ask for a reading really want to be manipulated. They want someone to help them make up their mind. If they didn't, they wouldn't need a reading."

Dorsey returned carrying a tray of food in one hand. She reached with the other to drag a chair to the table. Putting the plates down, she said, "You look like you need more than pies. Young uns like you need feeding well. We'll call it square, the reading for the food. Marlea will bring a jug of beer in a minute. Then we can get started."

Oisin looked at the plates in astonishment. Pies, bread, fruit, and vegetables piled high in front of him. His stomach rolled in anticipation of the feast. "Thank you. I am Oisin and that's Serena, and Michal."

"Dorsey, but I think you know that," she said, picking at a piece of bread. "I know you spoke to my day man, and you've talked to one of the girls."

"They speak well of you," Serena said, taking the dice, and shaking them in her cupped hands. "You have done some wonderful things."

"I do what needs doing. Thanks, Marlea." Dorsey took the two jugs from the waitress and then looked at Serena. "You eat something, dear, before these two scrape the crumbs off the plates. We'll have a mug of beer while we wait."

Oisin could tell by the way Dorsey watched them that she had something to say. He wanted to ask her outright but knew it wouldn't get them anywhere. She would control the pace of the information. He watched Serena nibble on a sandwich, her eyes focused on the innkeeper. Each woman sizing the other up.

Dorsey broke the silence. "I saw you watching Kael var Radborne. Are you on the run?"

Serena pushed the plates of food aside to clear the center of the table. "We noticed the way people reacted. He seemed to stir up the crowd. It's gotten noisy since he left."

"He stirs up a lot of emotions," Dorsey said.

Serena picked up the dice and held them out to Dorsey on her open palm. "Are you ready?"

She shook her head. "I'll not be pushed into asking my question the wrong way."

"As you wish." Serena placed the dice on the table. "When you are ready, pick them up, warm them in your hands before shaking them, and then drop them on the table."

"I know how it works, don't fret."

Oisin poured beer into all four mugs. There was still food on the table but he was full for the moment. "Will there be trouble?"

He nodded toward the table of four very drunk men. "They've been drinking since this afternoon. I see their friend is gone."

"More's the pity about that. He could have kept them in line. Now they are angry, drunk, and have no perspective. Don't worry about them. We'll make sure they don't end up in the dungeon."

Oisin nodded. He watched Michal who was still picking at the food. He wondered why the Romany didn't join the conversation. Should Oisin keep his mouth shut? Was this some kind of game, and he was interfering?

Michal put the last bite of food back on his plate. "What is it you want to say?"

Dorsey laughed. "No way to fool you, Romany. But let's do the reading."

She took the dice and rubbed them between her fingers, then cupped her hands. Oisin heard the dice rattle. She abruptly dropped them on the center of the table. The closest die to her was the fish. The one slightly behind was a closed circle.

"You had your question held close when you dropped them?" Serena asked.

"Yes."

"The fish has many meanings. I will tell you them until you nod to the relevant one." Serena waited until Dorsey nodded her agreement.

"The fish shows a sign of plenty if well managed." She waited, but there was no reaction from Dorsey. "The fish is a sign that you have many people around who rely on you. Your question probably does not have a direct answer. The fish will point you in many directions. Flexible and agile, the fish can be a sign of a change in direction."

Dorsey nodded.

"You are thinking of making a change. Something fundamental. A change in your life? Your direction? You will bring many people with you if you change. But choosing not to change may cause you to lose that influence."

Dorsey shrugged, but indicated that Serena should continue.

"If you choose to change, there will be support. An adventure with companions. The ring indicates probable success, if you bring your companions along. Not all, but those who are closest and most valuable."

Oisin hoped Dorsey couldn't read the clues that Serena was leaving behind as clearly as he could.

Dorsey snorted. "Do the dice say how to know who I can trust?"

"If you did not ask that question, these dice will not answer." Serena sat back. "The reading is complete."

"I need a second reading." Dorsey reached for the dice.

Serena snatched them away. "No, the dice need to be cleansed of the last question." She placed them on the table, put her right hand on top, then reached down to the stone floor with her left hand. "This will ground the dice and clear them for the next reading."

"Then I guess we need to drink some more beer." Dorsey poured. "We'll let the dice cool, while I think of a better question." She stood and walked back to the bar with the empty jugs.

"Do not get drunk," Michal said. "We need our wits about us for later."

"You think we'll get anywhere?" Oisin was not sure the interruption was a good thing.

"She's hooked," Serena said. "She was hooked when she decided to sit down. She was scoping us out, seeing if she can trust us."

"Why did you ask her so bluntly about what she wanted to say?" Oisin asked Michal.

"It was obvious she wanted to say something. I thought it worth a try. If she knows we can read her, she might just get to trusting us faster," Michal answered.

"She's already decided," Serena said. "The fact she is asking for a second reading is proof. She'll let me know her question."

"How can you be so sure?" Oisin asked.

"She is a woman who doesn't ask permission. She takes in the people the duke kicks out. She doesn't care what he thinks about that. This hasn't been about her making a decision, it's been about us showing we can be trusted."

Dorsey walked back to the table, this time carrying a jug of tea and fresh mugs. "You'll need to keep your heads about you if you want to do anything else this night."

"Thank you," Michal said, taking the jug. "It is time for your next reading."

"My question will be, can I trust my heart with this decision." Dorsey took the dice and repeated the warming procedure. The dice landed far apart. The closest showed the face of a sun, the farthest a straight line.

Serena leaned closer. "The sun represents your heart. It shines true. The answer is yes, you can trust your heart. The straight line is showing the path. You will be best served by going straight ahead, and not wasting time with evasion. The two dice say yes, trust your decision, and do not delay."

"Come back in two hours, through the door to the left of the Green Man." Dorsey stood and walked to the table of drunks. Two of the men were face down on the table, the other two were singing loudly, and off key.

CHAPTER THIRTY-SIX

It was dark by the time Michal led Oisin and Serena through the narrow door beside the fountain. The door had been unlocked. It opened onto a flight of stairs that led to a locked door. Michal knocked. No sound came through from the other side. He knocked again, and the door cracked open, a blue eye looked through at him.

The door opened wider. Dorsey gestured them to enter, locking the door behind them. Inside, the room was lit by candles and warmed by an open oven. Michal realized they were underneath the kitchen. Sitting on barrels, and leaning against the wall, twenty men and women looked at the newcomers.

"I assume you are planning something to do with the duke. You can trust these people," Dorsey said. "I'm not warranting they will join in whatever your plans are, but they won't betray you. And if they join, they will bring others."

Michal turned to face the people. "My name is Michal var Avinon. I am Romany. I have seen the Metas do brutal, unwarranted violence to innocent people. I believe it is time we took back the rule of the land."

"Plainly spoken," a woman in the dress of a baker spoke. "I

don't think anyone here will disagree. What can we twenty do against armed Meta?"

"Not just you," Michal said, pointing around the room. "You and fifty others. You with swords."

"Where are these swords? And where are these others?" A man with arms like a blacksmith asked. The others nodded and muttered.

"Some will be here tomorrow, some in three days. The swords are on the road. And before you ask, we act within the week." Michal didn't mince words. These were not reluctant recruits. He didn't have to convince them that things were bad enough to change. They lived with it every day.

"How do you plan on changing things?" a tall woman asked. She had the fair skin of someone who spent most of her time indoors.

"We take the duke by surprise in his castle. Where he feels safe."

"How will you get in? Are you planning to storm the front door?" This was from the waiter who had talked to them that morning.

Serena stepped forward. "We need information about the castle. There must be ways to enter other than the front door. Ways to bring in a small party, people who will cause a commotion and distract the guards, someone to let the larger party in through the main gate."

Dorsey held up her hand to silence any response. "Anyone who doesn't want to get involved leaves now. We trust you not to say anything, but it looks like now is the point of no return."

"You know damn well we're in, Dorsey. Don't interrupt again." The crowd laughed at the old man's words.

Michal relaxed. He hadn't realized how much tension he was carrying. In his heart, he had hoped that Dorsey was trustworthy. He never dreamed the woman could pull together such a strong group. Once again, they seemed to get what they needed too easily. He pushed aside the thought. "We will be joining with the other groups in few days. If we can work out the details, we plan to attack within the week. We want this resolved before the duke marries. With good planning, and a little luck, we can be finished before any of the brides arrive."

"The invitations have been sent. The women will be here in six days," the waiter said.

"Then we need to plan the attack in five." Serena looked around the room. "We need information on the castle. We need people who know the secret places to help on the initial attack."

"We all want to be on that attack." A stooped young man stepped forward. "We shouldn't keep ourselves anonymous. I'm Alric. The duke had his guards beat me for bringing him apples when he wanted plums. They broke me so badly I can't stand straight. I'll show you how to get in."

"Aye." A woman stepped out of the shadows. "I know how to move around the castle without being noticed. They killed my daughter. They just barreled past her on the bridge, and she fell. It was a stupid careless accident, one that wouldn't have happened if they cared for us."

"My brother can tell us more about the castle routine than anyone. He still works there," Alric said. "Will you come with me to see him? He couldn't come to the meeting but will be home by now."

Michal didn't want to leave these people, but knew they needed Alric's brother.

"I'll come," Oisin said. "We'll go now."

Dorsey tapped a beer keg and offered drink to the conspirators. "This'll be thirsty work."

Michal nodded goodbye to Oisin and beckoned the group to come closer. "Tell us what you know."

CHAPTER THIRTY-SEVEN

Oisin crept up the ladder, knowing that the slightest sound could wake the other guests. He could hear gentle snoring from the room across from theirs, and a sharp cry, from a child down the hall, that was followed by murmurs of comfort.

The light shone under the door of their room. Michal and Serena were back, good. He gave the door a quiet knock before opening it.

"I was getting worried." Serena stood from where she had been sitting on her make-shift mattress. "We've been back for ages."

"It's been less than half an hour," Michal said, the smile on his face softening the words. "Did you have luck?"

Oisin tried not to read too much into the fact that Serena missed him and worried about him. "The brother is with us. Tell me what you talked about in the meeting."

"You first," Michal said. "We have a couple of ideas. Your information might help us choose one of them."

"The brother knows the plans for the next week. He's the duke's secretary. He knows where the duke and Kael will be. He says they don't always keep to the schedule during the day, but at night, and in the morning, the schedule is reliable."

Serena pressed her lips together. "So, I guess we should start at night, or in the morning."

Michal shook his head. "No, we go in at night, early in the morning really. We wait until the duke is up and Kael is there and then we attack. It's perfect."

"Who will be with us?" Oisin could feel excitement and fear mingle in his stomach. This was going to happen, no longer just an adventure, this was a serious undertaking. "How big will the party be?"

"Inside, only five people, six maximum," Michal said. "We will have to hide, so the fewer the better."

"Who?" Serena asked. Oisin heard tightness in her voice. Perhaps they had argued about this.

"Me, Dorsey, Alric." Michal counted off the people. "Oisin and Ellis."

"And me," Serena said through clenched teeth. "I am coming."

"No," Oisin and Michal said.

She held up her hand. "I am coming. No arguments. If you try to leave me behind, I'll just come anyway."

"We need someone to lead the second wave." Oisin could hear the weakness of his argument in his voice.

"No, Dorsey can do that, or Zandor," she hissed at them. "Don't pretend that I am special and need protection."

Michal held his hand out and patted the air, signaling her to keep her voice low. "Be careful. We can't lose control."

She pressed her lips together again. Oisin knew that she was not going to let it go. He looked at Michal who shrugged. "Okay, you come with us." Oisin looked down at his hands, trying to make peace with the decision, knowing he couldn't change it.

"Will this brother be there?" Serena asked.

"If we need him to be, but I don't want to put him in any

danger if we don't have to. I think if he's usually with the duke in the morning, we should let him keep to that," Michal said.

"Okay when we meet with the others, what do we tell them?" Serena asked.

"Everything we can," Michal answered. "No secrets. We need to trust each other."

CHAPTER THIRTY-EIGHT

Kael stood at the door to the small house. It didn't look like the house of a traitor. It should be scruffier, more run down. When the woman had asked to meet with him so early this morning, he had almost told the guards to send her away. He was grateful to whatever whim of fate made him agree to see her.

She was clearly angry. Her body shook with it. Her language had been laced with obscenities. Kael couldn't bring himself to say the words even in his memory of the encounter. "He has been talking to people who are planning trouble. I don't know who they are," she said.

When Kael asked her why she thought so, the woman had answered, "He told that wife of his. She came to tell me he trusted her more than me, that he loved her more than me."

She had told Kael the man's name, and where he could be found. After that, her language had degraded rapidly into incoherent sputtering. The guards had taken her back to her house, hopefully she would calm down there.

Now both guards had returned and waited for Kael's instructions. They all stood in the post-dawn chill, the sound of insects filling the air with creaks, scratches, and buzzing. He nodded and the lead Meta banged on the door.

"Open up," the Meta shouted. "Duke's guard."

A voice called out of the window, "Wait. I'll be down in a minute."

Kael raised his hand to stop the Meta from banging again. "It is not our intention to raise the neighborhood. Is there any other way out of the house?"

"Not out of sight. The house backs into the wall. The only way out is door or window. We'll see him no matter how he tries to leave."

The door opened and a man put his head out. "Kael, what can I do for you?"

"You can let us in, Edmond," Kael said, taking a step forward. "We have questions."

The man rubbed his face, nodded, and opened the door wider. "Can I make you tea?"

"No, you can get your clothes on and come with us. Come quietly, and your neighbors will not know we have been here." Kael did not want to face an angry crowd. He had only entered the traitor's home in order to make the arrest.

"Is there some problem, sir?" Edmond started to look nervous. His eyes were shifting from Kael to the door, as if he was thinking of running.

Kael motioned to the Meta closest to the door, and he stepped to block Edmond's way. "You may get dressed, or you can come with us in your night clothes."

Edmond slumped. "I need a minute."

Kael motioned to the other Meta. "Go with him. We need to make sure he comes back down the stairs."

Kael stood in the dungeon looking at his captive.

He hated the smell of stagnant water, the constant drip of moisture from the rough ceiling, the overwhelming damp. If he stayed too long, his joints would ache. He'd already been here long enough for his sinuses to mimic the dripping moisture. He hated being in this position. He didn't want to torture anyone, let alone Edmond who had always felt like an ally when the duke was stubborn.

Kael moved closer to the only source of heat. The stove in the corner did nothing to warm the room; all of its energy poured into heating the two black pokers sticking out of the grille. As he extracted one of them to examine the rosy end, Kael wondered at the ease of the arrest. No claims of innocence, no questions, simply compliance. Now the traitor was tied to a chair in the dungeon, down the longest passageway, away from the other prisoners.

Placing the poker back in the fire, Kael moved to stand in front of Edmond. "Let's try this the direct way. Who were you meeting with? What are their plans?"

Edmond looked up at him, his face untroubled. "I don't know what you are talking about."

"Yes, well we know that's a lie." Kael motioned to a man standing in the corner next to the stove. The man nodded and wrapped a cloth around his hand before pulling a poker from the fire. He inspected the glowing end and looked at Kael.

"Not yet, Archer." Kael waved the man back.

"Look," Edmond said. "I really don't know what you are on about. If I did, I would try to help you. I have no desire to feel the heat of that poker, no matter how cold it is down here."

"Do you find this funny?" Kael motioned to Archer, who took the poker again and walked toward Edmond. He placed the poker two inches from Edmond's right hand and looked at Kael for instructions. Kael looked back to Edmond. "You met with a group of people last night. I wish to know who they are and what you were planning."

Edmond blinked, a few beads of sweat breaking out on his

brow. "I met with some friends. We were drinking to a new marriage. We were celebrating."

"Who are they?"

"What are you going to do to them? I don't want them to end up here for a few secret drinks."

Kael waved Archer away. "Perhaps your wife will be more helpful."

"No, she won't."

"Let's bring her in and see." Kael turned to go.

"She left on the last wagon yesterday. She's not here."

Kael realized the woman hadn't come down when they arrested Edmond. It hadn't seemed to matter at the time. "Well, then we'll just have to do what it takes to get you to talk."

"Ask what you wish," Edmond said. "I will give the answers I have. I cannot tell you things I do not know."

Kael sighed. He needed concrete information to get the duke to act on the threat. As it stood, the duke would simply fire this man as he had any others who caused problems. Kael was sure that Edmond would break, it was just a matter of time – time Kael wasn't sure they had.

CHAPTER THIRTY-NINE

Sitting at a table outside one of the taverns in the market square the next day, Oisin tried to quell his impatience. He didn't care for the idea of sitting and waiting for Jane, or one of the others, to find them. The rebellion was in motion, and if not properly managed, would get out of control. He feared that they would unleash an angry mob that would do more damage in one day than the Metas could in a lifetime.

"She didn't say when? Or, where?" he asked.

"No," Michal said. "It's the same answer as five minutes ago. Jane said they will find us, and so we have to be findable."

Oisin feared that by being findable, they were being too obvious. That the guards would ask questions. The fact that the guards didn't seem to notice, did nothing to alleviate his worry.

"Jane is over by the sausage stand," Serena said, turning back to the table. "She saw us."

"I need to speak to you, Oisin." The voice came from the table to his right.

Oisin looked at the man, it was Alric. "Make it quick," he said.

"It's my brother, Edmond." Alric's voice was barely audible

and his eyes were focused on the ground. "He's been taken by the duke's man. He's in the dungeon."

"I am sorry to hear that." Oisin looked at Michal, who nodded for him to leave. "Meet me at the bakery around the corner."

Oisin rose, waved goodbye to Serena, and then walked to the corner. He noticed Jane following a circuitous route to their table. He figured he had five minutes to get back before she reached the group.

Looking in the window at the shiny-topped pies and artfully shaped breads, Oisin's stomach was so tense that instead of hunger he felt nausea. If Edmond had been taken because of the rebellion, what could they do? No one would be safe if the man talked.

"They took him early this morning," Alric said as he stepped beside Oisin. "The fool couldn't keep his mistress and his wife under control. The mistress went to the castle, and the next thing Kael and two Meta thugs were knocking at his door."

"Could it be for anything other than the rebellion? You said he could be trusted."

"Yes, it could be. The stupid woman could have accused him of theft of the duke's property. It feels too much of a coincidence, though."

Oisin didn't know what to say, but he knew he had to say something. "What do we need to do?"

Alric rubbed his chin. "Regardless of why he's there, he won't tell about us. I guarantee he'll hold up long enough; he's a tough one. If they do torture him, the only two people he knows are you and me. We need to get out of town. When the rebels attack, they'll free Edmond."

"No," Oisin said. He knew what he had to do. "I will not allow him to be tortured to save me. I'll go in and get him. You find a way in and meet me at Dorsey's place after sundown. I'll go in when it's dark enough to give us cover."

"Your friends won't let you do that."

"They won't know. They will think I am leaving town. That's what they'll tell me to do."

Alric nodded and Oisin could see the grin on his face reflected in the window. "Okay, but I'm coming with you."

"No, just me." Oisin knew that more than one person could bring more attention than they needed. "You need to get out of town. We'll say I'm going with you."

"But he's my brother. I should be the one to rescue him."

"No. I am his leader. I am responsible."

Alric clapped Oisin on the shoulder. "At Dorsey's, then. I'll find you as much information as I can."

When Oisin arrived back at the table, Jane turned to him. "What happened? There's gossip that someone has been taken to the dungeon."

"Yes, Alric's brother was taken early this morning. It could be about something else, but –"

She cut him off. "Yes, but... I think we'd be naive to assume it was about something else."

"Alric says he won't tell them anything."

Michal and Jane both spoke. "We can't count on that."

"I know," Oisin said. "Look, he only knows me and his brother. The rebellion is safe. We'll get out of town. I figure we have until tonight; it will be better for us to leave in the dark. We'll get farther before we're missed."

Jane shook her head. "And, if he cracks before then?"

Michal put his hand on Jane's arm. "If Edmond had cracked by now, Oisin would be in the cell next to him. If he hasn't cracked yet, he has some resources and will likely last until night."

"That's speculation," Jane said.

"Yes, but that's all we have," Michal argued.

"Look, I'll keep a low profile." Oisin turned to Jane and changed the subject. "Let's talk about what you have to tell us."

"I suppose it wouldn't help to run around in a panic." She took a sip of her tea. "Just keep your eyes out. If the guards come toward you, don't jump and panic. It will only raise their suspicion."

"Okay," Oisin said. "So, what has happened in the last few days?"

"We brought the swords into the city. They are in our warehouse. I'll take you there later." She paused as two women walked by laughing and flirting with a couple of young men at a stall selling knives. "The people we recruited will be here in three days. They will come in small groups and not arouse suspicion. There are a lot of people heading this way in anticipation of making money off the duke's bride search."

"Have you made any arrangements for meeting places?" Michal asked.

"We have the warehouse, but we may need another place. Too many people going in and out of the warehouse will..."

"I know, arouse suspicion." Serena laughed as though they were joking and gossiping. "We have another place. We'll show you later, too."

"Should we go now?" Oisin asked. "It's getting a bit crowded here. I think it will be difficult to be alert if we can't see far enough in any direction."

Jane stood. "Come with me. I'll show you the warehouse and the weapons."

Oisin wondered if he could find a sword small enough to smuggle with him into the castle tonight. And take it without tipping off any of them that he wasn't going to slip out of town.

CHAPTER FORTY

Kael climbed the stairs to the duke's chamber. The afternoon was passing, and Edmond had not broken. He got no pleasure from torture. It often resulted in lies told to stop the pain. Perhaps time alone in the dark cell, with the damp seeping into his bones, would make Edmond reassess his willingness to provide answers.

The heat of the upper levels of the castle was slowly penetrating the chill, but not fast enough to provide relief to his aching joints. He composed his mind, gathering his arguments as he rose toward the room. The whisper of servants and scent of the flowers arranged in vases on each floor brought a feeling of home and a certain level of comfort back to Kael.

The door to the duke's chamber was ajar, and Kael could hear the duke talking and cursing. Kael suspected it was about the lack of a secretary.

Pushing the door open wider, he spoke, "Sire, is there something I can do to assist?"

"Where is that damnable Edmond? He has not been in to see me all day. I have no idea where I am supposed to be, or why."

"I asked Harley to assist you, did he not come?"

"I sent him away. He didn't know how to change the schedule. He simply kept repeating where I was supposed to go."

"I apologize." Kael stepped closer. "Where is the diary?"

"In the fire." The duke pointed; the sheets of paper containing his schedule were curled and black. There was nothing to rescue.

"I see."

"Answer the question. Where is Edmond?" The duke was screaming.

"I arrested him this morning." Kael paused, waiting for the reaction.

"You did what?" The duke's face turned a darker shade of purple. "Damn, you, Kael, why?"

"He has been plotting rebellion. I —"

"Do you have proof?" The duke's voice dropped to a dangerously calm level. "Tell me that you have concrete evidence. That you didn't inconvenience me because of rumor and conjecture."

Kael swallowed, hoping his next words would satisfy the duke. "I received a report that he had agreed to help invade the castle."

The duke stalked toward Kael. "From who?"

"A source very close to him. Someone who would have his confidence."

"Who? Stop evading me."

"His mistress."

The duke clenched his fists, his voice tight as he spoke. "You locked up my secretary, the man who helps me get through every day, the man who keeps people from bothering me with trivialities, on the word of a mistress." His control slipped and he roared. "Can you tell me, please, why she came to you?"

"She thought it was her civic duty." Kael kept his voice even, despite his sudden compulsion to flee.

"And." The duke's voice was calm again. Kael felt his knees shake. "Has he provided you with any useful information?"

"Not yet," Kael admitted. "It will take a little more time to soften him up."

"How long do you think you might need?"

Kael knew better than to be fooled by the reasonableness of the question. It was critical that he buy time. "The day is almost done," he said. "You have only dinner, and whatever evening entertainment catches your fancy. Edmond would be going home around this time, anyway. Let me have him until morning. If he hasn't provided information by dawn, I will release him, and he will have time to arrange your day."

"I do not like you taking this initiative. I will allow you this one night. If you do not have information by dawn, you will never mention this rebellion to me again. Are you clear?"

Kael paused to make the duke think he was considering the offer rather than being relieved that he was still alive. "If I cannot get information from him by dawn, I will not bring up the rebellion again without concrete proof."

"And, you will not take any more of the castle staff to interrogate to find that concrete proof." The duke had moved to his desk and was fingering the letter opener, his face turned away from Kael.

"Agreed." Kael forced the word from his tight throat.

"Now," the duke said. "Tell the cook I will eat in the main dining room, and the master of entertainment that I require music and dancers."

Kael bowed slightly to the duke. "Of course."

CHAPTER FORTY-ONE

Oisin worried about Edmond; he knew that the rebellion had been going too smoothly but would have been happy for that to continue. At any time having a collaborator taken by the enemy would be bad, but this close to the start of the rebellion, it was disastrous.

They'd met the original eight conspirators in the warehouse and returned to their room.

Michal looked worried. "At least we won't have to bring the swords through the city. That warehouse is close enough to the castle to be almost part of the storerooms."

Serena was pacing. "I don't feel good about leaving Edmond in the dungeon," she said. "That's two people in the dungeon. Remember, Inka's sister is there too. We should have someone on the first wave go free them while the others attack."

"Who?" Oisin asked. "You'll already be down one person, me. Who else will you take?"

"What about Jane?" Serena said.

Oisin shook his head. "No, it needs to be more than one person. And I think it should be people not related to the prisoner. The rescuers need to have clear heads."

"I hate to say this." Michal paused. "I think we should talk about this after Oisin leaves."

"You're right," Oisin said. "If I get caught, I can't tell them what I don't know."

Serena settled beside him. "I don't want to think about you getting caught. But if you do, they will torture you. If you have to tell them something, what will it be?"

Oisin shrugged. "If I get caught, I'll send them to Halm's town. I'll tell them we were planning to launch our attack there."

"Don't tell them anything," Michal said. "Think about when you were a kid, when you wanted to keep something secret from your parents. If you're anything like me, you were fine unless you started to talk. When I started talking, no matter how much I tried to control it, eventually I said something that gave me away. Something they picked up and went after until they got the truth."

"Okay." Oisin found himself concentrating on Michal's instructions. Because he wasn't leaving town, it was more likely he would be caught. He needed to understand anything he could about lying. He wasn't practiced at it, and Michal's advice sounded good. "I tell them nothing."

Serena moved closer to him. Oisin felt her arm go around his shoulder. "When will you leave? I want to make sure I say goodbye."

"I'll go after you sleep. I think the later I go the better."

She drew him into a hug. Oisin felt that danger was worth it, to have her so close to him.

CHAPTER FORTY-TWO

Kael entered the cell. He had been forced to join the duke for dinner, so his time with Edmond was short. He suspected the duke was trying to put obstacles in the way, as though this was a game, and the truth didn't matter as long as the duke won.

He stood at the entrance to the cell. "Edmond, how are you feeling?" He made his voice sound hearty and warm. "You were missed by the duke today."

"That is good to know," Edmond's voice returned from the dark room.

Kael laughed. "He could not read the schedule. He wanted to know where his damned secretary was."

"Ah, well I'm sure you will take over those tasks easily enough."

Kael felt his temper surge. The man was toying with him. He was far from broken. Walking over to the stove, Kael swung open the door, red light spilled from the opening. He could see Edmond sitting on the chair, facing away. From behind, Kael saw the blood at the man's wrists. He had been trying to escape. So, he was not as at ease as he had sounded. Good.

"Archer," Kael shouted for his assistant. When the man

entered, he beckoned him closer, whispering instructions in his ear. Archer grunted and scurried out of the room.

"So," Kael said to the back of Edmond's head. "You seem comfortable."

"It's a little cool for this time of year. But it is nice to find a place to meditate in the crowded city."

Kael listened for Archer's return. "It will be a pity if you have no peace. If something kept your focus away from the serenity you seek."

Archer returned. He carried a pail of steaming water and leather thongs.

"Thank you, Archer. Please drop the thongs in the water."

Kael took a ladle that was resting in the pail. "Take the thongs out, now. And be ready."

Moving close behind Edmond, Kael touched the man on the shoulder. He spoke quietly into Edmond's ear. "We don't want those wounds to become infected. This will sting a bit."

Kael poured the steaming water over Edmond's bloody wrists. The man hissed on an indrawn breath. "The salt will clean the wounds.

Archer reached and severed the ropes around Edmond's hands and quickly tied the wet leather. Kael nodded in satisfaction. "Not too tight," he instructed. "Leave room for the leather to shrink."

"I know... sir." Archer snapped.

"Thank you for your service, now go. Leave the candle." He waited for Archer to leave, and then walked around to face Edmond. "You must not try to fight the bonds this time. The leather will shrink to the size of your wrists, the salt will harden it, and if you struggle against them, they will cut through the skin. You may bleed to death before someone comes."

"Thank you," Edmond said. Kael could see how tightly he clenched his teeth. "I will achieve meditation faster without a physical task."

"Brave words." Kael smiled. "Now, one more thing, and I'll leave you to your peace."

He picked up the pail and poured half of it over Edmond's shoulders, knowing the heat would evaporate from the water rapidly, leaving the man shivering in the dark. He took the rest of the water and carefully doused the fire in the stove.

"Now, you will have no distractions as you consider the wisdom of maintaining your silence." Kael took the candle and left the room. He did not close the door as he left, leaving it open would leech the heat from the water faster.

CHAPTER FORTY-THREE

Oisin started to pack his clothes as Michal and Serena settled for the night. They had brought a small meal of bread and sausage to their rooms, and Oisin had taken a portion, ostensibly to eat on the road. He was going to leave as soon as the house quieted.

"You should take the money," Michal said when Oisin handed him the purse. "We can make more. You have the earning potential of a rock now that you are on your own."

Oisin laughed. "Thanks so much for your confidence." He tried to think of a way to refuse to take any money. Knowing he would either be in the dungeon, a prisoner, or back with them in a day. He didn't want them to go without because of him. "I will be fine. It's just over a day's walk to my father's house. There's no reason to worry. By the time any danger comes there, it will be over but for the elections."

Serena shook her head. "I don't like the idea of you not having a few pennies. You eat like a horse. If you try to subsist a day on that one sausage sandwich, they'll find you lying in a ditch passed out from hunger. And what about Alric? He may not be able to last a day without food."

"Look, we're not that delicate," Oisin said, opening the purse.

"There's twenty pennies here. You need at least that to get through the next three days before... before it starts."

"We'll do another performance tomorrow," Michal said. "We can get by."

Oisin couldn't think of another logical argument. "I'll take two pennies. It's not like there are any places to spend money on the way. It might be nice to buy some tea in the village before going up to the house."

"You will take care, won't you?" Serena stared at him as she asked. "I don't want to win this and find we've lost you."

"I will take care. You'll be surprised at how quickly the time will go before you see me again." He made himself stop talking. He was skipping too close to the truth. He realized now how valuable Michal's advice about lying was — don't offer any information.

"It's dark outside now," Michal said. "You can probably leave in an hour. Is that when you said you would meet Alric?"

"Yes, by the fountain at the Green Man. He knows a way we can slip out without the guards seeing us."

"Maybe we can fill the time by talking," Serena suggested.

"No." Oisin wanted them asleep before he slipped out. "It will feel too much like a wake. You're both tired. Try to sleep."

"I want to say goodbye when you go," Serena said. "I want to know you get out safely. I'll see you to the Green Man."

"No," Michal and Oisin said.

"He has to go alone," Michal finished. "The more traveling back and forth we do, the more dangerous it becomes. All we need is for the guards to detain one, or both, of us for something stupid. He's right. Try to sleep."

Michal rolled himself in his blanket and turned away from them. Oisin felt like he'd been given privacy with Serena, and was grateful for Michal's discretion.

"I won't be able to sleep," Serena whispered.

"You will. I don't want you getting yourself killed because you didn't get enough sleep." Oisin patted her bedding. "Get in the covers. I'll sit here until you drop off."

She wrapped the blanket around her shoulders. Oisin put his own on top. "You might as well have this one too, I won't need it."

"Oisin, don't get killed, I'm not finished with you," she said as he tucked the covers around her.

"I'm not done with you either," he whispered.

CHAPTER FORTY-FOUR

It had taken less than ten minutes for Michal's breathing to turn into a gentle snore. Serena tossed a few times, but the extra heat of the blankets had done what Oisin hoped. Her body went slack as a child's in sleep as her breathing deepened.

He waited what seemed like an hour, watching her sleep, trying to imprint the image on his brain. The night sounds of the inn had slowly drifted away. The last sound being a mother singing a lullaby to a fretful child.

Oisin stood and picked up his travel bag. He wouldn't need it, but they would be suspicious if he left it behind. Alric would be waiting at the Green Man by now. Oisin figured he could hide his bag near the inn before they went to the castle.

Opening the door just enough to slip out and avoiding the creak it made when it was three quarters open, he slipped out onto the landing and closed it gently behind him. The ladder was lit by the flicker of the fire in the common room. Oisin stepped over the middle two rungs that usually squeaked. His eyes adjusted as he descended, and he was able to make his way between the tables without knocking anything over. The front door was off the latch. He slipped through into the dark street, ears straining for the least sound: footsteps, voices, anything.

He hitched the strap of his bag onto his shoulder and walked toward the square, keeping close to the wall to avoid casual notice by the Meta guards patrolling the city at night. The night guard was supposed to keep the city safe from drunken brawls and quiet from carousing. But Oisin had heard enough tales of beatings for running errands after dark, to make sure he avoided contact with them.

He was particularly alert for any Meta walking with purpose in the direction of the inn. He could only hope that Edmond had kept quiet.

When he reached the square, he was grateful that the moon was just a dim glow. The stalls that filled the center of the market were empty of goods and people. Oisin stood in the shadow of a doorway scanning the open area. If he could simply cross the square, he would be at the Green Man in less than a minute. The problem was, the three guards sitting on the edge of the center fountain. They were relaxing and talking to each other, not particularly alert, but there was no way Oisin would be able to hide if he crossed the square.

Looking to the right, where the shadow of the buildings gave him just enough room to move, he saw that he could get halfway around before having to cross open space. Looking to the left, he saw there was no hope, the alleyway was in shadow, but the buildings past it were painted with moonlight. The Green Man was closer if he went left, but it would be a stroll in full sight of the Meta.

The long way around then.

Taking another glance, he moved slowly to the right, making sure his movements were smooth and careful. He put away the worry of how he would manage after he ran out of shadow, hoping something would occur to him, or simply occur, by the time he got there.

Two of the Meta stood and faced the third who remained sitting on the fountain. "That stone is cold enough to freeze the dinner in your gut," one of the standing Meta announced. "I don't know how you can stand it."

Oisin stopped and waited, realizing how difficult this would be if the Meta had been more interested in keeping their own language a secret. They may have saved the effort of learning Human Standard by making the humans learn Metase, but now they lost the opportunity to keep secrets.

The sitting Meta said something, and the other two laughed.

"It's a quiet night," the second standing Meta said. "I don't know that we're going to get any fun."

"Don't worry," the first one said. "I heard a few loud voices coming from the Goat's Breath, they'll be out soon. We'll have some fun before sunrise."

The three Meta laughed again. Oisin's stomach clenched. He hoped the drinkers at the Goat's Breath Inn stayed put. Maybe they would pass out, and not stumble into what looked like a plan to ambush anyone who came near the guard.

He inched along until he reached the edge of the shadow. If he moved forward now, the seated Meta would see him. The others stood with their backs to him, and if they didn't move, only one would see him. Realizing he was holding his breath, Oisin let it out slowly through his nose.

The open distance was only five buildings.

He could cross in a few seconds. Once past, he would be in a deeper shadow and could reach the Green Man fountain with little trouble. If only that damn Meta would stand up and face away. Oisin forced himself to calm. Patience was the key, just like hunting rabbits.

The Meta were still talking, but had lowered their voices, he couldn't hear the words. Looking at the space he needed to cross, he saw halfway was a tavern. If he could get there, he could use the scattered tables as cover, keeping low. To get to the table he needed only a second. If he didn't make noise, he could get to the last building without trouble.

"I'm busting," the seated Meta said. Then he stood and turned his back to urinate into the water. Oisin smiled and crouched low, making it to the cover of the tables with no sound. He sent a silent thanks to the tavern owner who had not cleared the tables into the common room for the night.

He hugged his bag to his chest as he moved from table to table. The Meta finished relieving himself and moved away from the fountain. The others followed him. They were walking toward the alleyway next to Oisin's hiding place.

Oisin froze.

"I'm not going to sit waiting for some drunks to come out, or not," The Meta who had urinated said as they passed the table. "Let's go see if there are any humans sneaking home."

Oisin waited until they were out of sight before moving. He ran, crouched over, until he arrived at the small fountain with the carved leaves and man's face. Grateful the Meta hadn't been resting at this fountain, he was even more grateful he had never as much as touched the water in the central one.

Two people sat on the ground with their backs to the fountain, Alric and Dorsey. "I thought they would catch you for sure," Dorsey whispered.

"I almost thought they had," Oisin admitted. "I could feel a hand about to touch my shoulder the entire time."

"Come inside," Dorsey said. "You'll need a minute or two to settle before you go up to the castle."

All three entered the stairwell leading to the basement room. Oisin was glad of the opportunity to steady his breathing and talk above a whisper. "Michal and Serena think I've left the city. I need to leave my bag somewhere; will you take it?" He held out the bag to Dorsey.

"Aye, leave it with me. I'll make sure you get it back." She held out her hand. "Now, what is your plan?"

Alric looked at Oisin who answered, "I guess we go in, find Edmond, and get him out. All without getting caught, obviously."

"Obviously," she said, chuckling. "What weapons did you bring?"

Alric reached into his pocket and withdrew his hand clutched around a metal bar. "A bit of extra power in my punch," he said.

Oisin pulled out the sharp knife Jane had given him earlier. "I hope it will be enough."

Dorsey sighed. "I hope you won't have to use them." She pointed at Alric's metal bar. "That will more likely break your hand at the first punch. And Oisin, be careful, a knife is a treacherous weapon. It's as likely to cut you as it is to cut your attacker." She picked up two short clubs from a lower step and passed them to Oisin and Alric. "These will stun a Meta for a few minutes. Try to hit them on the side of their head, just above the tip of their ears."

Oisin took the club and hefted its weight. "Thanks, I'll still take the knife. You never know when it might come in handy."

"And, this." Dorsey picked up a small bundle of cloth. "If Edmond is hurt, you might need to bind his wounds before you can move him. These have been soaked in liniment. Tell him it will sting so he's prepared."

Alric took the cloth and slid it into a pocket inside his jacket. Oisin noticed that Alric was wearing black clothing, nothing that gave off a reflection, nothing metal showed to make noise. Michal had advised Oisin on how to dress for sneaking in and out of a building. Alric must have known someone like Michal.

"How are you getting in?" Dorsey asked.

Alric tucked the club into his pocket before answering. "The lower channel; we can hide out for a while there if need be. It is only a few feet from the entrance to the dungeon. We can come out the same way. There's not likely to be a guard there. They don't like the smell."

"When you are done, come back here," Dorsey said. "I'll leave a key in the mouth of the Green Man beside the door. The room will be warm. I'll put a bath down there and keep food available."

Oisin realized how deeply committed Dorsey was to the cause. She had made all the arrangements that Oisin had not even thought about. If it had been up to him, they would be thinking about where to go as they left the castle. He had a lot to learn about planning it seemed. Well, how many revolutions did a man have to organize anyway?

"Good luck to you," Dorsey said. "Go on now and take care."

Alric grinned at her and said he would expect a jug of beer to be waiting too.

CHAPTER FORTY-FIVE

Oisin and Alric crouched in a hedge outside the entrance to the dungeon. Oisin breathed through his nose to avoid gagging on the smell from the sewer. The grounds had gone quiet a half hour ago, and Alric whispered that Oisin should be ready.

"Are we going in the water?" Oisin whispered back. "If we go inside stinking of sewer, it will be hard to pass unnoticed."

"Yes, it will," Alric breathed in his ear. "Do you think I might have planned around that?"

"Yes," Oisin said. "But what did you plan? I would like to know what I'm facing."

Alric turned, still crouching. "There is a walkway in the channel. It's above the water, most of the time. Be careful not to slip. See where the bank curves around the wall?"

Oisin looked where Alric pointed. The wall was the near side of the tunnel. The grass curved around as though it went inside. It didn't, though, the grass was bordered by stone, and the path into the tunnel was paved. Lanterns stood on poles along the side of the lawn.

"We go carefully across the grass and get on the path. The light from those lanterns will shine just inside the opening. About ten feet in there's a side passage. It leads to the dungeon. The guards use it to toss bodies in the sewer from time to time. They block the flow of the water until it overflows and someone has to clean it out."

"So, the plan is we go down that path, find Edmond, and bring him out the same way."

"That's the plan all right," Alric said. "Now, stretch your legs a bit before we go. Can't have you cramping up and falling in."

"Don't they have guards?" Oisin couldn't push aside the thought that there was an ambush waiting inside.

"It's usually not guarded. The Meta don't think anyone would want to crawl through the dark sewer to break in. There's a jailer, Archer's his name. He makes sure everyone is locked in."

Oisin stood from the crouch and winced at the burning in his leg muscles. He stretched while looking around to make sure no one had seen them. "I need to make one little change to the plan," he said. "There's a woman in there. The sister of one of our people. We need to find her and bring her out too."

"We can bring out the whole dungeon's worth after the fight," Alric said and then looked at Oisin's expression. "I suppose it won't hurt to find the woman. Ready?"

Oisin nodded and followed Alric. The ground was wet and slippery, and he had to step carefully to avoid sliding on his backside into the foul waste. The only good thing was that the smell was no worse as they entered the tunnel.

When they were inside Oisin relaxed. The footing was still slippery, but they were no longer on an incline. The path was straight, and the light from outside showed him enough ahead to see the path was well maintained. He hoped they wouldn't have to find the side passage by feel.

Alric put his finger to his lips and pointed to the tunnel. He mimed tiptoeing and started forward.

Oisin followed, trying not to touch anything. The tunnel darkened faster than he expected, then he realized his body was blocking the light from outside. Alric's presence was a darker patch in the gloom ahead.

A splash sounded beside Oisin, and he jerked toward the wall, and then recoiled from the dampness soaking through his sleeve. They reached the side passage and turned, following the tunnel for several paces, walking slowly and stopping to listen every few steps. Oisin noticed the sewer smell fade the farther they went, that or he was simply getting used to it.

As they reached the opening, Oisin heard footsteps and almost bumped into Alric, who had come to a complete stop. A human passed the entrance to the passage. The man didn't look sideways. If he had, there was no way he could have missed seeing the two of them frozen in place.

The man muttered as he walked. "Leave him be then go check on him. Let him stew then make sure he isn't dead. Make up your mind Kael. He's not going to talk. I've seen his type before."

Alric looked out of the tunnel after the man had passed. Oisin leaned out to watch the man's candle flicker all the way down the corridor then pass to the right. They withdrew to the passage again. Crossing to the other side to avoid being seen as the man returned.

Oisin mouthed the words, "It's Edmond."

Alric nodded and waggled his hand, mouthing what looked like, maybe.

The light flickered as the man returned. "Passed out, but still alive. Hope that's what you wanted, Kael. It'll have to do until morning. I'm for my bed."

They waited for the man to move out of sight and stepped out into the darkness of the tunnel. Oisin's eyes adjusted, but no more than to allow him to see doorways as they passed them. He wondered how he would find Inka's sister.

CHAPTER FORTY-SIX

Oisin followed Alric to the end of the passage. The door in front of them was open and the room was a deeper black than the hall. Cold crawled out of it, freezing Oisin ankles.

"This is it," Alric said. "Can you hear me, Edmond?"

"Alric?" The voice seemed to come from the center of the room. "Get out before they see you. Damn." Edmond's last word came on hiss of pain.

Oisin felt Alric's elbow hit his arm. The man was searching for something in his pocket.

"Finally," Alric whispered.

Oisin heard a scratching sound then closed his eyes before the light flashed. He couldn't afford to get blinded. "Get inside. Someone might see it," he said pushing Alric toward the door.

Oisin remembered to keep his eyes squeezed tight until he thought the flash had subsided. When he opened his eyes, he saw Alric holding a tiny lantern. It gave off only enough of a glow to light a circle two feet around. "A bit of warning would have been nice."

"Sorry, I didn't think," Alric said, moving to his brother.

Edmond was tied to a chair in the middle of the room. Oisin could see the man was damp, his face pale except his cheeks and nose, which were a feverish pink.

"Give me that pig sticker you brought." Alric held out his hand. "Hold Edmond so he doesn't fall. They've tied him tight."

Oisin crouched down in front of Edmond. Placing his hands on the man's shoulders, he braced himself to take the weight. "Okay."

Alric started with the ropes binding his brother's chest and feet to the chair. The sharp knife sawed through quickly. Oisin slid his hands under Edmond's armpits as Alric raised his brother's arms. The wrists were bound tightly. Oisin couldn't see how Alric would be able to slide the knife between the leather and the skin.

"This is going to hurt," Alric said. "I'm going to have to cut you. We'll bind the wound, but there's no other way."

"I know. Just do it." Edmond pressed his lips together.

Oisin watched Alric slide the point of the knife into the side of his brother's wrist, taking care to miss any veins. Alric flicked the blade sharply, the leather parted, and blood flowed.

Edmond stood, but seemed to lose the strength in his legs. Oisin took hold of him and threw the uncut arm around his own shoulders. He looked over at Alric and said, "I've got a handkerchief in my pocket, it's clean. Pull it out, wrap it tightly around Edmond's hand, and then find some way to secure his arm so the wound is above his heart. It will stop the bleeding. I don't think Dorsey's cloths are a good idea. We don't want him screaming when the liniment hits the wound."

When Edmond's arm was bound with the handkerchief, Oisin nodded to Alric to lead the way out.

Oisin was ready to step into the corridor with Edmond when Alric extinguished the lantern and plunged them into darkness. "Wait until your eyes adjust again before we head out."

"For crying out loud, Alric, don't keep doing that." Oisin's stomach was twisting with the stress, the sooner they could get out of here the better.

He tightened his hold on Edmond and followed Alric out of the cell. He remembered it was a hundred paces to the side corridor on the way in. It would be more going back because he had to shuffle with Edmond's weight. Oisin counted fifty steps before he bumped into Alric's back. Edmond groaned quietly at the jolt.

"Careful," Alric whispered directly into Oisin's ear. "There's someone ahead."

Too easy, I knew it. Oisin glanced around — nowhere to hide.

A gravelly off-tune voice floated down the corridor. "If I were your − agh what's the damn word − lover, I... uh oops, you would be my love..." A giggle followed. "Ah, who needs to be sober if you have to be sitting down here all night?"

"Go back," Alric hissed. "Maybe we can slip out after the guard leaves."

Oisin turned around, trying not to put any more strain on Edmond. The singer started again; his voice closer. Oisin was grateful for the darkness, without it they would have been seen already.

"Don't worry about me," Edmond said. "Get yourselves safe."

Oisin held him tighter. "No chance. We came to get you, and that's what we'll do."

The singing started up again and now it was punctuated with the sound of boots hitting stone in an irregular pattern. "If you... um if we were to dance... Now that's a nice idea. A dance would help fill the night." The steps turned into a shuffle that seemed to go along with the slurred words of the song.

Oisin turned the corner into Edmond's old cell and lowered him onto the chair. When he was settled, Oisin turned to Alric. "What now?" he whispered.

"I can go out and try to deal with him."

"No," Oisin whispered. "We go together. Edmond will be fine here." *Unless we're captured.* Oisin couldn't see anything they could use as a weapon. Then he remembered the clubs Dorsey gave them. "Have you ever hit a Meta?"

"I don't know if I can aim right in here. If we don't hit him on the right spot... well it won't be good."

Oisin listened. "I don't hear him."

Alric leaned around the corner of the door and beckoned Oisin to follow.

The singing was still going on, but it was muffled. They crept toward the sound. They kept tight to the wall to take advantage of the shadow that deepened at its foot. When they were close enough to see the shape of the guard, they both came to a stop. He was slumped on the ground, back against the opposite wall. He was three feet on the other side of the opening to the sewer.

"If we were..." The guard snored and then grunted. "To... If we were..." The fragments of song were punctuated with snores.

Oisin pulled Alric away and back to the cell. When they were inside, he whispered, "We don't need to get past him. If we are quiet, we can get into the tunnel."

"I'd feel better if he was completely unconscious." Alric looked at his brother. "Can you carry Edmond and be quiet enough?"

"Maybe." Oisin realized maybe wouldn't be enough. "Probably. Yes, if Edmond can keep quiet I can too."

"Let's go then," Edmond said. Before struggling to his feet.

Oisin shook his head and then wrapped his arm around Edmond. "Not so fast. I've got you."

They moved as quickly as Edmond could manage a slow steady shuffle. Oisin cringed at the sound of their feet on the stone floor. Ahead, the sounds were more snore than song, but the Meta had not completely passed out.

When the guard came into sight, Oisin paused. He was too close. If they continued shuffling it might wake him, and it was too slow. He tapped Alric on the shoulder. When he turned, Oisin pointed to Edmond's feet, then to Alric.

Oisin waited until comprehension dawned.

Alric grinned and bent to pick up his brother's feet. They slipped past the guard and into the tunnel. Oisin had to fight the urge to run when they were out of sight.

When they were back in the bushes outside the sewer, Oisin laid Edmond down. "I need to go back to see if I can get Inka's sister." Oisin kept his voice so low he barely made a sound. "I can move quietly by myself; the guard won't know I'm there."

"Be quick. The longer we're here the more likely we'll get caught," Alric whispered back. "Go the other way and you'll see cells lining the wall. There's probably more light, but there might be sober guards."

Edmond reached out and held Oisin's arm. "Who are you searching for?" His voice was rough.

"A woman, she's been in there for almost three weeks."

Edmond grunted quietly as he shifted position. "Only one woman in the cells. She's not being punished. The duke heard she was a musician, and he wants her to perform for him. She said no. She's well taken care of. The duke doesn't want her harmed. If she won't change her mind about performing, he'll find some leverage."

Alric looked at Oisin. "I say leave her there. No sense bashing the wasp's nest if you don't need to."

Oisin considered. If they rescued her, it may cause the duke to do something rash. But they were taking Edmond so that was already a risk. "Won't the duke come looking for you?" he asked Edmond.

"Kael is the only one who's come to the cell. If the duke cared, he would have been there. I get the feeling the duke didn't approve of Kael taking me."

"Make up your mind, Oisin," Alric said, looking to the tunnel mouth. "We need to be gone from here long before dawn. Dorsey will be waiting to help get Edmond out of the city."

Oisin looked over his shoulder at the entrance to the tunnel. Shaking his head, he bent to help Edmond up.

CHAPTER FORTY-SEVEN

Kael had risen at dawn to finish questioning Edmond. If he wasn't ready to talk, he would have to let him go. There was no time to conduct the torture he had been avoiding. The duke would expect Edmond to be back on duty after breakfast at the latest.

As he approached the stairs leading to the dungeon, the duke stepped beside him. "Ah, there you are. I thought I would come with you to hear what Edmond has to say."

Kael hid his discomfort behind a warm smile, and said, "As you wish, Sire." Now it would be humiliating if Edmond didn't tell the truth about the rebellion. Kael tried to remember the reasons he had decided to work with this alien. Yes, making sure he ruled effectively and efficiently. Where had it all gone wrong?

They walked down the stairs side by side. The duke chatting about his plans for a large hunt while the bridal parties were in residence. Kael made noises intended to show he was listening while he thought about how he could get the truth from Edmond.

At the foot of the stairs, the duke stopped Kael from entering the dark hallway. "Wait, I wish to look in on the musician. She hasn't agreed yet to my request for a concert. Perhaps being the musician for the wedding will be sufficient incentive."

"The woman is over here." Kael led the way. "The jailer tells me she meditates for most of the day."

At this end of the prison, the cells were in good repair. Each small room had a door with a window covered with a grille. The rooms were dry and furnished with a table, a chair, and a cot. Farther down, the cells became increasingly less habitable.

"Elliene," the duke called softly through the grille as though calling to a pet. "Are you awake?"

There was a rustling of cloth before the woman spoke, "I am. Are you come to release me?"

"Will you play the violin for me?" the duke asked.

"I do not perform concerts, sire," Elliene said. "I play only for family. I would not be able to play before strangers."

"Silly woman," The duke snapped. "There will be a wedding in a week. Prepare yourself to play for me."

The woman did not answer.

The duke turned to Kael. "Lead the way. I am interested in seeing how you have handled my secretary. To see if the inconvenience I have endured was worth it."

Taking a torch from the wall, Kael focused on success. Edmond would speak.

"Kael," the duke said, his voice heavy with menace. "You remember our agreement, I hope."

"Yes, Sire. If I am unable to get concrete evidence, I will leave the subject of rebellion alone."

"Good."

They reached the end of the corridor, and Kael stood aside gesturing for the duke to enter.

"What kind of joke is this?"

Kael looked up at the duke's words. The cell was empty. Cut ropes and leather straps lying in an ashy pool of water.

"Archer!" Kael bellowed. "Sire, it seems we have had a prison break."

"Are you sure he didn't simply walk out?" The duke's tone was dangerously sarcastic. "The door was open when we arrived."

"He was bound too tightly to escape by himself." Kael could hear Archer's footsteps. He rounded on the man as he entered the room. "Where is the prisoner?"

"He was here when I checked on him," Archer said, looking at the chair. "Ain't no one been here since."

"Are you suggesting he disappeared?" The duke laughed. "I had no idea my secretary was also a magician. Although that does explain his ability to get me through a busy day."

"Don't know about that." Archer shrugged. "I know he were here. Now he ain't. You can make of it what you want. There were a guard down here, maybe you should ask him."

"Check the other cells." Kael gave Archer a rough push to the door.

"It seems you will have to put aside your rebellion," the duke said. Then he raised an eyebrow. "Unless you have already received the information you need?"

Kael tried to think of any information that might be enough to sway the duke. It was unbelievable that he was so blasé about the idea of a rebellion. Did he think the humans so cowed they didn't even consider fighting? "I think the fact that Edmond has escaped shows there is unrest."

"Fool." The duke shook his head as though he didn't believe how stupid Kael was. "It proves that Edmond has resourceful friends. It does not take a rebellion to release a friend from prison. These cells are not meant to be impregnable. Most of the doors don't even have locks. There are probably twenty ways to break in and out. Let's get somewhere warmer and have breakfast."

Kael followed the duke back up the corridor. As they turned the corner, Archer was walking toward them, shaking his head. "Everyone else is still where they should be."

"Well, Kael. You have had a busy night. You've lost me a secretary, and given up a useless campaign. Your first duty after breakfast is to find me a replacement secretary. One who is as good as Edmond was. Until you do, you will fulfill that function. I suppose you should also find out how Edmond escaped. Rebellion or not, we can't have people coming and going from prison as they please."

CHAPTER FORTY-EIGHT

Serena sat looking at Oisin's bare mattress. She had hardly thought of him in the nine months she'd been on the road with Michal, happy to put that part of her life behind her in exchange for the adventure of being free. Now, she felt a missing spot in their room where he should have been. Something cold sat beside her heart. She hoped it wasn't a premonition. She needed to see him again, needed to know he would be all right in the new world they were creating.

"He'll be okay," Michal said, his voice gentle. "It will all be over in a few days."

"I know, but it's the next few days that count, isn't it?" Serena tried to push away the feeling of doom that lay in her gut. She sighed. "I am tired of waiting."

"I know, me too, but there is nothing we can do until people get in place." Michal leaned against the wall, tossing scarves into the air. "We could eat."

"I'm not hungry. We just ate lunch."

"We could perform in a few hours. It would be something to do."

Looking around the room, she rolled her eyes. "I could clean up, I guess."

"It would be nice not to have to tiptoe around your clothes." Michal dodged the shoe she threw at him, not losing control of the scarves. "I know you are worried about Oisin."

"It's not that."

"You've been touchy all morning. Face it, you love the guy."

"I haven't been touchy. I'm bored that's all."

"Okay, if you say so." Michal tossed the scarves into a pile in the corner. "You know he adores you. But I know you don't want to talk about it. We'll do something else. Your juggling needs work. Grab those shoes."

Serena stood and picked up three shoes, the odd one's mate would be somewhere, she thought. Tossing them one at a time, she started a rhythm then strolled around the room juggling. "I know he loves me. It's not about love."

"Heads up." Michal threw one of the scarves at her. "If it's not about love, what is it about?"

Serena stopped walking and started turning in place, the shoes and scarf moving in a figure eight. "We've been friends for as long as I remember. What I feel is just friendship."

"Sure." Michal slid off one of his bracelets and threw it at Serena.

"Hey," she yelled, but managed to change her juggling to add the metal ring. "Okay, I can juggle all these things, I can do it walking around and spinning in a circle. What else do I need to learn?"

"Nothing, you are —"

Michal was interrupted by a knock on their door. He motioned for Serena to drop the objects and stand behind him. Opening the door, he looked down to see a young boy panting on the threshold. "What do you want boy?"

"Dorsey says come to the Green Man," the boy panted out. "She says it's important."

Michal looked up and down the hallway. No one was there. "Okay, we'll go. Wait here." Shutting the door, Michal turned to Serena. "Get your stuff. Where's the purse."

Serena held up the almost empty purse. "Do you think something has gone wrong?"

"I don't know, are you ready?"

She covered her hair in a bright blue scarf and nodded.

Michal opened the door and reached into the purse pulling out a small half penny. "Here boy," he held it out.

"No, Dorsey paid. You don't have to." The boy turned and ran down the stairs.

"That's a relief," Serena said. "We can buy a couple of mugs of tea for dinner."

Michal followed Serena up to the Green Man Inn where Dorsey was waiting for them beside the fountain. She motioned them to the side door, opening it and leading them onto the tiny landing.

"I've news for you," Dorsey said. "Go on down."

They descended the stairs and walked into the warm storage room. Standing by the stove was Alric.

"Surprise," he said, pointing to a man who looked so much like him he must be the brother. "This is Edmond."

"You are supposed to be out of the city," Michal said. "I'm glad you got your brother out of the dungeon, but it's not safe for you to be here."

"Edmond didn't tell Kael anything," Alric said. "We're fine. You'll need all of us for the rebellion."

"It's okay, Michal." Oisin stepped from behind the crates, rubbing his hair with a towel.

"Oisin," Serena shrieked and ran to hug him. Then, pulling back from the hug, she landed a punch on his arm. "What the hell do you think you are doing here?"

"You hugged me." He rubbed the spot where she had hit him.

Michal tried to sort out his feelings. It was good that Edmond was free, who knows how long he would have lasted in the duke's care. Having Oisin around would make Serena happy, and Alric would be helpful when they got into the castle. How could they be certain that the duke didn't find anything out?

"Tell us the story," Michal said. "How did you rescue him? How did you get back here?"

Oisin recounted the story and added the information about Inka's sister. "She will be fine until we can release her. I think we should make sure that all the prisoners are given amnesty after the rebellion."

Michal nodded. "I guess we should get Edmond out of town. Dorsey can you arrange it?"

"Already in the works," she answered. "That friend of yours, Zandor, he's agreed to slip Edmond into the secret compartment of one of his wagons. He'll be safe by evening."

"We'll pass on the news to Inka about her sister." Michal shook his head. "You were crazy to do this, I understand why, but you were still crazy."

CHAPTER FORTY-NINE

Kael stood in the duke's chamber waiting for orders. He had updated the schedule for the day, based on what he was sure was a whim on the duke's part designed to annoy him. He had met with the household staff to confirm details of the preparations for the visiting families and, now, he waited for the duke to provide him with the last-minute decisions.

"I heard from the head guard that you ordered them to search for evidence of the escape," the duke said, staring out the window.

"Yes, sire, I was concerned that the castle was vulnerable. I asked that they search the grounds for weaknesses."

"They reported to me." The duke turned. "There were footprints around the sewer tunnel. It's hard to believe anyone could bring out a prisoner through there. Three guards fell into the sewage before they could even enter the tunnel. There is access to the dungeons through there."

"We should set guards to watch the tunnel..." Kael began.

"It is already done," the duke snapped. "I have reassigned the other guards."

"But there may be other weaknesses," Kael said.

"Why am I worried about weaknesses? There is no threat to the castle, is there?" The duke smiled, but it didn't reach his eyes.

Kael knew he was being tested. "No, there are no threats."

The duke smiled. "Then the guards can go back to their other duties. Agreed?"

Kael swallowed a sigh and said, "Yes, sire."

The duke chuckled after Kael closed the door. He enjoyed making the man squirm. He would be glad to be gone but would pay the world to see Kael's face when no brides turned up and there were no Meta in the castle, city, or on the world. Perhaps he would rise to the opportunity and take charge.

He wished the humans luck; they would need it to be successful. They had no skill. None of them seemed to care that their duke ignored evidence of rebellion. Of course, if he really believed the humans had enough backbone between them to raise a rebellion, he would crush it.

Such a weak world was not fit for Meta.

Allorn was not due to report until tonight, but the duke didn't care to wait. He took the key from the desk drawer and warmed it to tune the right vibrations before going through the passage to the shuttle chamber. As he walked, he mulled over the preparations. "Hmm, the outside tunnel entrance should be cleared by tomorrow. If there have been no issues with the repairs, it is time to send out the messages to the other families."

He approached the end of the tunnel and heard commotion coming through. *What now?* His temper gave him more strength than he expected, and he pushed the door so hard it slammed against the wall. "What is the problem?"

The technicians were huddled in a group; they turned as one. The duke saw them raising glasses of what looked the good wine from his cellar.

"Ah, commander." Allorn stepped out of the group. "I thought you would approve a little celebration. I liberated a bottle of wine to celebrate the finish of the repairs."

The duke smiled. "You are done? We can finish with this back-water world? Is there another glass? I would celebrate with you."

"I was going to bring you a glass when I reported. It seemed unkind to make the others wait. They've worked so hard on clearing the rubble." Allorn escorted the duke to a small table and poured a glass, emptying the bottle.

"It is hard to believe we are so close to leaving," the duke said. "I will not be sorry to go, although I think we will take as much of this wine as the intelligence will allow."

"I will ask when we next connect. The intelligence is discon-necting for the time we move the shuttle."

"When do you do that?"

"Tomorrow night. We will need the help of some of the guards," Allorn said, pointing to his scientists. "Strong arms and backs are in short supply."

"I will assign all but four of the guards to assist. It will seem suspicious if all of them are gone, but I need little in the way of protection for the next few days. You may keep the guards to ensure the shuttle is safe until needed."

"We appreciate the help," Allorn said, raising his glass in salute. "To freedom."

CHAPTER FIFTY

Michal put their last coin on the table at the Green Man. "Dorsey," he said, with a smile. "Can we get some tea?"

She laughed and slid the coin back toward him. "Just remember who took care of you after things change. How about entertaining my customers tonight?"

Michal grinned back. "Happy to be of service. Of course, I'll remember you when I am rich and famous."

Dorsey walked away, signaling to one of the waiters to serve them. He nodded and went to the kitchen, returning a few minutes later with a tray laden with steaming bowls of stew.

"Your charm is useful for more than making the maids blush," Serena said as she dug into the hearty meal.

Michal closed his eyes and inhaled the rich aroma of herbs and meat. His stomach rumbled loudly. He looked around the room. "What do you think of juggling the things we find on the customers?"

"Dorsey needs to introduce the act," Oisin said. "I don't relish getting dragged into a brawl because someone misunderstood your intentions. Do you think there are enough people here to make it worthwhile?"

Michal looked around the room again. Two other tables were occupied and they were in the far corner. "Not, yet. The room will probably fill up in the next hour or so."

"Okay, so the money problem is solved if more people show up. How are we going to get everyone together?" Serena asked.

"Zandor is supposed to join us here," Michal said spooning some of the stew onto a chunk of bread. "I see Alric just came in."

Oisin nodded. "So, you think we should get them together? It would help take the burden off us. I don't know if you've noticed, but we haven't prepared ourselves. I don't know how to use a sword, how about you?"

Michal laughed and waved for Alric to join them. "I thought I'd stay with a shorter knife. I'm pretty good with it, and if I have to fight, I like to get in close."

"I could use some instruction," Serena said.

Alric dragged a chair to their table and joined them. "Instruction in what?"

"Sword play, or fighting, anyway," Oisin said. "Our education didn't involve combat skills."

"I can show you the basics," Alric said. "I learned as a kid. My dad wanted to make sure I could defend myself from bandits. He was a trader and often found himself on the road. He figured I'd follow in the business. I never thought it would come in handy."

"There's not much time. When?" Michal asked.

"Tonight? Downstairs. We'll ask Dorsey to let us use the room." Alric picked up the beer jug swirled the contents. "Let's get ourselves another beer."

"Do you have swords to fight with?" Oisin asked.

"Swords are tricky, and not for the novice. I can get my hands on a couple of short blades that should do the trick for you and the lass. She'd be hard pressed to hold a sword, they are not light," Alric answered, flipping some coin to the waiter for the beer.

Michal looked up and saw Zandor pause by the bar. He nodded and reached for another free chair to add to the table.

"That's Zandor coming over. We can work out the last details. After that, you can take Oisin and Serena downstairs for training. I'll do the show alone."

Zandor sat next to Alric. "If it's funds you need, boy, I will provide. I don't like the idea of you making a show of yourself. It's too dangerous to be noticed. If the guards decide they don't like the look of you, you might end up in the dungeon."

"We can look out for ourselves, thank you all the same." Michal tried not to sound disrespectful, but he didn't like to take charity. He always provided for himself, sensitive to the reputation his people had of taking what was not theirs.

"No offense intended," Zandor said. "Who is this man?"

Alric held out his hand. "Alric var Trent, late of the duke's household, at your service."

"Zandor var Ivan, trader. I have a friend's daughter to rescue, what drives you to the cause?"

"Many things, most recently, my brother tortured," Alric said. "Now, to the business at hand. What are the plans?"

Michal looked around. The inn was filling up, but no one was paying attention. No one was close enough to hear if they kept their voices low. "We go in at night. Two days from now."

"How many in the party, and who?" Zandor asked.

"We've thought about this, but we didn't have all the information we needed. So, we talked about six, eight maximum," Michal said. "We will need to hide somewhere in the castle for the night. More than eight will be difficult to hide. We need to split up, one party to the duke's chambers, one to the door."

"Eight is best," Alric said. "Five to the duke. He has guards outside his door. You'll need to fight. The other three to the door."

"Who, then," Oisin asked. "Who goes in, and who goes to the duke?"

Michal moved the plate and mug away, placing his elbows on the table and leaning into the center. He waited for a group of four men to pass them on the way to a back table. "Me, Oisin, Serena, Alric, Zandor for sure."

"Serena should not go in," Zandor said. "It is not the place for women."

Michal waited for the explosion. Serena never let that type of comment pass. He watched her face, lips firming and brow furrowing, she seemed to be swallowing her first reaction.

"I go," she said.

"But," Zandor started to argue.

"I go. Now let's talk about the other four." Serena stared at Zandor, as though challenging him to continue.

"I suppose that is the end of it," Zandor said, and then laughed loudly and heartily. "Ah, if only I were thirty years younger."

"I'm sure you were quite the catch," Serena said.

"The other four," Oisin brought them back to the topic.

"One of them needs to know the castle," Michal said. "Alric will go with one group and the other will need directions from him."

"Well, for the other three, I suggest Allen, Alec, and since we are including women, Inka," Zandor said.

"Inka will want to get her sister out," Michal agreed. "She can come, but I don't want to count on her to fight."

"She won't need to know how to fight to get her sister out. Oisin and Alric did fine without fighting," Serena said. "So, does that mean ten in the party? Five for the duke, three for the door, two for the dungeon?"

"It's getting out of hand," Michal said. "Let's start again. If we bring Inka, and she goes to her sister, do we need two people? Can we show her how to get to the dungeon and out?"

Alric nodded. "Let me offer a suggestion. I know the castle inside out. We can't get this Inka into the dungeon the same way we got in, because there are guards positioned at the channel entrance now."

"So, Inka doesn't come," Michal said. "I don't want to be worrying about her running off to her sister."

"No, that's not what I meant." Alric held up a hand. "We can get her close and show her the entrance. When the fighting starts, the guards will leave, and then in she goes and gets her sister out."

"Okay, that makes sense," Serena said, and then looked at Oisin. "Do you think she will be able to get in and out by herself?"

"It's pretty easy when you know how. Alric can show her tomorrow," Oisin answered.

"The grounds are open during the day," Alric said. "We can take a picnic lunch and pretend to be courting. How do I meet her?"

"I'll take care of that. Meet me tomorrow about ten at the market fountain," Zandor said.

"Okay, that's solved," Oisin said. "Now, we need enough people to attack the duke in his quarters. If we have the element of surprise, how many guards will there be?"

"Usually three, but some of the guards have been sent away. We should still count on three, I think," Alric said.

"Okay, how big is the space? Can we get five people in there to fight?"

"A corridor runs to the foyer," Alric said. "You can't sneak up on them, but it's a short corridor. If the attackers move very quickly you can get into the foyer and stop the guards reacting. It should be pretty easy to get five of us in with the guards and still be able to do what's necessary."

"Can you give us directions? So that we don't need you with us?" Michal asked.

Alric nodded. "It's straight forward from the center hall. I think I know where we can hide eight or so people. Both parties will need to go through the central hall. I can show the attacking party to the stairwell, and then lead the group to the door to the courtyard."

"Okay," Michal said. "Will there be guards inside?"

"No. The duke doesn't like having guards in his private rooms. What time do you think we should start the attack?"

Michal closed his eyes and tried to imagine the castle with people going about their business. "As early as possible. We don't want to have to fight through the castle staff. It would be best to do it before breakfast. When the duke is getting ready for the day. As early as we can get people to the courtyard."

"You don't need to come in through the courtyard," Alric said. "There are other doors where people can gather."

"How many, without bringing the attention of the guards?" Zandor asked.

"If we have enough, we can hide people down side alleys and they can rush the doors. We'll only need me to open the door," Alric said.

"No," Michal said. "No one goes alone. We can't assume that it will go smoothly."

"Okay five people to the duke, three to the door," Serena said. "Alric will coordinate the instructions. Where should people meet?"

"The best door is off the south of the castle. There's room for twenty people to gather without causing concern from the wrong quarters. There's three alleys that open onto the little square, that's another thirty."

"That's enough," Michal said. "Zandor, how many of your people will be here by tomorrow?"

"Half are already here," he answered. "The other half will arrive over the next two days."

"Okay," Michal said. "Alric, are you sure you can do this? You will be training Oisin and Serena, you'll be meeting Inka and taking her to the entrance to the dungeons, meeting the other members of the group, and giving directions to everyone."

"Not a problem." Alric flipped his fingers. "I have organized and managed enough banquets for the duke at short notice to be able to do more than five things at the same time, while going days without sleep. Don't fret."

"Well, you have all the hard work." Serena laughed. "All we have to do is..." She looked around. "I guess all we have to do is finish it."

Zandor stood and made his goodbyes.

Michal shifted in his seat, pulling silken scarves from his pockets. "It's time for you three to go. On your way out, tell Dorsey to announce the juggler."

A half hour later, Serena sat on a barrel and watched as Oisin hefted the knife that Alric had handed him. It was about eighteen inches in length, most of it a double-edged blade. She held its mate across her lap. The metal was icy in her fingers.

She listened to the instructions Alric gave. Be wary of the knife, it will as likely cut you as your intended victim. Hold it in your fist, fingers down, the head toward your body, point away. Stab not slice. She looked at the blade and considered its destiny, the metal gleamed, and she almost felt a hunger from it. It was a weapon designed to harm and to kill. She wished it was a kitchen knife, something with a useful purpose.

The sound of Oisin's feet shuffling on the stones of the floor as he moved, practicing the stab and run motions with Alric, and the murmur of the men's voices faded into the background. The heat of the room lulling her into a half dream.

She imagined facing the duke, imagined being the one to sink her blade into his body, the one to take his life and bring an end to his brutality. Her hand on the haft of the blade started to tremble. She had never taken a life, hadn't even killed a chicken for dinner. What if she couldn't do it? What if at the crucial moment, she faltered?

"Serena," Oisin's voice cut through her dream. "Are you okay?"

"What? Yes," she said.

"I called you four times." Oisin touched her hand. "Are you sure you are okay?"

"What if we don't kill him?" The words were out before she could stop them. "I shouldn't jinx it, I know, but what if they stop us?"

"It will all work out," Alric said. "We have it all worked out. It's a good plan. Not to worry."

"We never planned for anything to go wrong," she said.

"Come on, stand up," Alric ordered. "Let's see if you can use that blade. Working your body might help put aside your worries."

She stood and followed Alric's instructions. The blade fit her hand well, and she had no problem following the moves. It did nothing for her worries.

"Have you ever killed someone?" she asked Alric.

"No," he said. "Are you worried no one will be able to do it?"

Relieved he had named the fear, she nodded. "If we can't, what is the plan?"

"If you can't kill him, you will have to keep him in a cell until someone works out how to deal with him." Alric shrugged. "Killing is final, but it's not the only option."

Oisin stepped over and put his arm around her. "I don't know if any of us have killed before, but remember we'll have Zandor and his crew with us. It's possible they will be able to do it. If not, starting a new life without taking one is a good thing."

"I suppose," she said.

CHAPTER FIFTY-ONE

The next afternoon, Michal waited at the fountain for Alric to appear. They were going to check out his recommendations for entering the castle. Michal wanted to know how the meeting with Inka had gone. It felt like that would be the omen. If Inka was confident she could get in to rescue her sister, then it was a good omen. If she felt it was too dangerous...well perhaps it would not be a bad omen.

The sound of laughing broke into his thoughts. Three children raced by in a flash of skirts and arms. He hoped they would be free to run like that for their whole childhood. He looked around him, hoping to see Alric, but only catching the eye of a Meta guard strolling into the square, laughing.

He stood and started to make his way around the fountain. Alric would see him as long as he stayed in the center, but he thought perhaps he would be conspicuous sitting in one place for any amount of time.

"Feeling restless?" Alric asked as he approached Michal. "I feel it too."

"I don't like waiting. It's like someone, or something, is

looking for a chance to screw up the whole plan. How did it go with Inka?"

"She's a lovely lady," Alric said. "We found a place for her to hide. There is only one guard on the grounds, and he is more asleep than alert. I think the duke has his household stirred up for this wedding, and the only guards outside are being punished for something. Inka will wait until the guard is distracted before going through to her sister."

"Okay." Michal felt a layer of anxiety lift from his shoulders. "Let's get to the warehouse and pick up Zandor. He'll want to know all about this gathering place."

The two men started toward the far northern corner of the market. Leaving behind the calls of the vendors and the enticing smells of food, drink, and flowers from the stalls.

"I thought Serena and Oisin would be with us today," Alric said as they entered the alleyway.

"I made them practice their fighting again," Michal said. "Serena is starting to worry too much about what might happen. Practicing helps keep her mind off it."

Alric nodded then asked, "If it comes to it, will you be able to finish him?"

"I don't know." Michal didn't like admitting weakness, but he'd been worried about the same thing. "I wonder if it's better that we don't. Finish it, I mean."

"What do you mean? I don't think we can cancel it now." Alric started walking again.

"I mean if we put him in a cell rather than..."

"It will be tricky," Alric said. "In a cell, he is available for rescue and reinstatement."

"Serena told me what you said last night – that the details will take care of themselves in the end. Do you think it's true?"

"Well it's not how I would plan this, but yes, I believe they will work themselves out one way or another." Alric motioned with his chin to a wide doorway across from them. "That's the warehouse?"

"Yes." Michal's eyes flicked to a smaller door within the larger one. It cracked open enough for a man to slip out. "There's Zandor."

They waited at the corner for the merchant to join them. Michal worried at a hangnail, the nerves in the pit of his stomach dancing like flies.

"Let's go," Alric said. "We need to see what you think about the gathering place. Do you have the final numbers?"

Zandor shook his head. "Nothing's changed. We agreed eight people inside. One is Rafe, the farmer, you sent. He came with his people yesterday. He'll be a good addition to the attack."

"I wasn't sure he would make it," Michal said. "When I saw him in the Green Man while entertaining, I made sure he knew where to find you. What about the other three?"

"Dorsey, George, and Mary," Zandor said. "The others are forming small squads."

"You seem to have lost your objection to women being in the midst of things," Michal said.

"It seems I learn fast." Zandor laughed. "Mary and Dorsey were not as kind as Serena. I feared for my life when I objected to them joining in the fun, as they put it."

Michal echoed the laughter and slapped Zandor on the back before they set out.

Alric led them away from the sunny entrance to the warehouse toward the shaded side of the city. Michal felt the chill across his shoulders as they passed from the light. The foot traffic they had been mingling with started to drop off, and there were offices facing the street, and a few bookstores, no food vendors, no warm smells to ease the bleakness.

"Will people be able to gather without suspicion?" Zandor asked, giving words to Michal's thoughts.

"By the time they come, these stores will be closed. There are a few apartments above the stores, but the residents will likely be asleep. Meta don't wander down here at night. No drunks for them to torment," Alric said as they turned to the right. "We'll put together a map, and you can copy it for each group."

"How many do you have ready?" Michal asked.

"There are forty people ready at the warehouse. Declan and Rafe say all their people have come. I think we'll have a few more by tomorrow morning," Zandor answered.

"It will be too late by tomorrow morning," Michal said. "Can we slow down a bit?" Alric had steadily picked up speed as they passed through the streets. His stooped back not slowing him down at all.

"Sorry," Alric said. "I guess I got excited. Going by these back streets is the long way around, but Edmond and I used to race through here as lads."

"It's okay, but I don't think we need to race to the battle." Michal looked at Zandor. The older man was red in the face and breathing deeply. How would he fare in the fight? "Let's stay here for a minute."

Alric leaned against the wall, glancing up to the top. "That's the castle. We still have to get halfway around to the gate. It faces the outside wall."

"Do deliveries come this way?" Zandor asked, his color returning to normal as his breathing slowed.

"No, the deliveries come to an outside gate in the wall across the way from the door we're going to. Coming through the back streets is the best way for a large group to sneak up."

Zandor, who had been leaning on the same wall, pushed himself away from it and waved Alric ahead of him. "Let's finish this. I want to make sure it will work before I hand over the responsibility to others."

Michal brought up the rear as they walked the wall. Despite the lack of windows, he felt eyes crawling over his back. The passage became narrower, only wide enough to let two people pass. He worried that if they were caught it would be a slaughter. He was about to speak when the passage opened out into a small square. Three other alleys opened off the square and two doors faced each other. One door in the outer wall, wide enough for a wagon. The other about a third as wide cut into what seemed the solid bank of the castle grounds.

Alric drew them to lean against the castle wall. "That's the gate. All deliveries are made during the day, the duke thinks he can hear the workers, and won't let them disturb his sleep."

"Where do those streets go?" Michal asked.

"Two of them go to work rooms, the laundry is that way." Alric nodded to the opposite passage. "They are all dead ends, don't worry."

"The workers won't be there?" Zandor asked.

"No one is allowed to work in this area until the duke is awake. Only the kitchens, and they are at the end of a long corridor behind that door, which leads to one of three places: the kitchen, the front hall, and the garden."

"It looks like it will work," Zandor said.

CHAPTER FIFTY-TWO

"Kael," the duke bellowed. "Where are you?"

Kael entered the main hall of the castle. The duke was standing next to a long table, which was covered in a red cloth. He was picking at the cloth, disturbing the stacks of paper that had been placed there in preparation for the day's judgments.

"I'm here, sire." Kael reached out a hand and straightened the cloth, patting a pile of paper back into a neat square. "What is it you need?"

"I have made a decision," the duke announced. "About the wedding."

Kael waited, expecting a decision about the color of the dining room linens, or a specific dish the duke wished.

The duke continued, "I have decided to leave tomorrow afternoon to meet the women in their own environments."

Kael blinked; not sure he had heard correctly. "The women will be already on their way. Surely it is too late to change your plans."

"I am the duke," came the sharp answer. "I sent messengers this morning to tell them to expect me in a few days. If I leave tomorrow, I can be done within the week."

"I..." Kael swallowed. "We will prepare your travel things. I'm sure we can have you on the road by late afternoon."

"No, by morning," the duke said. "I do not need much. Let's make this a stripped-down adventure. Just me and the guards, we'll move quickly. Take them by surprise."

"Are you saying you don't wish a cook, or a laundress, or me?"

"Exactly." The duke smiled and nodded as if Kael was a particularly dim student who had finally caught on to a simple lesson. "Just me and the guards, as I said."

Kael knew there was something more to the duke's action than a need for speed. The only explanation he could come up with was that he was still being punished for talking about the rebellion. He knew there was a plot going on, but the duke wouldn't listen, and now he was punishing him, and all the people who had worked so hard to get ready for a large contingent of Meta to visit. Keeping his frustration out of his voice was a monumental task. "Very well, I will see to it."

CHAPTER FIFTY-THREE

Michal waited with the others at the door to the castle kitchen. There was no handle on this side, but Alric had paid a boy to unlock it. They needed to get in fast and relock the door, so no one had a chance to get suspicious.

"Who's leading the others?" Serena asked in a whisper.

"They're broken into small groups of three or four," Zandor answered as quietly. "We have people stationed at the turns to lead them through the maze of streets. Don't fret, they will be in place."

The sound of shuffling feet on stone made Michal's skin crawl. He wished they could be quieter, but *Gadje* weren't trained to be quiet. No matter how stealthy they tried to be, they always made enough noise to announce their presence to a deaf man. He closed his eyes and breathed deeply, then opened them to see Alric tense then nod. The others shifted and the sounds made Michal want to scream at them to be quiet. He touched Zandor's arm and put his fingers to his lips. Zandor nodded and repeated the action with Serena who stood in front of him. The sounds died out over the next few moments as the signal passed.

Alric stood beside the door, a hand pressed where the latch would be. The boy was to lift the latch then give the door a slight push, enough to be felt, but not to open it. Michal waited for Alric to nod. They would wait a minute for the boy to leave, and then slide inside. Michal hoped he would feel calmer when they were in, hoped that the tension he felt was mostly about being exposed, and that when they started, he would be focused on the action, not on his fears.

Nodding, Alric slid the blade of his knife in the crack, levering the door open. Michal held his breath expecting guards to come pouring out of the door. No one did.

Alric stood back and motioned three of their party to come close, Oisin, Serena, and Rafe watched him point to the right, and then hold up four fingers. Michal had insisted he remind them where to go before they entered. They needed to be in and through the space quickly – no time for second thoughts.

The first three disappeared, Alric motioned for the next three and gave them instructions to go right and through the fourth door. Then Michal and Zandor joined Alric at the door, slipping through and waiting for him to close and latch it before joining the others of their team in the storage room at the far end of the corridor.

They closed the door and lay flour sacks across the gap at the bottom, so they would be able to speak quietly without danger of someone walking past hearing them.

"Let's go over it again," Michal said. "When we go upstairs, you wait for a count of five hundred, then go and open the door. Two of you guard the one who goes to the door."

"Dorsey will open the door," Mary said. "If there's trouble, she can fight without a blade."

"I guess hefting trays of food and beer has come in handy, after all," Dorsey said, flexing her arms. "If I can reach someone, I can fell them with a single blow, human or Meta."

"I hope it won't come to that," Michal said, smiling to cover his nerves. "We'll attack the guards outside the duke's chamber," he continued. "When we get in, we need to be sure that we have people at our backs."

"They will be," Dorsey said.

CHAPTER FIFTY-FOUR

"Four bags are not enough, sire," Kael said. "You will need different clothes for each household."

They had been discussing the details of the duke's bridal tour since the sun bleached the night sky. The duke's demands that he travel light had been a point of conflict. Kael was standing firm, he could not in all conscience let the duke travel for a week in one set of clothes.

"No," the duke said. "Let them see me at my messiest. I do not wish a bride who only wants me at my best."

"If you would delay your travel for a day." Kael tried to keep the pleading from his voice.

"No." The duke threw his mug of tea across the room to smash in the hearth. "I believe I have made myself clear. The guards and I leave in two hours. I have sent all but the two outside my door to the gathering point outside the city. It should be a matter of minutes to put together a few bags and see me off."

"The only guards in the castle are outside your door?" Kael felt the weight of worry over the rebellion smother him. "Two guards? Who knows this?"

"Stop your fussing, man. There is no need for more. And I do not wish to hear anything about that damn, nonexistent rebellion."

The sound of raised voices filtered through the door.

"Stop," came the muffled voice of one of the guards. "Put down your weapons."

"I don't think its non-existent, sire." Kael ran to the door to try to catch the rest of the words. As he approached, something thudded against it. Kael looked around. "Sire, help me," he said as he ran to push a wardrobe against the door.

CHAPTER FIFTY-FIVE

"Stay back." Michal put his arm up to stop the others following him and Oisin. "Only two guards, but not a lot of room. Let us go in, but be prepared to jump in if need be."

Serena watched Michal and Oisin take their blades in hand and step around the corner of the hallway into the small foyer. She poked her head around the corner and felt Rafe lean against her to watch.

The two guards were talking while they rested against the wall beside the intricately carved door that led to the duke's chamber. They didn't notice Michal and Oisin, until Oisin called out, "Stand aside and we will spare you."

The closest guard looked up and suddenly his stance became more alert and threatening. The other followed suit, and shouted, "Stop, put down your weapons."

Michal rushed toward them, Oisin a step behind. Serena gripped the handle of her blade and started to step forward. She felt an arm slide around her waist and hold her back. "Let them be, girl. They don't have much room. If you get in the way, it might come to tragedy."

She nodded, swallowing her fear and impatience.

Michal attacked the guard on the right; Oisin took the guard on the left. Serena watched as they exchanged blows. The movements rapid and hard to follow, it was nothing like the practice bouts. One of the combatants would swing their blade across the body of the other. The defender would dodge and swing his own blade.

Serena didn't understand how they could react so quickly and accurately. It must have been less than a minute since the fight had started. None of them had drawn blood, but the guards were starting to gain an advantage.

"See how they're moving back to back?" Rafe whispered. "That's what years of training do. Those guards aren't thinking about how to fight. They are just fighting."

"It doesn't look good." Serena heard the tears in her voice. "When do we help them?"

"It'll be easier to help when the guards have finished getting into position," Rafe said. "When they are back to back, there will be more room for someone else. Let me go in first."

"Are you that much more experienced than the rest of us?" Serena whispered, keeping her eyes on the action across the foyer.

Zandor stepped from behind them, staying far enough away from the action to not get in the way. "I think he is," Zandor beckoned them to stand beside him. "Perhaps the guards will lose heart if they see that there are others waiting to attack."

Serena flipped the blade handle in her grip so that she would be ready to fight as soon as the opportunity arose. "It seems not," she said. The guards paid them no attention, focusing on their current opponents.

"Well," Zandor said. "I trust Rafe, who was the captain of the council guards almost thirty years ago, to guide us when it comes to attack."

"I didn't realize you recognized me." Rafe laughed. "They are doing fine. I'll step in soon. The boys are tiring. Zandor next, as soon as I get one of them free. Then when it looks like there's an opening, if we don't finish them off, Serena steps in."

Standing, her eyes riveted on the fight, Serena wanted to push Rafe in to get Michal or Oisin out of danger. She had known it would be dangerous, but knowing and seeing were two completely different things.

The guards had settled into a rhythm of slash and block that looked like it could go on forever. Michal and Oisin each faced a guard, backs to the wall. Serena saw an opening, why didn't Rafe step into the side, making it a three-point attack on the guards.

The guards took a half step toward their opponent, a small advance that seemed intended to cause Michal and Oisin to back closer to the wall. Michal stepped forward into the advance cutting his guard on the chest, causing the Meta to retreat the half step.

Oisin stepped back again as his guard continued to advance. Serena could see that one more step would leave him no room to maneuver the blade. She felt Rafe shift beside her, but he was going to be late.

She watched the guard shift his weight to take the next step as she flew across the space screaming, pulling her right arm across her body to expose the full length of the blade in front of her. She reached the guard as he turned to face her. Her arm plunged forward as if it had a mind of its own. She felt the resistance of the guard's leather shirt and threw her body against the pommel of her blade. Her weight made the difference, and she heard a gurgle from the guard, then felt leather against her hand, then warm liquid.

"Look out." She heard Rafe call as he stepped between her and the other guard who had turned away from Michal to attack her. She dropped to the floor to get out of the way.

Above her the guard was impaled from both front and back as Michal's and Rafe's knives passed through his body.

CHAPTER FIFTY-SIX

Michal slumped to the ground. The two guards were dead. He watched Rafe and Zandor drag the bodies to the back of the foyer. It seemed to him that hours had passed. He was shaking with exhaustion, but he knew it had only been minutes since they had attacked.

The other group would be opening the door downstairs. They would soon have reinforcements. By the noise of heavy furniture being moved behind the door, it was not going to be easy to get it open.

"Are you hurt?" Rafe asked.

"No." Michal levered himself up and groaned. "Oisin?"

Rafe helped Michal stand. "The lad is fine, and so is the lass. Let's see what we can do about getting in to deal with the duke."

"There's a barricade," Michal said. "It sounded heavy. And there's at least two people in there. My guess is the duke and Kael."

Oisin groaned. "Let's see if we can speak to them. Can someone go and check on the others? It looks to me like the fight here is pretty much over."

"Zandor has gone," Rafe said. "Let's see what we can do about this."

Michal watched Rafe as he picked up one of the swords and held it gingerly by the blade. He went to the door and used the pommel to rap on the wood. "Open the door." He turned back to them and shrugged. "Worth a try."

Michal put his ear to the wood. "Someone is arguing in there. I can't make out the words, but they're shouting."

Serena was running her hand along the seam of the door. "It opens inward, but there's a gap here." She pointed to the center of the double doors. "I think I can pop the latch with a blade."

Michal handed her his knife. She slid the thin blade between the two halves of the door, moving it up and down to find the latch. "Here," she said, stopping the movement. "It's lifting." She started flicking the blade up and down. Michal could hear a metallic clank each time she lifted. The latch was bouncing in the shoe. If she could get enough momentum, it would flip around, and they would only have to deal with whatever the barrier was.

"Damn," she said. "I can't get enough force behind it." She turned and passed the knife to Oisin. "Try it."

Oisin slid the blade in. He raised his arm and flicked his wrist. The sound of metal rubbing on metal ended with a clang. The latch was off.

Serena stepped back as the men leaned on the right-hand side of the door. Michal felt it shift an inch, but no more. Then he heard voices.

"Sire, help me."

And the door slammed shut again as the barrier was forced back into place.

"There's a wardrobe or something across the doorway," Rafe said. "And, you were right, Michal, that was Kael's voice."

"We'll need something to use as a ram." Oisin looked around. "There's not much room to swing one. It will have to be short and heavy and easy to pick up."

"Zandor's back. I'll go find something and get enough of the others so we can batter the door." Rafe left them.

Michal gestured to the others to sit. "We might as well get comfortable. I don't think those two are going out the window."

Serena sat with her back against the wall, keeping her gaze away from the dead guards. Trying not to think about the feeling of her blade slicing into flesh, she wiped her hands on the fabric of her trousers. They would have to be thrown away.

"Thank you." Oisin slid down the wall next to her. "You saved my life."

"I don't want to talk about it." Her voice caught in her throat.

Wrapping his arms around her shoulders, Oisin pulled her into his embrace. "I know."

"No." She pulled away. "I never want to think about it ever again."

Zandor crouched in front of her. "Serena, you will have to talk about it. You must not let this fester inside you."

Serena pushed her face into Oisin's chest. He patted her back and kissed the top of her head. "It's okay."

The sound of running feet announced the arrival of the reinforcements. Rafe led a group of four others who carried a stone bench between them. "Stand away," he shouted. "This bloody thing is heavy."

The four men ran at the door, managing to swing the bench back a foot then shove it, crashing into the door before letting it go.

"Well," Zandor said, "it's better than it was."

Serena couldn't quite agree, the door was splintered, and they had managed to move the piece of furniture back a foot, but not enough to let them through.

CHAPTER FIFTY-SEVEN

Kael leaned against the wardrobe, knowing that his weight would make little difference in the end. He stared at the duke who was rifling in the drawers of his desk. "Sire, help me hold this back. The guards will come soon. I'm sure someone has run to get them. If we only hold back this attack for a short while."

"You fool," the duke said. Pulling out a drawer and tipping it upside down. "The guards are not coming."

"If you had only..."

"Kael, don't you dare say I told you so."

"No, sire. Please, come and help me hold them back."

"I have to find the key," the duke shouted. "I can escape through the tunnel. Stop talking."

"It's gone quiet out there," Kael said, watching the duke pick through the pile of contents from the drawers. "What key?"

"Shut up you fool." The duke walked toward Kael. "Shut up."

"Open the door," a man's voice called.

The duke stopped in the middle of the room. "So, it seems my guards are dead."

"Perhaps not, sire." Kael couldn't understand the duke's mood.

He should be fighting. He should be trying to break down the door and fight the rebels himself.

"They would not have surrendered. They would not have run away. They would fight to death." The duke pushed him aside. "Get the bed over here."

Kael looked at the massive bed. There was no way he could move that without help. He turned to the duke as the sound of the latch lifting came from the door. "Help me do this, sire."

The duke turned to Kael, and then to the door, and, for some reason, to the far wall. "Yes," he said. He didn't seem to be answering Kael, but he walked away from the wardrobe toward the bed.

Kael stepped to the head of the bed. "Take the other side, sire."

The duke walked to the desk and tipped it over.

The door crashed against the wardrobe.

"Sire," Kael said. "Help me."

The duke reached under the top of the desk and pushed the drawer out to shatter against the floor. "Ah, here is the key. I should have thought of this. The damn drawer has been broken, it slipped underneath." Out of the splinters, he took what looked like a medallion.

Kael could hear the people on the other side of the door talking. It sounded like there were hundreds of them out there.

The duke rubbed the medallion between his hands and Kael heard a low hum fill the room.

"Sire," Kael said, stepping toward the duke. "Help me."

The duke spun around and slapped Kael across the face. "You fool. I cannot wait until I am rid of you and your stinking kind. You are a coward. A traitor to your people. I don't believe the things you've done just because I had a whim. I used to make things up to see how far you would go." He laughed. "Get away from me. You disgust me by your presence."

The duke continued to speak, but Kael couldn't hear anything else. He felt like he was in a hollow tube. It was cold. He could hear the blood rushing through his heart. His line of sight narrowed to the object in the duke's hand.

"How can you say I disgust you? I warned you this would happen." To Kael, his voice sounded like it was coming from outside.

The duke turned away rubbing the medallion between his hands. Kael could hear him laughing, a gentle chuckle that hurt worse than the slap.

"Speak to me," Kael said, his voice rising in volume. "Don't turn your back on me."

The duke shrugged and started toward the wall beside the fireplace. Kael stepped toward the duke, picking up the broken desk leg. "Speak to me," he screamed.

The duke didn't turn back when he said, "Oh, shut up. Your voice is grating on my last nerve."

Kael raised the desk leg and swung with all his might against the duke's head. The duke dropped to his knees, purple blood pouring from a wound in the side of his head. Kael raised the desk leg and hit the duke again, and again, finally stopping when the duke's head was a bloody pulp.

Kael was panting and dizzy. Sounds returned. He could hear people talking outside the room. They were discussing what they had heard, wondering who had killed whom.

"Wait," Kael's voice came out hoarsely. "Step away from the door."

"What has happened?" The same man's voice asked.

"Step away, and I'll move the wardrobe," Kael said, thinking they would know soon enough what had happened and not wanting to put words to what he'd done.

He heard arguing and then a woman said, "Okay, we're stepping back."

Reaching over the wardrobe, Kael used the bloody desk leg to reach and push the splintered door closed. He moved around the wardrobe and placed his back against an undamaged part of the door. He raised his foot and pushed at the furniture, moving it a few feet, enough to let the door open, and people into the room.

CHAPTER FIFTY-EIGHT

When they entered the duke's chamber and saw what Kael had done, they locked him in a side room. It was one thing to be grateful that he had removed the duke, and another to trust him.

Serena sat at the dining table in the main hall of the castle. Forty of the rebels sat at the table ready to discuss the next steps. They were all as hungry as though they had fought together. But the only battle of the rebellion was the one at the duke's chamber.

She didn't know what Michal would tell them. She knew he would want her to report on Kael, so she had spent an hour with the man asking for information. He tried to tell her what he knew but admitted that the duke had been playing him for a fool, and he didn't know what was truth, and what lies.

The first information had been verified. There were no Meta in the castle, in the city for that matter. Serena hadn't been able to sift through the stories. She decided she would simply relate the facts, leaving interpretation to others.

Michal stood and the quiet conversation stopped.

"Today the humans have retaken Mont Kinner. Soon we will take back all of Free Faith."

The crowd cheered. Serena saw Inka sitting next to a smaller paler version of herself, and then noticed Edmond sitting at the back of the room.

"We need knowledge," Michal was saying.

"Make Kael speak," a man called from the side of the room. "He will know all that is important."

Serena stood at a nod from Michal. "I have spoken to Kael. He is willing to tell all he knows but it seems the duke has been feeding him false information. Kael does not know what is true. I will tell you what he told me and perhaps we can find the truth in the facts." She picked up her mug of tea and moistened her throat. "He isn't sure whether the story of a bridal search is true, but he thinks the Meta are all travelling somewhere. And the guards are gone. He says that the way the duke was acting, there must be a secret door in the chamber from his room."

She sat and waited for someone to ask questions she couldn't answer.

"The part about the guards is true," a boy called. "I was assigned to carry supplies. They are camped four miles outside town."

"I assume they will come looking if the duke doesn't show up," Michal said.

"I don't know if the bride thing is true, but I know the duke was planning a journey," a stablewoman said. "I packed some bags into the carriage this morning."

Zandor stood. "We need to decide what we should do, regardless of what the duke's plans were."

"True," Declan called. "Who will lead us in the meantime? We should have a temporary council or something."

"Michal," the stablewoman called. "He should lead us."

Michal stood and gestured for silence. "I have no interest in leading, temporarily or otherwise. I have no skill for it, and I yearn for the road."

Rafe stood. "Until we can convene a new council, I suggest

that Zandor lead a committee of merchants and tradesmen. Who will sit with him?"

Serena looked around the room, three of the castle servants stood and two of the rebels who came with Zandor. She elbowed Oisin. "Stand up. You will be good at this."

"No, these are smart, strong people." Oisin elbowed her back. "I have no place here."

"Yes, you do." She pinched him. "Get up or I'll stick you with a fork."

"Yes, ma'am." He chuckled and rose.

"Good," Rafe said. "Now, what do we do next?"

Zandor looked at the whole room. "We need information. We should send scouts out. Who will go?"

Serena watched as three young boys and a girl stood. "Good, decide between yourselves who goes in which direction, but go out for half a day, a day at most, and come back. You are looking for anything unusual, perhaps more than just the guards are camped nearby. Don't get into a dangerous situation."

The kids ran out together chatting.

"I think now we need someone to act as guards at the gates in case the Meta come back."

Five of the stable lads jumped up and took offered swords before leaving.

Zandor nodded. "Now, let's discuss what we do next."

CHAPTER FIFTY-NINE

Michal stretched and looked out over the balcony. He had finally slept after the long rounds of discussion about what to do, and when to do it. He was immeasurably grateful that there had been no argument to put him in power. Just sitting through the discussion was enough to confirm he would not be a good politician.

The events of the last two weeks had started him thinking about his family. How his father was not as bad as the duke. Perhaps if he tried, there was a peace to be gained with the old man. A way to stay with the people he loved without antagonizing his father.

He could feel rain in the air. Whatever was to come would be done soon, and life could start again for the people who had lived through the last twenty-five years.

Leaning on the stone wall he watched the people in the court-yard at their business. Mostly it was people reuniting with friends and family from the dungeon. They had released all the prisoners and offered them food, a bath, clothing, and a night's rest in bed. Some of the castle servants had been sent through the town passing on the news of the end of the Meta rule, and the release of the prisoners. A pigeon had been sent to each of the other towns.

He saw an old woman throw her arms around a bent old fellow. Even from this distance, he could see the tears running down her cheeks.

The cook had set up a table and covered it with food. Zandor and the other council members wandered among the crowd talking, shaking hands, and giving the occasional hug.

Michal watched three of the runners from last night enter the courtyard and look around them. He left the balcony and ran down the stairs to hear the news.

"Two parties of meta," the girl gasped out. "They are headed toward the guards. The guards are camped in the same place they were the day before."

Michal sighed. "We'll need to get everyone ready to fight, then."

"They don't look like they are coming here," the taller boy said. "They are settled around the camp with the guards."

"How many do you think there are?" Zandor asked.

"We know," the other boy said. "Ian is watching them now. They don't seem to be keeping guard, and we were able to get close. There's ten little kids, five older kids and over seventy males and about sixty females."

"That sounds like all of them," Rafe said, frowning. "Now what does that mean?"

"There's no humans," the girl announced. "None. It's only Meta."

Michal worried about the other boy. "Why did you leave Ian there? We told you not to take risks."

The taller boy bristled. Michal recognized the emerging man warring with the boy he still was. "It wasn't a risk. He's hidden. We thought he could give us early warning if they started to move."

"Good thinking," Michal nodded. The boy blushed.

CHAPTER SIXTY

Serena was frustrated. This constant discussion was difficult to deal with after the rush of action yesterday. The council did not have enough facts to make a decent plan and they couldn't get everyone to agree to any action based on supposition. Every council member had an opinion about what the few facts they had meant.

She stood and waited until she had the attention of all of them before speaking. "The only person who might have an idea of what all this means is Kael. We should bring him here and ask him what he thinks."

"How can we trust him? He was as bad as the Meta. Always bullying us, and reporting infractions to the duke," one of the men she didn't know said.

"He killed the duke," she said. "Whatever happened, at the end he killed the duke. I think that buys him some of our time."

Oisin stood beside her. "I agree. We don't have to take his advice but listening might help. And, perhaps, he's had enough time to think about what he has to offer us."

"Let's bring him here, then," Zandor said. "Serena is right, we don't have to believe. It can't hurt to listen."

It took no more than ten minutes for one of the new castle guards to bring Kael to the meeting. He had been allowed to bathe and change, no trace of the gore from his attack remained. The man had lost his arrogance and seemed smaller to Serena, smaller and older. He stood beside Zandor, head bowed, hands linked before him. She pushed away the feelings of pity. No matter what he looked like now, this was the same man who tortured Edmond.

Zandor told Kael what they knew. Kael looked up startled when Zandor said how many Meta were camped.

"What is your interpretation of the events?" Zandor sat back arms crossed.

Kael cocked his head. Serena could almost see the wheels turning. "The child was correct," he started. "That number, if they counted accurately is the total of the Meta, less the two guards and the... the." He took a deep breath before continuing. "The duke."

"Why would they all gather with no humans?" Rafe asked.

"I have come to think this bride search was always a ruse," Kael said, his words measured. "The duke sent all but two of the guards away a couple of days ago. He wasn't concerned about an escaping prisoner, and he constantly dismissed my warnings of rebellion."

"And how do you explain that?" Rafe asked.

"I assume the Meta had need to gather, perhaps a succession decision. The other Meta might prefer a leader who has offspring."

"I don't think the Meta are much for camping. It's hard to believe they would need to gather in the countryside to make that kind of decision, and how would they know the duke is dead?" Serena asked.

"You are right," Kael said. "They prefer the convenience of a roof and walls."

"Do you have anything constructive to offer?" Zandor asked.

"I can no more make a conclusion of the information than you can," Kael said, his tone harsh. "My suggestion, if you are interested, is to spy on the camp and get more information."

Serena agreed with him. Tired of listening to the suppositions and guesses, she rapped on the table for attention. "The man is right. We need to take a small party to see what is happening."

"I agree," Michal stood. "It's time to find out what's going on. We cannot sit and wait for them to act."

"A small party then," Zandor said. "Me, Michal, Oisin, and Serena."

Rafe held up a hand to stop the conversation. "You are the head of council. You cannot go on these adventures. It seems fitting that the three of them go, they started this adventure. I will join them, and Kael will come with us."

"Kael goes back to his cell," Zandor said.

"Kael comes with us," Oisin said. "He may bring knowledge that will catch an interpretation we will miss."

"Then you will also take one of the guards. I don't trust him." Zandor's tone left no room for argument.

CHAPTER SIXTY-ONE

The young scout, Allie, had led them to the clearing, and now Oisin waited patiently for her to speak.

"The Meta camp is about a mile into the forest." Allie pointed across a meadow. "Ian was hiding in a group of bushes when we left. He may have moved by now."

"We go in and get as close as possible," Michal said. "Untie Kael's hands. I don't want him tripping and alerting the Meta."

"If he runs?" The guard asked.

"Kill him," Michal said. "Let's go."

Oisin took up position behind Serena and followed the group into the woods. Allie led them quietly until they reached a small brook. She stopped, put her fingers to her lips, and then held up her hand to indicate they should stay. She slipped to the left and was out of sight so fast that it seemed like she disappeared.

Forcing himself not to slap at the insects that buzzed about the party, Oisin peered after her. He could hear the water burbling along in the brook and knew the Meta should be in hearing range, but no sound of laughter or talking drifted to them. It was eerily quiet of anything but normal forest sounds.

There was a shift of branches and leaves and Allie stepped

into sight, a small boy a step behind her. "Ian says the Meta are gone," she said.

"They upped stakes and left an hour ago. I was waiting for a bit to see if they came back before coming to tell you."

"Which way did they go?" Michal asked.

"Into the forest. I couldn't follow because they kept watch. But something happened last night that you should know," Ian said.

Oisin saw the boy pale when he started to tell them. He reached out and placed a hand on Ian's shoulder. "Just tell us. It will be easier when the words are out."

"The castle huntsman arrived, just after dark. They caught him and dragged him into the center of the camp. I don't think he intended to come across them. I think he was investigating the noise and looking for poachers."

"Go on," Oisin said, moving to put his arm around the child.

"He told them the duke was dead. They didn't believe him. They crushed his hands and he still told them the truth. They killed him. I didn't know what to do."

Oisin patted the boy on the shoulder. "You did the right thing. Don't worry, you did exactly the right thing."

"What do we do?" Serena asked.

Before anyone was able to answer, Oisin felt the ground vibrate, and then a humming came from behind them. The humming grew to a bone shaking vibration. Oisin looked around, bending his knees to try to keep his balance. He couldn't see what could possibly be making the sound.

The vibration calmed as quickly as it rose and was replaced with a roar. Oisin looked up. Overhead a large dull, gray machine rose and flew over their heads before shooting into the sky. The silence that came after the machine left made Oisin wonder if he had been deafened.

Then a bird called in the trees and Serena whistled.

Oisin turned to Rafe. "All that planning, and we didn't ..."

"What? Have your rebellion?" Rafe grinned. "Oisin, there's more to life than fighting the enemy. What do you think would have happened if the Meta had just left? How long before we realized they were gone?"

"Not that long. A day or two at most."

"Aye and when do you think we would have gotten around to deciding who was in charge? You and your friends put together the future. Be happy you didn't have to kill a lot of Meta to do that."

EPILOGUE

Michal walked through the open gate into the town of Mont Kinner. It had been a year since the Meta flew back to space where they had come from. After the week of celebration and organization, he had left Oisin and Serena and returned to his family.

As he passed into the sunlit market square, he thought it had been a good year. His father made him do a penance for disobedience, nothing too onerous. Alana had married in the interim and had a fine set of twins. Lissendra was not married. Michal courted her, and they were set to wed in a month. He still didn't get along with his father, but he was able to avoid open warfare.

"Michal," Dorsey shouted as he entered the market square. "I heard you were coming. Welcome. Will you stay at the Green Man?"

"I will certainly come for a fine meal," he called back. "But I have been invited to stay with Oisin and Serena. I hear they have a nice house near the castle."

"That they do." Dorsey laughed. "That they do."

Michal hitched his travel bag higher on his back and made his way through the market. The familiar stalls were decorated with branches of evergreens and carved and painted baubles. This was the first Liberation Day celebration. Stall owners offered free samples to people passing. A woman stood by the fountain singing while a man played a cello beside her. Each corner of the market had a street entertainer. Michal felt the joy pour out of the people around him.

The stores were open, and people wandered from shop to shop, carrying bags and boxes. Michal smiled at the bustle and hurry of the crowd. He approached the end of the street and saw Serena standing on the doorstep of a large house. She caught sight of him and ran to meet him.

"Finally," she said wrapping her arms around him. "Oisin is still at council, but I expect him back any second. Come in and have a glass of the new wine."

Michal laughed and hugged her in return. "So, you've settled for being a wife. But I don't see any chains attached to you."

"Cheeky." She slapped his arm. "I realized that no one would put chains on me unless I let them. No, I'm too busy with the new school to be tied to the kitchen. I have a cook and a house-maid. Can you believe it?"

"I can," Michal said. "I never thought Oisin was the type to tie you to the kitchen. How is your son?"

"Michal var Oisin is doing well, thank you." Serena grinned. Michal could see the pride shining from her eyes.

"And your school, how are the students doing?"

"They seem to have a good handle on the juggling, but most of them are not good at attracting an audience or doing any other acts." Serena shrugged and took Michal's bag, handing it to the girl waiting by the door. "Thank you Mirea. They mainly want to entertain their families, but one or two are serious. I think we'll have a couple of good street entertainers by summer."

"Good work. I'd like to see them while I'm here." Michal followed her into the side room.

"They asked me if you would. You are a bit of a celebrity to them." She bent over a cradle and lifted out a bundled baby, kissing the top of his head before passing him to Michal.

Michal winked down at the baby who had Serena's green eyes and Oisin's blond hair. "Who would have thought we'd be here a year after raising a rebellion?"

"No one," Oisin said as he entered the room. "I remember thinking we wouldn't survive the night."

"How is the council?" Michal noticed his friend looked older, and more a man than a boy.

"Not interested in the Romany." Oisin laughed, taking his son from Michal. "You earned a bit of privacy last year. Zandor was elected as permanent council head, well permanent until the next election in five years. The big surprise is Kael."

"He's part of the council?" Michal took the mug of wine from Serena and sniffed the glass.

"It took some time, and there are those who will never trust, or forgive him, but he's become invaluable. He really has a talent for organization."

"Enough business. Taste the wine," Serena said. "It's good, you'll like it."

WANT MORE?

Use the QR code to check out more Science Fiction books by P A Wilson.

Or check out the sneak peek for RESCUE! book one in the Humanity Found series.

If you enjoyed reading Breaking the Bonds, please consider helping other readers to find the story by leaving a review.

CHAPTER 1

Jocaster sat in the back of the room as befit his rank and standing. If he hadn't listened to Pen, and they hadn't been caught, they would be in the center of the room. But they were both under punishment for the antic. He reminded himself that this was a briefing, not a life sentence. If he was lucky they would get out of the room without making things worse.

"You'd think this would get more interesting," Pen said, reaching back to tighten the pins keeping her hair under control. "We'll be making rendezvous in three days, and we're still not planning a welcome party." She elbowed him. "You get special assignments; are you keeping secrets from me?"

Jocaster kept his eyes on the captain, sure that he would notice the inattention and apply another level of punishment to his hell. "Pretty sure there's no party. We don't have the excess supplies. Maybe later."

"You aren't bored?"

"I am, but if we mess up on one of the tiny details, *Zeus Rising* might collide with us rather than connect. Then where will *Dark Prospect* be?"

"Our ship can take a few bumps," Pen said. She didn't sound convinced to Jocaster.

"Be quiet. I don't want to find myself in the brig for insubordination."

She sat straighter and the conversation ended.

Jocaster smiled. He'd met Pen when he was on an undercover operation and they'd been friends since. She was adventurous and spontaneous. Half the time he went along with her plans to make sure she didn't do something fatal. Everything about them was opposite. She was blond, fair skinned and blue eyed. He was dark skinned, green eyed, and bald by choice; his hair tended toward wild if he didn't shave it, and an officer with an afro the size of a small moon would send a different message than he wanted.

No matter what trouble they got in, the captain never seemed to take away the plum assignments. He knew the value of their partnership, even if it upset the order on *Dark Prospect*.

The daily list of outstanding tasks for the rendezvous was winding down. The captain moved to the front of the room as the duty officer covered her final bullet points.

When the captain stood alone at the front of the room, everyone shifted slightly in their seats. No one had been slouching, but they all came to a bit more attention.

"I know this was tedious," the captain said. "I'm here today to remind everyone of the purpose of our current mission."

He nodded to someone and a chart of the local area of space filled the wall behind him. Jocaster looked at all the blank darkness that crowded the edges of the image and encroached a lot farther into their position than he'd expected.

"This map contains our knowledge of the area, and what *Zeus Rising* has transferred to us. As we receive data from the remaining ships, many of the gaps will fill in. Until now, we've been satisfied to roam through space as individual communities. Now, we are joining together for a reason. In the last joint report from the ships close enough to send more than a short update, we learned that what started as a thirty-ship search for a new home away from the enemy has become a twelve-ship retreat from death. Our vessels are aging, and we need to find that new home."

The captain paused, but Jocaster knew there would be no questions.

"Sir," Pen said, raising her hand.

What trouble is she starting now?

The captain nodded at her. "Yes, Lieutenant Tromarin?"

Pen stood. "I think we all agree that this coming together is necessary," she said. "A question has been bugging me for a while and I can't figure out an answer."

"Ask away, Lieutenant." The captain smiled as he said it. Jocaster wondered if it was fondness or forbearance. Pen did have a reputation for keeping her cheekiness just this side of insubordination.

"When we find a planet, and I would love to be able to settle, don't get me wrong, but,"

"Spit it out, Lieutenant. We don't have time for the fluff."

A chuckle ran around the room.

"Yes, sir. The enemy has trouble finding us now that we're scattered, but they still do — find us, that is. Aren't we presenting an easier target by coming together, and an even easier one when we set up on a world?"

The captain nodded. "I'm sure you aren't the only one thinking that, but thank you for being bold enough to ask."

There it is again. Doesn't he know that he is encouraging her by doing that?

Pen sat.

"We know the dangers. But right now, if a ship is attacked, there is no one there to help. There is no haven for any survivors. No one uses the escape pods because there is no escape. Together, we hope to present a stronger resistance. Perhaps a deterrent.

And by the time we find a home, we hope to have outrun the enemy — or at least have a long head start. Does anyone know the plan for what we do when we set down? It was our mission from the start."

Pen stood again. "The ship will be taken apart to provide for our needs on land. Shuttles can completely gut the ship in three days. The shell can be used for raw materials if we have time, but if not, it can be vaporized."

She sat.

"Teacher's pet," Jocaster muttered.

She smiled.

"We've agreed to alter the plan slightly." The captain nodded again, and another image replaced the stars. It was a list of components.

"When we find a suitable home, we will scavenge all the items except for some samples that we need to be present when we destroy the ships. To be safe, two volunteers for each ship will move them to a different area of space, blow the ships to leave enough trace for the enemy to believe we are all destroyed. The volunteers will return in shuttles; it will be a long journey, and potentially a fatal one."

Jocaster stood, and when the captain acknowledged him, he asked, "have we identified any planets that might support us?"

"Good question, Lieutenant."

The captain's approval removed Jocaster's fears that their last escapade had damaged his reputation beyond repair.

"We, the other captains and I, will begin that process in earnest as soon as we have combined our information."

Another hand went up. Julie Ackerman, junior Lieutenant. A good partner in the war games Jocaster played in addition to the training simulations. "Sir, may I ask a question?" The captain nodded. "Is there room for any survivors in case of an attack?"

The image behind the captain changed again. The twelve remaining ships and a number beside each.

"As you can see, some of our colleagues are in worse shape than *Dark Prospect*; the enemy is not the only threat out here. We have an inventory of the skills that have survived on each ship, and everyone can meet basic requirements. If we don't make changes to our mission, we will not live to see a new home."

Julie was still standing. She clearly wanted more. Pen wasn't sure that the captain had even considered taking on survivors, but now that the subject was opened, she wondered, too. She didn't ask. Pen figured she'd embarrassed Jo enough for one session. The enemy had been chasing them for generations, and no one had ever lived to tell what they looked like. An attack was always a surprise, and always an obliteration. If the price for meeting new people was a boring reminder of what they lived with every day, then so be it.

"So, Junior Lieutenant, the answer is: we'll do what we need to. We hope never to face it, but there is room on *Dark Prospect* for as many as we need. It could mean short rations and tight quarters, but there are so few of us that we cannot refuse shelter. We need the genetic material, and if that's not enough for you, we will not hold onto our humanity if we leave our companions behind."

Pen noticed Julie clench her hands where they rested behind her back. Her face didn't reflect anything but respect; her body gave away the fact that she strongly disagreed. Pen wondered what she thought would happen if people needed help. Would she be happy to watch frozen corpses float by the screens?

The meeting was coming to a close. Pen leaned in to whisper to Jo, but her snappy retort was silenced as a cadet entered. The boy was in a hurry and didn't stand on protocol. He ran to the front of the room and interrupted the captain with a few whispered words. The captain stared at the boy and asked him to repeat the message. When the boy complied, the captain paled.

Pen's body tightened in preparation for whatever the message brought. She felt Jo come to attention beside her. The entire room went quiet, the small noises made by so many people in a confined space dropping away.

The captain sent the boy away and turned to address the officers. "*Zeus Rising* met the enemy on their way to us. Survivors fled in the escape pods. We have information that they made landfall on a nearby planet. We are going to rescue them. Return to your stations and wait for further orders." He marched from the room without waiting for any response.

Pen stood and fumbled for support. Everyone was suddenly talking. She needed to absorb the information. A rescue team? A planet? "We have to be part of this," she said, taking Jo's arm. "Imagine, landing on a planet. Not a holographic representation, a real planet."

He guided her to the wall where the eddying crowd was thinning. "And rescuing the crew and passengers of *Zeus Rising*," he reminded her. "This isn't a joyride. The mission is too important for us, for humanity, to let an inexperienced team go."

Pen grinned. "Yep, but everyone is inexperienced. No one has made landfall before. In the eight hundred years since we left earth, no one has gone more than a kilometer from the ship." She grabbed his arm tighter. "That means we are as useful as anyone." She was already planning how to worm her way into the meeting so she could volunteer.

"Pen," Jo said. "I don't think the captain thinks the same way. He'll assign it to more senior officers."

"You mean older, right?" She huffed. "We should go and tell him that it would be a mistake. Being younger is a good thing. We're more adaptable."

"I'm not walking up to the captain and telling him how to do his job. If we're lucky, we'll be included."

"So, just let them decide and maybe leave us out of it?"

"Yes, that's exactly what I mean." Jocaster looked directly into her eyes. "Don't get us into any more trouble."

Pen admitted that Jo was right to be worried. She knew he could lead a rescue team, and she knew there would be an opportunity to show the captain that Pen Tromarin wasn't someone who lived in Jo's shadow. "I promise," she said. "I won't do anything that might keep us away from the mission."

CHAPTER 2

The wait for information was killing Jocaster. He paced outside his quarters, ignoring the communication beeps from Pen. Two hours had passed since the report. The only action from the ship was to announce a change in course. They were heading toward the last coordinates of *Zeus Rising*. No rescue team prepping, no call for volunteers. The captain, the senior officers, and the civilian leaders were secluded. All this time and the survivors were alone.

"Lieutenant Bryman, report to the captain's quarters."

Jo spun on his heels and ran. He was going to be on the rescue mission! Pen would be jealous. Of course, if he had an opportunity, he'd volunteer her. It wouldn't be the same on a mission alone.

There were two ensigns standing at the door to the captain's quarters. They snapped to attention as Jocaster approached.

"Go right in, sir," the one on the left said.

Jo nodded, pretending a nonchalance he didn't feel.

Inside, the captain and the civilian leader stood next to a printout. The captain beckoned Jocaster over and pointed to the chart. "This is where the survivors were headed. We got another short transmission an hour ago. Most of the people got out."

Jocaster stared at the chart. The system was a binary with five planets. The survivors were headed for the fifth one. It was a long way from the two suns. "They should be able to survive," he said. "At that distance, the planet would be hospitable, if not long term habitable. What did they say when you told them rescue was on the way?"

The captain exchanged glances with the civilian leader. "Roger and I think it best we not communicate that."

"I don't think we've met," the civilian leader said, holding his hand out for shaking. "Roger Whitnal."

Jocaster shook the man's hand. "We did, actually," he said. "I attended a lecture you gave on settling new worlds. You were kind enough to answer a couple of questions."

Whitnal smiled, but Jo could tell he didn't remember. "I hope my answers were helpful. You are probably wondering why we decided to maintain silence."

Jocaster had been, but knew he needed to impress the man. "I assume there is a good reason. It doesn't matter, we're going to rescue them, right?" Was this what the captain wanted? For Jocaster to carry the news to the rest of the crew that they were not going for the survivors?

The captain cleared his throat. "We don't have time for politics, Roger. Lieutenant Bryman doesn't need to figure out what we're asking." He turned to Jocaster. "Lieutenant, we didn't respond because we fear that the enemy may have remained in the area. They could also have this information. The rescue party will be heavily armed, and we need a leader who will step outside regulations, if necessary."

Jocaster clasped his hands behind his back, images of his last few escapades flashing through his mind. How much did the captain know about them?

"We want you to lead the team. We need you to pick who goes along. I'll make sure you get who you request," the captain said.

"You want me to lead them?" Jocaster needed to hear the words again. He'd meant what he said to Pen. He wasn't ready. He couldn't be responsible for that many lives.

"Yes," the captain said. "You have shown an ability to work through situations that others get mired in. Five years ago, you uncovered a scheme to cheat the officer qualification test. Since then I've kept my eye on you. I think you are the best choice."

"But there are more qualified candidates," Jocaster said.

"No, there are not," the captain replied. "Just older. Between you and Lieutenant Tromarin, you have plenty of experience working without oversight. She will join you, that's the only stipulation."

Pen will be no use in talking the captain out of this plan.

"I also have one request," Whitnal said. "I would like you to include Asher Jones in the crew."

"His qualifications?" Jocaster wasn't going to bring any spectators. He needed the room on the shuttle for survivors.

"Asher is combat trained. He is also well versed in conflict management."

"Excuse the question, sir," Jocaster said to the captain. "This isn't a negotiation, we're going in to bring the survivors back, right?" *Had he lied in the briefing?*

"You may find that the survivors need convincing, Lieutenant," Whitnal answered, ignoring Jocaster's clear expectation that the captain would speak. "I assure you he will not be a burden."

His mind was too busy trying to accept that he was the right leader for the mission to argue about one team member. He had no room for passengers. He'd deal with his concerns directly with Jones. "How many shuttles? We need room for survivors — we don't know how many."

This time the captain answered. "You will have two of the

landing shuttles. There's room for a four-person crew and fifty passengers — sixty if you need to push it. We think there are two hundred, possibly more on the planet. They landed somehow. You can use their shuttles. Worst case scenario, you make more than one trip back. The rest of the force will be ready to defend against an attack, if one comes."

The landing shuttles were supposed to take the entire complement of the starship to a new home planet. Two of them was a sacrifice. "Thank you, sir. I will choose the crew and be ready to go in three hours. Will we be close enough to the planet by then?"

"We'll be close enough for you to launch, but you will have a six-hour flight to the planet. The shuttles move faster than *Dark Prospect* in the short term. We will continue to move toward a rendezvous point as you complete your mission."

"If you will excuse me, I have preparations to make." Jocaster waited for the captain to dismiss him. "Mr. Whitnal, if you can have Asher Jones meet me in the armory in twenty minutes, I will be ready to assess him."

He marched through the door without waiting for the answer. Maybe Pen could help him believe he could do this.

If you want to know more, use the QR code to grab your copy of RESCUE!

FREE EBOOK

Claim your copy of Running the Game when you use the QR code below to sign up for my newsletter and cheer on Pen as she vies for a commission in the military.

ALSO BY PA WILSON

For more books by P A Wilson

Use the QR code below or go to pawilson.ca

ABOUT THE AUTHOR

Perry Wilson is a Canadian author based in Vancouver, BC who has big ideas and an itch to tell stories. Having spent some time on university, a career, and life in general, she returned to writing in 2008 and hasn't looked back since (well, maybe a little, but only while parallel parking).

She is a member of the Vancouver Writers Social Group, The Royal City Literary Arts Society, and The Surrey Writing Workshop. Perry has self-published several novels. She writes the Madeline Journeys, a fantasy series about a high-powered lawyer who finds herself trapped in a magical world, the Quinn Larson Quests, which follows the adventures of a wizard named Quinn who must contend with volatile fae in the heart of Vancouver, and the Charity Deacon Investigations, a mystery thriller series about a private eye who tends to fall into serious trouble with her cases, and The Riverton Romances, a series based in a small town in Oregon, one of her favorite states. Her stand-alone novels are Breaking the Bonds, Closing the Circle, and The Dragon at The Edge of The Map.

For more information
www.pawilson.ca
pawilson@pawilson.ca

 X

ACKNOWLEDGMENTS

People think that the process of writing is solitary. That's not the case for me. I have help from so many people it would be hard to acknowledge everyone, but I'll give it a try.

The support and inspiration I get from my writer's groups is incalculable. The Vancouver Writers Social Group opens my mind to other ways of telling a story. The Royal City Literary Arts Society gives me the opportunity to meet and share with other writers who have more knowledge than I do. The Other 11 Months group is where I learn about getting the words on the page. And my critique group who helps me find the best parts of the story I want to tell. Thanks to all of the members of these great groups.

Last of all, but definitely a huge part of the process, my beta readers. These are the people who love stories and are willing, and more than able, to tell me if my finished story is ready for you, my readers.